The Easter Sepulchre

The chronicles of Hugh de Singleton, surgeon

The Easter Sepulchre

The thirteenth chronicle of
Hugh de Singleton, surgeon

MEL STARR

LION FICTION

Published by
Lion Hudson Limited
Wilkinson House, Jordan Hill Business Park
Banbury Road, Oxford OX2 8DR, England
www.lionhudson.com

ISBN 978 1 78264 306 7
e-ISBN 978 1 78264 307 4

First edition 2020

A catalogue record for this book is available from the British Library

Printed and bound in the UK, June 2020, LH26

For Ana
Our "Angel Unaware"

Acknowledgments

Several years ago when Dr Dan Runyon, professor of English at Spring Arbor University, learned that I had written an as yet unpublished medieval mystery, he invited me to speak to his fiction-writing class about the trials of a rookie writer seeking a publisher. He sent chapters of Hugh de Singleton's first chronicle, *The Unquiet Bones*, to his friend Tony Collins at Lion Hudson. Thanks, Dan.

Tony has since retired, but many thanks to him and all those at Lion Hudson who saw Hugh de Singleton's potential.

Dr John Blair, or Queen's College, Oxford, has written several papers about Bampton history. These have been valuable in creating an accurate time and place for Hugh.

In the summer of 1990, Susan and I found a delightful B&B in a medieval village north of Lichfield named Mavesyn Ridware. Proprietors Tony and Lis Page became friends, and when they moved to Bampton some years later they invited us to visit them there. Tony and Lis introduced me to Bampton and became a great source of information about the village. Tony died in March 2015 only a few months after being diagnosed with cancer. He is greatly missed.

Glossary

Anchorite: one who lived in seclusion, generally to practice religion alone.

Angelus Bell: rung three times each day – dawn, noon, and dusk – announcing time for the Angelus devotional.

Apple moise: a fruit pottage made with apples, breadcrumbs, honey, almond milk, and spices.

Arbolettys: a cheese and herb custard, made with eggs, milk, butter, parsley, sage, and ginger.

Archdeacon: a priest whose duties involve assisting a bishop in ceremonial functions and administration.

Bailiff: a lord's chief manorial representative. He oversaw all operations, collected rents and fines, and enforced labor service. Not a popular fellow.

Beadle: a manor officer in charge of fences, hedges, enclosures, and curfew. Also called a *hayward*.

Boon work: the extra hours of labor service villeins owed the lord at harvest and other specific times of the year, beyond normal service, which was called week-work.

Burgher: a town merchant or tradesman.

Candlemas: 2 February. The day marked the purification of Mary. Women traditionally paraded to church carrying lighted candles. Tillage of fields resumed this day.

Capon: a castrated male chicken. They could grow quite fat.

Chauces: tight-fitting trousers, sometimes of different colors for each leg.

Clerk: a scholar assigned to assist a clergyman.

Coppice: the practice of cutting trees so that a thicket of small saplings would grow from the stump. These shoots were used for everything from arrows to rafters, depending on size.

Corn: a kernal of any grain, not the "corn" (maize) of American usage, which was unknown in Europe at the time.

Coroner: a manor official whose duty was to inquire into any death thought unnatural.

Cotehardie: the primary medieval outer garment. Women's were floor-length, men's ranged from thigh to ankle-length.

Cotter: a poor villager, usually holding five acres or less. He often had to work for wealthier villagers to make ends meet.

Cresset: a bowl filled with oil and a floating wick used for lighting.

Crown: a coin worth five shillings or sixty pence.

Demesne: land directly exploited by a lord and worked by his villeins, as opposed to land a lord might rent to tenants.

Deodand: any object which caused a death. The item was sold and the price awarded to the king.

Dexter: a war horse, larger than pack horses and palfreys. Also the right-hand direction.

Dibble stick: a simple stick used to make holes for the planting of peas and beans.

Dighted crab: crab meat soaked in wine vinegar, made into a paste with sugar and spices, then replaced in the shell and boiled.

Donatist: one who held that sanctity in a priest is necessary for the effective administration of the sacraments.

Easter Sepulchre: a niche in the wall of a church or chapel where the host and a crucifix were placed on Good Friday and removed Easter Sunday morning. Often closed with a velvet curtain.

Eels in bruit: eels cooked in a sauce made of white wine, onions, parsley, sage, breadcrumbs, pepper, and cinnamon.

Farthing: one-fourth of a penny. The smallest silver coin.

Fast day: Wednesday, Friday, and Saturday. Not the fasting of modern usage, but days when no meat, eggs, or animal products are consumed. Fish was consumed by those who could afford it.

Fewterer: the keeper of a lord's hounds.

Fraunt hemelle: an egg, pork and breadcrumb pudding

Garderobe: the toilet.

Gentleman: a nobleman. The term had nothing to do with character or behavior.

Gittern: a small, round-backed type of lute.

Groom: a household servant to a lord, ranking above a page and below a valet.

Hall: the chief room in a castle or manor house.

Heriot: an inheritance tax paid by an heir to a lord, usually the deceased's best animal.

Hypocras: spiced wine. Sugar, cinnamon, ginger, cloves, and nutmeg were often in the mix. Usually served at the end of a meal.

King's Eyre: a royal circuit court presided over by a traveling judge.

Lady: a title of rank for a female. As with "gentleman," it had nothing to do with character or behavior.

Lammastide: August 1, when thanks was given for a successful wheat harvest. From "Loaf mass".

Leach lombard: a dish of ground pork, eggs, raisins, currants, and dates with spices. The mixture was boiled in a sack until set, then sliced for serving.

Lombard stew: a pottage made with pork, onions, almonds, red wine, and spices.

Lychgate: a roofed gate in a churchyard under which the body of the deceased was rested during the initial part of a burial service.

Marshalsea: the stables and associated accoutrements.

Maslin: bread made with a mixture of grains, commonly wheat and rye or barley and rye.

Matins: the first of the day's eight canonical hours (services). Also called *lauds*.

Michaelmas: September 29. this feast signaled the end of harvest. Last rents and tithes for the year were due.

Mortrews: boiled pork ground to a paste and mixed with eggs, bread crumbs, and spices, then simmered briefly.

Mortuary: a fee paid to the village priest by the heirs of a deceased parishioner.

New year: take your pick! Most fourteenth century English celebrated 25 March as the beginning of a new year, but some of the wealthy gave New Year's gifts on 1 January.

Page: a young male servant, often a youth learning the arts of chivalry before becoming a squire.

Palfrey: a riding horse with a comfortable gait.

Passing bell: the ringing of the parish church bell to indicate the death of a villager.

Pax board: a wooden board, frequently painted with sacred scenes, which was passed through the church during a service for all to kiss.

Pears in compost: pears cooked in red wine with dates, sugar, and cinnamon.

Penny: the most common medieval English coin. Twelve pennies equaled a shilling, although there was no coin worth a shilling.

Pomm dorryse: meatballs made of ground pork, eggs, currants, flour, and spices.

Pork in egurdouce: pork served with a syrup of ground almonds, currants, dates, wine vinegar, sugar or honey, and spices.

Porre of peas: a thick pea soup made with onions, spices, and sugar.

Pottage: anything cooked in one pot, from soups and stews to a simple oat porridge.

Pottage wastere: a stew made with whelks, rice flour, ground almonds, and spices.

Pyx: a container for the host – the communion wafers.

Rebec: a fiddle with three strings played with a bow.

Reconquista: the liberation of the Iberian peninsula from Muslim conquerors.

Remove: a dinner course.

Reeve: an important manor official, although he did not outrank the bailiff. Elected by tenants from among themselves, often the best husbandman. He had responsibility for fields, buildings, and enforcing labor service.

Rice moyle: a rice pudding made with almond milk, sugar, and saffron.

Rood screen: an often elaborately carved screen separating the chancel and the nave.

Sackbut: an extended trumpet, like a trombone without a slide.

Scion: a new shoot sprouting from the base of a tree.

Shilling: the value of twelve pence, although there was no one shilling coin. Twenty shillings, or 240 pence, made one pound, although there was no one pound coin, either.

Sinister: the left-hand direction.

Solar: a small room in a castle, more easily heated than the hall, where lords preferred to spend time, especially in winter. Usually on an upper floor.

Sole in cyve: a popular fast day dish amongst the wealthy. Sole was served in a yellow onion sauce made with white wine, breadcrumbs, onions and spices.

Sops in fennel: bread toasted, cubed, then covered with a syrup of olive oil, fennel, onions, saffron, and sugar.

St. Beornwald's Church: today the church of St. Mary the Virgin. In the fourteenth century it was dedicated to this obscure Saxon saint who was said to be enshrined within the church.

Stewed herring: filleted herring, stuffed with breadcrumbs, parsley, thyme, pepper, currants, onions, and sugar.

Stockfish: the cheapest salted fish, usually cod or haddock.

Stone: fourteen pounds.

Subtlety: an elaborate confection, made more for show than for consumption.

Tenant: a free peasant who rented land from his lord. He could pay his rent in labor on the lord's demesne, or (more likely in the fourteenth century) in cash.

Toft: land surrounding a home often used for growing vegetables.

Valet: a high-ranking servant to a lord.

Verjuice: the sour juice of crab apples used to flavor pottages and beverages.

Vicar: a priest serving a parish but not entitled to its revenues.

Villein: a non-free peasant. He could not leave his land or service to his lord, or sell animals without permission. But if he could escape his manor for a year and a day he was free.

Void: dessert – often sugared fruits and wine.

Weald (the): a neighborhood to the immediate southwest of Bampton village, a possession of the Bishop of Exeter.

Week work: the two or three days of labor per week (more during harvest) which a villein owed his lord.

Whitsunday: White Sunday – ten days after Ascension Day, seven weeks after Easter. Pentecost Sunday.

Yardland: thirty acres. Also called a *virgate* and in northern England an *oxgang*.

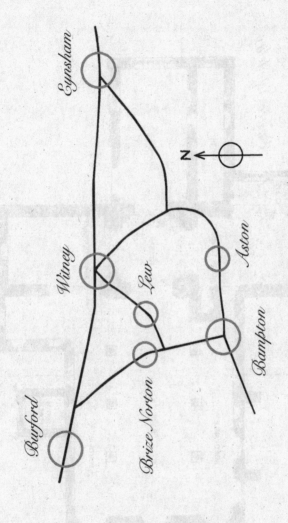

Eynsham

Witney

Lew

Aston

Bampton

Burford

Brize Norton

N

13

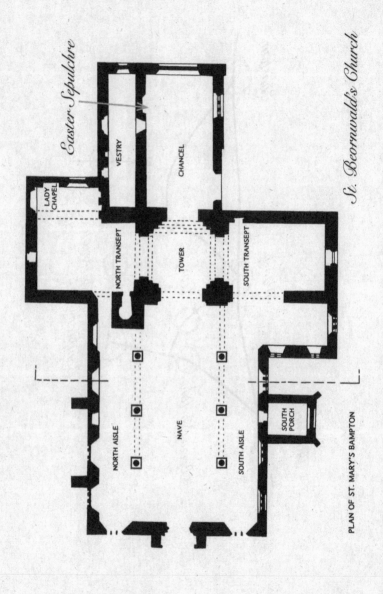

Easter Sepulchre

St. Beornwald's Church

VESTRY

CHANCEL

LADY CHAPEL

NORTH TRANSEPT

TOWER

SOUTH TRANSEPT

NORTH AISLE

NAVE

SOUTH AISLE

SOUTH PORCH

PLAN OF ST. MARY'S BAMPTON

14

Chapter 1

John was feverish and so was my Kate, so I attended the Maundy Thursday mass with only Bessie to keep me company. The new year had begun but a few days before, and the calendar said that spring was to be in the air. The calendar lied. A low sky spat frozen rain upon my fur coat as Bessie and I hurried to St. Beornwald's Church.

Father Simon placed the host into the pyx as the service concluded, and Bessie and I scurried home to escape the hard pellets of ice that stung our cheeks. The year of our Lord 1374 had begun badly. It was sure to improve. I have been wrong before.

I returned to the church alone for vespers on Good Friday. Bessie and John – Bessie is nine, and John but an infant – regularly pass coughs and dripping noses back and forth. This time 'twas John's turn to send a flush to Bessie's cheeks and redness to her nose.

When the mass was completed, Father Thomas took the host from the pyx, wrapped it in a linen cloth, and placed it, along with a crucifix, within the Easter Sepulchre where, like the Lord Christ, it would remain buried 'til Easter morn.

The Easter Sepulchre at St. Beornwald's Church is unlike that of St. Anne's Church in Little Singleton, where I was born. The church there is small and plain, as is the Easter Sepulchre. 'Tis but a wooden frame covered with a linen cloth, as a burial shroud, whereas the Easter Sepulchre at St. Beornwald's Church is a niche in the north wall of the chancel. Inside the niche is the wooden structure where host and crucifix may be placed, then the whole covered by a cloth deftly embroidered with scenes of our Lord Christ's passion.

John Younge, St. Beornwald's sexton, moved to the chancel as Father Ralph and Father Simon joined Father Thomas at the Easter Sepulchre to light candles. The chancel was soon glowing.

'Twas John Younge's duty, along with the priests' clerks, to keep watch over the Easter Sepulchre 'til Easter morn. This was a great honor, he had told me a few days earlier. Alone in the church, the nave and aisles dark but the chancel bathed in candlelight, a man might inspect his soul for the betterment of the days remaining to him. Younge would serve the first watch of the night. I saw him from the porch as I departed the church, standing squarely before the Easter Sepulchre, arms folded across his chest, determined in his duty.

* * *

Kate's rooster woke me at dawn on Saturday, as he does each morn, competing for the honor with the Angelus Bell ringing from the tower of St. Beornwald's Church. Had he not, the pounding upon the door of Galen House moments later would have. I crawled from our warm bed, my joints complaining – they never used to – drew on chauces and cotehardie, and stumbled down the stairs.

'Twas Father Thomas who had bruised his knuckles upon my door. When I opened it he said abruptly, without a greeting, "Odo's gone missing. We've searched the church, but he's not to be found."

"Your clerk?" I said stupidly, because so far as I know no other Odo resides in Bampton or the Weald.

"Aye... Odo."

"Was he not one of the watchers at the Easter Sepulchre?"

"Aye. He was to attend to the duty after John."

"He did not do so?"

"He did. Peter Bouchard said Odo arrived to take up his post in good time, but when Ernaud went to ring the dawn Angelus and replace Odo, my clerk was not there."

"Perhaps he left his duty early, when he heard Ernaud ring the Angelus Bell? He would know that his replacement was present within the church."

"Nay. Ernaud saw from the base of the tower that Odo was not where he should be before he rang for the Angelus devotional.

Father Simon arrived moments later to conduct the devotional and together they called out for him, Ernaud said, but there was no reply."

"'Twas a cold night," I said. "Perhaps he became chilled and sought his bed."

"So I thought, and went to his chamber to reprimand him. If the Lord Christ could die for Odo's sins the fellow could withstand a cold night for but a few hours to do honor to his Savior. But he was not there. His bed was cold."

Here was a puzzle. 'Tis an honor to stand guard at the Easter Sepulchre, and one that John Younge and Peter Bouchard, Ernaud le Tournier, and Odo Fuller – sexton and clerks – defend vigorously. Others of Bampton, good men and true, have volunteered to watch, but these four will not share the honor.

"You have begun to search for Odo?" I said.

"Aye. Ernaud and Father Simon came to me and Father Ralph. I combed the church and when 'twas light enough examined the churchyard. He was not there. Where might he be?"

"Where indeed!" I replied. My wits were gradually returning after being roused from my bed so precipitously, but not so much that I could devise a response to Father Thomas's question.

I stood in the doorway scratching my head, which was empty of intelligent thought, when Kate came down the stairs behind me. Her hair, the color of an oak leaf in autumn, had been hastily tucked into her linen kerchief.

"Might he have visited the tithe barn?" she said. She had heard our conversation and now offered a solution. "Did he need to replenish stores at your vicarage?"

Father Thomas stroked his beard and spoke. "Mayhap, m'lady. Alan, my cook, cares for that usually. But I will question him. He may have asked Odo to do an errand for him."

"But you think not," I said.

Alan had not done so, and as with all others we spoke to that morning had no thought as to where Odo might be.

By the third hour the church, churchyard, tithe barn, and vicarages had been searched over and again. Odo was not found.

I told Father Thomas that I intended to return to Galen House, break my fast with a loaf and ale, then seek the castle and bring back with me some of Lord Gilbert's grooms so as to widen the search.

* * *

I am Hugh de Singleton – Sir Hugh, since Prince Edward saw fit to offer me a knighthood for services I rendered to him – surgeon and bailiff to Lord Gilbert, Third Baron Talbot. Lord Gilbert had returned to Bampton Castle but a fortnight past, after spending the winter at Goodrich, another of his possessions.

When I walked under the castle portcullis I saw Lord Gilbert striding toward the castle marshalsea. Lord Gilbert enjoys a good meal, and that, along with practice in the arts of war, has given him a brawny form. His face is brown from looking into the sun from the back of a dexter. He has skilled pages, grooms, and farriers to care for his horses, but as with most of his class considers himself an expert judge of beasts, their care, and their ailments. No doubt he intended to peer over some stable groom's shoulder.

I hailed my employer and hastened to where he stood awaiting me. If I intended to take half a dozen or so of his grooms from the castle to seek Odo Fuller I should tell him why.

"Father Thomas's clerk, you say?" Lord Gilbert said when I told him of the missing man. "Has he ever shirked his duty in the past?"

"Not that I've heard. Father Thomas is a friend, and has confided in me in the past, but has never complained of Odo's work or his loyalty. Indeed, if the clerk had given him reason to do so the priest would have sent him packing and Odo would be seeking other employment."

"True enough. Father Thomas is not one to suffer incompetence," Lord Gilbert agreed. "Well, take whom you need, and inform me when you find the fellow. Must be somewhere near."

With that conclusion he bade me good day and continued toward the stables. I sought Arthur Wagge, a groom in Lord

Gilbert's service who had proven himself useful to me in seeking felons and suchlike rogues in the past, and Uctred, another groom who had also been of assistance. I found Arthur with two other grooms at the castle sawpit, where the three of them were sawing planks for an extension to the castle larder. No doubt they were pleased to be released from this arduous labor. I told Arthur to find Uctred and two more grooms, then the six of them were to proceed posthaste to St. Beornwald's Church. And I told him why. Arthur tugged a forelock and set off to find Uctred. I hastened from the castle, crossed the bridge over Shill Brook without stopping to gaze into the stream – a thing I often do – and went to the church.

Priests, clerks, and sexton were milling about the porch, exchanging suggestions as to where Odo might be and why he would be there. When I came near I told them that six of Lord Gilbert's grooms would soon arrive and we must organize a search that would see the entire village examined.

When Arthur, Uctred, and four others appeared, I sent the searchers out in pairs, as what one man might disregard, the other might see. With Father Thomas I divided Bampton among the searchers so that no place would be overlooked while some other street or house or barn might be examined twice. The searchers were told to assemble at the church with their reports when the noon Angelus sounded.

Peter rang the noon Angelus as Arthur and I walked under the lychgate and into the churchyard. Father Simon and Father Ralph and their clerks had preceded us, and Uctred and the other three of Lord Gilbert's grooms soon appeared. No trace of Odo had been found; no inhabitants of Bampton nor the Weald had seen the clerk since Friday.

"Has Odo enemies?" I asked Father Thomas. "Mayhap he has not gone away, but some other has done him harm."

"What enemies would a clerk make?" the priest replied, shaking his head. "Odo was honest with me and, so far as I know, with all men."

"Honesty is known to cause trouble," I replied. "There are men who prefer deceit. Has Odo had reason to consort with deceitful folk, either willingly or unwillingly, so that they might despise his truthfulness?"

"Not that I know of. He'd have spoken of it to me, I think, had he done so. His life was this church and service to it, and to me. How would such a life bring Odo into conflict with evil men? That is your thinking, is it not? That Odo has not gone off of his own choice, but some other man has had a hand in his disappearance?

"And if some rogue did injure or slay Odo, would there not be some sign of the evil in the chancel? He was there, we know, when he took Peter's place at the Easter Sepulchre. He would not have departed the chancel and ignored his duty for some light reason."

"We have not sought any sign that harm came to Odo while he stood guard," I said. "Such a thought did not occur to me, or to you, I think. Why should it? What mischief could come to a lowly clerk as he stood watch at the Easter Sepulchre? Mayhap it is time we considered that possibility."

Father Thomas spun on his heels and entered the porch, but I grasped his arm and said, "Wait. Many men have already stood about the chancel and before the Easter Sepulchre. If more of us do so, whatever sign there is of evil done to Odo may be obscured, if 'tis not already."

"What do you intend?" Father Thomas said.

"I would like to examine the chancel alone. The sky is beginning to lighten, and the candles also provide light. Windows and flames may permit discovery of things not seen or expected this morning."

"Very well. I see your point. I and Father Ralph and Father Simon will observe from the rood screen while you search the chancel."

They did – as did Arthur, Uctred, and the other grooms. These fellows felt themselves a part of the mystery and were interested now in seeing the matter to its conclusion.

I walked past the rood screen and cautiously peered at the flags before my feet. Stone does not preserve footprints. I cannot say what I thought I might discover there on the floor of the chancel, but whatever it might have been I did not at first find it. This elicited sighs of disappointment from behind the rood screen. However, undeterred, I decided to give it a second pass. This time, as I slowly walked past the Easter Sepulchre I saw, between the sepulchre and the high altar, a tiny dark dot upon the flags before the altar. The speck was about the size of the nail upon my little finger. 'Twas no wonder neither I nor any other had taken note of it in the dim light of early morn. Even the flames of a dozen or so candles would not make the spot plain to a casual observer.

I kneeled for a closer look and from the rood screen Father Thomas said, "What have you found?"

"I am unsure," I replied. As I spoke I remembered that in Galen House I had a tool which might allow me to better examine the spot before my eyes. I stood, walked to the rood screen, and spoke to those who stood near it.

"I must go to Galen House, but will return anon. Please allow no man to enter the chancel. There is a mark upon the flags which is suspicious and I have at Galen House an instrument which may help me learn what is there."

The speck was dark brown and I feared it was a dried drop of blood. The past summer I had seen Master John Wycliffe and Abbot Gerleys of Eynsham Abbey using a glass that enlarged the letters upon a page. I had purchased one of these lenses, and now it occurred to me that the instrument might allow me to better identify the stain I had found.

"Have you found the clerk?" Kate asked as I entered my home.

"Nay, and I fear we may not."

"You may not? Why so?"

"I may have found a drop of dried blood near to where Odo would have stood while watching over the Easter Sepulchre last night."

"You may have? How will you know?"

"I have come for the glass I bought last summer. It may tell me what my eyes alone cannot."

The glass was within my chest in our chamber. I hurried up the stairs, withdrew the glass, and clattered back down again. Kate was where I had left her, at the door, a worried expression upon her face. Perhaps she was anxious that I would do myself some injury if I did not take more care upon the stairs.

"Will you return soon for your dinner?" Kate asked. "I have prepared stewed herring and rice moyle."

Until Kate spoke of it I had not thought of my empty stomach, being too much involved with the matter of Odo Fuller's disappearance.

"I will not be long," I said.

At the church I produced my glass and Father Thomas spoke. "I've heard of such things, but I've never seen one before."

"The work of the devil," Father Ralph said. "Making of things what they are not."

"Nonsense," Father Thomas replied. "The words on a page are not made other than what they are by being enlarged so that men of great years may yet read them. I wear shoes so as to protect my feet and make them more useful. Are shoes the devil's work also? I warm myself at the fire. Shoes and fire are man's creation. God did not light these candles the better that we may see. Men did. You suggest that what men can create is the work of Satan?"

Father Ralph sniffed in reply but said no more.

I passed the rood screen and bent to find the speck upon the flags. 'Twas not readily visible, but after a moment's searching I saw it, dropped to my knees, and held the glass over the spot. With a fingernail I cautiously scratched at the dried matter and watched through the glass as some of it flaked away. Here was a reddish-brown drop of dried blood, I was sure of it. The glass helped make clear what I had suspected.

One drop of blood. If Odo was slain here (if indeed he had been slain – and I hoped not) then why so little gore? Certainly he was not stabbed. Had this been so he would have left his blood spattered about. Strangled? Then there would have been no bloodstain at all. Struck upon his head? Aye, that would answer. A blow upon a man's skull might slay him and cause little bleeding. If Odo was knocked upon his head, what was the weapon? A felon might take his club with him after his evil deed, and that would likely mean he had entered the church intent upon striking Odo down, and so brought the weapon to the church with him. I glanced about the chancel and high altar, peering into dim recesses, and even opened the door to the vestry. But that chamber had already been searched in the morning and I found nothing new.

My eyes were drawn to the altar, and the two great candlesticks there. They were silver, heavy, and costly; a gift to the Church of St. Beornwald from Sir Aymer de Valence many years past. The candles upon these candlesticks were lit, providing light as I approached them. A blow from one of these could propel a man into the next world. They were as long and thick as my arm.

"What do you see?" Father Thomas asked.

"There is a speck of blood upon the chancel flags."

"Then some evil has happened here."

A glance at the candlesticks told me nothing. To more closely examine them I would have to extinguish the candles so that I might handle and turn the candlesticks in the light of the windows and other candles illuminating the chancel. I did so, and at the base of the first candlestick I lifted I found another brown smudge, and a hair.

"Come," I said to Father Thomas. "Odo has been struck down."

The priest hurried to where I stood at the high altar.

"Look here." I pointed to the base of the candlestick. This is blood. And Odo is fair-haired, is he not?"

"Aye, he is."

"Do you see the hair caught in the blood? 'Tis not dark."

"It is difficult to know," Father Thomas said, "from just one hair. But it does seem the hue of Odo's hair. What has happened here?"

"It seems some man struck Odo down while he stood watch at the Easter Sepulchre," I said.

"But where then is he? Did his assailant drag him away? Was he perhaps smitten unconscious, but forced to accompany his attacker? Or was he slain? If so, where is his corpse?"

These were all laudable questions, for which I had no answers.

"Here is another question," I said. "How would some man enter the chancel, filled with light as it was from the candles, and seize a heavy candlestick with which he could then strike Odo? The clerk would surely have seen the man enter."

Father Thomas glanced about him, as if to reassure himself that what I said was so.

"It must be," the priest finally said, "that whoso attacked Odo – if this is truly what happened – was known to him."

"I agree, unless Odo was dozing and did not see or hear his attacker enter. Odo is a small man, and not accustomed to labor or combat. A large man might overwhelm him, I think."

"Aye," Father Thomas agreed. "And even if Odo thought himself in danger he would not forsake his duty to stand guard at the Easter Sepulchre. He was not a man to shirk an obligation, especially an obligation to the Lord Christ."

"Was not a man? Already we speak of him in the past," I said.

"The blood upon the floor and candlestick causes me to believe his life is ended," the priest said. "If I am wrong, why can we not find him? If he lives, why has he not shown himself? Would some man bludgeon him over the head, then drag him away and keep him hidden but alive?"

"I can think of no reason for doing so," I said.

"Neither can I," Father Thomas agreed.

We spent the remainder of the day – but for the two other clerks and John Younge, who returned to watching over the Easter Sepulchre and occasionally glancing over their shoulders – searching for Odo Fuller.

We might not have troubled ourselves. Odo was found the next day, Easter. But unlike the Lord Christ he had not risen from the dead.

CHAPTER 2

Easter Sunday dawned clear, as is appropriate for such a day of joy, and Kate's rooster outdid himself in exuberance. But when we departed Galen House for the church 'twas yet cold, so Kate bundled Bessie and John against the chill. She was determined that above all days, disregarding coughs and dripping noses, our family would worship the risen Christ together.

We were not alone. A parade of Bampton townsfolk joined us on Church View Street and filled the nave of St. Beornwald's Church. It was clear to all in attendance that Odo Fuller was not present to accompany Father Thomas as he and the other vicars of St. Beornwald – Father Simon and Father Ralph – as well as their respective clerks, entered the chancel from the vestry and approached the Easter Sepulchre. Most folk of Bampton knew of the clerk's disappearance, having been asked by those of us who had scoured the town the previous day whether they had seen Odo.

Father Simon approached the velvet curtain that had covered the Easter Sepulchre since Good Friday. He drew aside the curtain to bring forth the host and crucifix, but instead stepped back and stumbled to his well-padded rump. A muffled gasp came from several dozen throats as those in the nave who could see past the tower and rood screen to the chancel saw the priest fall.

I saw Father Simon rise, speak to Father Thomas, and point to the Easter Sepulchre, but due to the murmuring of congregants in the nave I could not hear his words. Father Thomas turned to follow Father Simon's pointing finger, as did Father Ralph. The two priests stood as if frozen. They crossed themselves as they gazed into the Easter Sepulchre.

Father Thomas turned from the Easter Sepulchre and approached the nave. His eyes darted about the congregation, and settled upon me. He gestured vigorously that I should join him. Doing so required much pushing and shoving, as other

25

folk had begun to realize that all was not as it should be and were clustered at the base of the tower, the better to see into the chancel.

I stepped past the rood screen and Father Thomas grasped my arm.

"'Tis Odo," he whispered. "Within the Easter Sepulchre."

I did not ask whether alive or dead. I knew. Some man had delivered a blow to the clerk's pate with a candlestick, then hidden the corpse where it would not be found for many hours. We had combed the church and village seeking Odo while his corpse lay under our noses. Who would commit such sacrilege as to conceal a corpse in such a holy place? The same person who would slay another, made in the image of God. In all our searching for Odo it had not occurred to me to draw aside the curtain and peer into the Easter Sepulchre. I could not conceive of such blasphemy as to hide a corpse there.

His hand yet grasping my arm, Father Thomas drew me to the Easter Sepulchre. I saw there, below the wooden frame upon which host and crucifix rested, the black-clad form of a man bent to a fetal position. I could not see the man's face for 'twas pressed against the wall. But I knew, as did the priests, who this must be. Who else of Bampton or the Weald had gone missing?

"Shall he be drawn out?" Father Thomas asked. "Or do you wish to examine him as he now is?"

I could see no value in crawling over the corpse and under the wooden frame. What would I see that I could not see better if Odo were pulled out flat upon the chancel floor?

Father Thomas told the clerks, Peter and Ernaud, to lift Odo from the Easter Sepulchre. I doubted this was a task they thought they would perform when they assumed their vocations. The clerks hesitated, looking to each other as if hoping the work might be avoided. It could not be. The priests were not about to go upon hands and knees to drag the corpse from the enclosure. The clerks reluctantly did so.

When Odo's body was laid out upon the flags 'twas plain to all who stood over it what had caused his death. A dent above

26

his right ear was surely the result of a blow that had caved in the clerk's skull. I knelt beside the injury for a closer look.

"What do you see?" Father Thomas said. "Is there a clue to who has done this?"

"Nay. I thought perhaps we might learn if the felon was right- or left-handed by the location of the wound, but not so. The dent is at the side of Odo's head, not front or back."

"I don't understand."

"If Odo was struck from behind, the assailant was right-handed. If from the front, the felon was left-handed."

"Ah."

"Most men," I said, "are right-handed. So it is likely your clerk was struck down from behind."

"He turned his back to some enemy?"

"Perhaps his back was turned while he was looking at something else and he was unaware that someone had crept up on him. Or, possibly, his back was turned to some man he thought a friend. Would you turn your back to a foe if you knew he was there?"

"But why would a friend slay Odo?"

"Not a friend, but perhaps a man Odo thought was a friend."

"There is a difference," Father Thomas agreed. "Men may be duplicitous, appearing to be a friend when actually consumed with hate and vitriol. But who could hate Odo so much that he would do such a thing?"

"He was your clerk. You would know better than any other who might have done this murder."

Father Thomas raised his palms and silently looked about him. He glanced to Father Ralph and Father Simon, their clerks, and then to the press of faces beyond the rood screen. Onlookers had fallen silent in the presence of death. I saw Kate, holding John, among the congregation. Her face was white and drawn. Bessie I could not see; she was hidden behind the legs of the shocked assembly.

"Had Odo anything upon his person worth stealing?" I asked. "Did he wear a chain about his neck, or own a ring another man might covet?"

27

"Nay," Father Thomas replied. "Odo was a simple man, content with his station and his few possessions."

Why will a man take the life of another? Revenge for some slight or past evil done. Greed. Jealousy. A fit of passing anger. An accident. The desire to possess what another has. I considered these and cast them aside as motives for the murder of Odo Fuller. But if not these, what, then? One must certainly be true.

As far as Father Thomas knew, the clerk had no enemies who sought revenge against him. He owned nothing worth stealing. What man would be jealous of a celibate clerk? Assuming Odo was faithful to his vow. What if Odo had interrupted some other felony and perished because he tried to stop an evil directed at some other? Or at some thing? Was there another man keeping watch Friday night at the Easter Sepulchre? As far as I knew there was no rule prohibiting other men from joining the duty. Did Odo die trying to prevent an attack upon another? If so, the intended victim would know the slayer. Why would such a man remain silent when he, as all of Bampton, would know that Odo was missing and assiduously sought? I dismissed the thought and considered alternative scenarios.

Might Odo have died trying to prevent theft? What in St. Beornwald's Church might a man steal? The two great candlesticks that had adorned the high altar for many years had not been taken. Indeed, one of them had been used to slay Odo, then set again in its accustomed place. What of the other candles and their stands? More than a dozen had been lit two days past to illumine the chancel and Easter Sepulchre. I had not counted, but surmised the number. I turned to Father Thomas.

"How many candlesticks were brought to light the chancel upon Good Friday?"

The priest was dazed at the sight of his clerk stretched out upon the flags. My words brought him back to the present time and place.

"Uh... how many?" Father Thomas looked to his fellows for assistance.

28

Father Ralph spoke. "Peter and I brought three."

I looked to Father Simon, who said, "Ernaud and I provided two."

"Odo and I supplied two candles also," Father Thomas added.

"And how many, other than the two great candlesticks upon the altar, and the additional ones you brought in, are found within the church at all times?" I asked.

"Twelve," Father Ralph replied. "For the twelve apostles."

"Were these of silver, or some more base metal?"

"A few were silver. Most were pewter," the priest replied. "Three were wooden."

I addressed the priests together. "So nineteen candles lighted the chancel Friday evening when John Younge took the first watch, not including the great candlesticks upon the altar. How many are present now?"

The priests, clerks, and I peered about the chancel. I watched Father Simon count upon his fingers. Few of the congregation had departed the nave. Those closest to the rood screen could surely hear the words we in the chancel spoke, and could see Odo's corpse stretched upon the stony floor. I saw some of the watchers also counting candles.

"I count sixteen candles," the clerk Peter announced.

"Fifteen," Father Thomas replied.

Ernaud and Father Ralph spoke next. "Sixteen," they said, nearly in unison.

"Aye," Father Simon agreed. "Sixteen."

"I will count again," Father Thomas said.

My count was also sixteen, but I, the clerks, and the other two vicars waited 'til Father Thomas completed his count.

"I was amiss. Sixteen candles remain. Three are missing."

"They will not be the wooden candlesticks," I said, "nor even pewter. Silver will be gone, and likely the better, larger silver candlesticks. You will recognize those that appertain to the church, and those you brought to add to the number. Inspect the candlesticks remaining and see if the missing can be identified."

They were. Two of the missing candlesticks were possessions of St. Beornwald's Church. The third was not a candlestick at all but a fine silver cresset belonging to Father Ralph, which he had set upon a stand in the chancel Friday at noon.

"Was it a thief who did this murder, then?" Father Thomas said. "All men knew Odo would likely be alone in the small hours of the night, with much valuable silver surrounding him."

"So it seems," I replied. "But I wonder that the felon took but two candlesticks and the cresset. He could likely have carried away more, especially if he came to the church intending the theft. He might have supplied himself with a sack and got away with nearly all of the silver candlesticks."

"He did not come with a weapon," Father Thomas observed. "Else he would not have needed to use one of the great altar candlesticks to strike down Odo."

Here was a puzzle. The vicar spoke true. If the felon came to the church intending theft why had he no weapon with which to threaten and subdue Odo? Or did he arrive armed with, perhaps, a dagger, but chose rather to smite Odo with the heavy candlestick rather than pierce him?

Had Odo been stabbed, there would have been a great pool of blood upon the chancel floor to tell of the felony, and a trail of gore would have led to the Easter Sepulchre. The blow to Odo's skull had left but one small drop of blood – at least only one that could be found. The slayer may have cleaned away what other bloodstains he caused. But with what?

I glanced over Father Ralph's shoulder and saw my Kate peering anxiously past the rood screen. John wriggled in her arms as if discomfited and I saw Bessie's head, as my lass pushed between those who crowded against the rood screen, eager to see what strange activity her father was about.

Kate could see Odo's corpse upon the flags and knew that I would be tasked with discovering the cause of this death and the perpetrator. There was little reason for her to stand gazing into the chancel when I would return to Galen House in due course and tell her all. At that moment John sneezed. The explosion caused the infant to cry out and tug at his ear. This seemed to lend resolution to Kate's mind. She caught my eye, nodded toward the porch, took Bessie's hand, and retreated through the mob of gawkers. When I returned to Galen House I would make a compound to soothe the little lad.

Lord Gilbert was not present, being accustomed to attending mass in the castle chapel – even at Eastertide – with his valets and grooms, his chaplain conducting the worship. He must be told of the murder, so I sent Ernaud to the castle to inform him and invite his presence at the scene if he chose to attend. He did not. He had noble guests it would not be politic to abandon. Instead he replied that he expected to receive a full report as soon as possible.

Odo lay upon his back, unmoved since Peter and Ernaud had dragged the corpse from the Easter Sepulchre. This thought caused me to glance into the niche. The host and crucifix lay untouched. No man, vicar, clerk, or layman was now interested in ceremony.

The three vicars stood silent, resting their weight first upon one foot, then the other. Each seemed to await instruction from the others. Their hesitancy was understandable. How many priests have the experience of opening an Easter Sepulchre to a corpse?

Father Thomas finally broke the silence. "Odo must be washed and prepared for burial. John, seek a pallet and with Peter take him to my vicarage. Odo has no female relations near. I will ask Mariot and Beatrice to do this."

Mariot is the wife of Bartram Thrupp, Father Thomas's cook, and Beatrice is the sexton's wife.

Onlookers in the nave heard Father Thomas's instructions, understood that the celebration of the mass was concluded before it had begun, and that the likelihood of further excitement had diminished. They began to drift away, some lingering in the churchyard to exchange opinions of what they had seen and heard.

While the sexton was away seeking a pallet I knelt beside the corpse for one further examination. I sought some sign of struggle which in my first examination I might have missed. I found what I sought.

What I had assumed to be dirt under Odo's fingernails was dried blood. Two nails upon the right hand had scored some man deeply enough to draw blood – likely upon his face. Father Thomas saw me hesitate as I examined the dead man's right hand. "What have you found?" he asked.

"Somewhere there is a man with two parallel scratches across his cheek deep enough to draw blood. Look here."

I held Odo's right hand before Father Thomas and pointed out the dark stain beneath the nails. The other two vicars also bent to examine the dried blood.

"All we need do," Father Ralph said, "is seek some man of Bampton or the Weald whose cheek is disfigured and we will have the felon. 'Twill be his left cheek, or I miss my guess."

This conclusion seemed reasonable.

John Younge arrived with a pallet, then he and Peter Bouchard placed Odo's corpse upon it and departed for Father Thomas's vicarage. All within the chancel crossed themselves again as the dead clerk was taken away.

All this time the crucifix and host had remained within the Easter Sepulchre. Father Ralph retrieved the objects and laid them respectfully upon the altar as Father Thomas followed his deceased clerk through the nave to the porch, thence to leave the church. Father Simon, Father Ralph, and I were the last to depart the church, our footsteps echoing through the empty nave.

CHAPTER 3

I hurried to Galen House for two reasons: my concern for my infant son, and my empty belly. I wished to make a preparation of the crushed leaves of hound's-tongue in oil of lavender to soothe the child, and I had enjoyed no loaf this morning to break my fast.

Kate and Adela our servant had prepared leach lombard, and as I sat at our table Kate sliced a thick wedge of the ground pork and fruit confection for my dinner. There was also a wheaten loaf with parsley butter, and ale the baker's wife had fresh-brewed. When the meal was done I was content. Even John and Bessie seemed comforted, although my Kate was yet puffy-eyed, red of nose, and feverish. She ate but a small portion of the leach lombard.

I had hired Adela to assist Kate after Prince Edward knighted me and gave me a sixth part of the revenues of a deceased knight, Sir Giles Cheyenne, whose murderers I had discovered. Adela is the oldest daughter of a poor cotter of the Weald. Her mother has taught her well the domestic arts and she is a great help to Kate. She will be a good wife to some young man, but I hope that day does not arrive too soon, else I must find another servant.

Kate protested, but I sent her to bed after dinner, declaring that Adela was quite competent to care for Bessie and John while I conferred with Father Thomas regarding the search for Odo's slayer.

I departed Galen House leaving instructions for Adela to put Bessie and John to their beds for naps. I found Father Thomas and the other vicars and clerks making plans for a wake. The bishops frown upon the feasting and drinking of such events, but carousing at such a time is a custom difficult to expunge, and I suppose Father Thomas assumed the Bishop of Exeter, within whose diocese Bampton and the Weald are found, would not learn of the revelry so long as matters did not get out of hand.

As Odo was a clerk he had little wealth with which to pay the vicars and their curates to pray his soul from purgatory. Perhaps the Lord Christ will overlook the lack. Or perhaps there is no such place. For services I rendered Eynsham Abbey some years past the abbot presented me with a Bible. I have read the book through several times and find within it no mention of purgatory. I must write no more of this matter. The bishops would be displeased to learn of my views, and an unhappy bishop is capable of great mischief, especially if his revenues are in danger, as they would be if men no longer believed it necessary to hire priests to pray them or other folk out of purgatory and into heaven.

"We will keep careful watch this evening," Father Thomas said, "when folk come for Odo's wake, and tomorrow at his funeral, for any man with reddened marks across his cheek. Such an injury will soon heal. We must seize the felon quickly, before it does."

I agreed with the assessment. The trail of a felon, like pottage over an untended fire, soon grows cold. Discovering who slew Odo Fuller was the vicar's responsibility more than mine. Odo served under the Bishop of Exeter through Father Thomas. The Church of St. Beornwald, its vicars and curates and clerks, minister to the folk of Bampton, as do I, but are not of my bailiwick.

Even death will not completely alter the routine of worship. I had heard the noon Angelus Bell ring, and as the sun dropped below Lord Gilbert's forest to the west, Ernaud went to the church to ring for the evening Angelus. Father Simon accompanied him to conduct the brief devotional. Both men soon returned to Father Thomas's vicarage, and residents of Bampton and the Weald followed. The house could not contain all who appeared. The overflow spilled into the toft, men and women drinking Father Thomas's ale and consuming loaves his cook had procured from Osbert Baker. Too much ale soon led to raucous jesting and twice an exchange of blows. Little harm was done. Drunken men seldom have the wit to aim their fists well.

When loaves and ale were all consumed, the merriment ended and folk staggered off to their homes. 'Twas near to midnight, well past curfew, when the last of the revelers disappeared into darkened streets. Bampton's beadle had attended the wake so knew why folk were prowling about in the dark.

All the time during the wake I had watched those who attended and saw no man whose face bore marks drawn across a cheek. I told Father Thomas of this before I departed for Galen House and my bed.

"I also watched for such wounds," the vicar said. "I saw nothing. Perhaps the man knew the scratches would identify him so did not attend. Or in the darkness we missed the injury."

"Aye, perhaps. 'Twill be daylight tomorrow. A man with a lacerated cheek will not be able to hide it as at night, and if he does not attend Odo's funeral we may have there a clue."

"Aye. We may seek those who do not attend, to learn if any one of them shows sign of meeting Odo's fingernails."

* * *

Odo had no female mourners to wail after his corpse as it was taken from the vicarage next morning to the lychgate. The procession was therefore mostly silent, although no less doleful. As there was no free ale, there were fewer mourners following the corpse to the church and it was difficult to list and remember those who did not attend. But of those who did, and those who did not (whom I and the vicars later examined), none showed evidence of Odo's fingernails slashed across his face.

After the mass, John Younge and two others set to work with spades in the churchyard at a sun-drenched place where Father Thomas had sprinkled holy water to indicate where Odo's grave would be. The spot was but a few paces from my father-in-law's burial place. Robert Caxton died nine months past and Kate yet grieves his loss. My parents died when plague first came to England many years ago, and Kate's mother died when Kate was a lass. So now Bessie and John have no grandparents to dote on them and bounce them upon a knee.

I departed the churchyard with the other mourners while John Younge and his assistants filled Odo's grave. I intended to return to my home, consume my dinner, and resume the obligations I owed Lord Gilbert. The vicars of the Church of St. Beornwald could seek a felon as well as I, and considering that the slain man was in holy orders and his death took place within a church 'twas the church that must seek justice.

* * *

Wednesday about the second hour I was sharing a maslin loaf and cheese with my Kate – whose fever and chills were much reduced – when Father Thomas again pounded upon the door of Galen House.

"Have you news of Odo's slayer?" I said when I opened to the priest.

"Aye. We have taken a man to the castle and Sir Henry has placed him in the dungeon 'til he may be taken to the bishop's court in Exeter."

"Who is under arrest?"

"Ernaud... May I come in?"

I had forgotten myself for interest in the solution to Odo Fuller's murder. I invited the vicar into my hall, motioned to a bench, and called to Adela for two cups of ale.

"Ernaud? What is the evidence against him?" I asked as Adela brought the ale.

Father Thomas lifted the cup to his lips, rolled the liquid about his mouth, then in seeming approval swallowed.

"He claims innocence."

"Of course. Why would he slay another clerk?"

"I do not know that. But there is some evidence that points to him. Father Simon found the missing candlesticks buried in the toft behind his vicarage. He noticed freshly turned earth and wondered at it, for he had not yet plied a spade to ready the soil for onions and cabbages and such, which he should have done some weeks past. Nor had Ernaud or any servant, to his knowledge."

36

"Ah, the missing candlesticks! And Father Simon believes that Ernaud buried them there?"

"Aye, that's what is believed."

"So you are suggesting that if Ernaud is indeed guilty of such a felony the motive might simply have been greed?" I asked.

"So it seems."

"It seems? So, what other motive might he have had? If indeed he is the felon..."

Father Thomas's eyes narrowed. "Indeed. There is surely more to consider. Ernaud is no fool. Would he slay a man for silver candlesticks then bury the loot where it could be so readily discovered?"

"He was there, in the chancel," I said, "when we counted the candlesticks and learned that two, and the cresset bowl, were missing."

"He was. So he would have known we would seek the stolen silver."

"Was the cresset found also?"

"Nay. No sign of the cresset bowl."

"Why not sneak off in the night and bury the loot some place where it could be safely hid," I suggested, "in a ditch off Bushy Row or in the forest beyond the tithe barn?"

"Just so."

"Ernaud, you said, is no fool. But even wise men occasionally do foolish things. The most profound Oxford scholar can look back upon his youth and recall deeds he laments... and some lamentable deeds more recent."

"I do not disagree," Father Thomas said, then fell silent.

"You have more to say, have you not?" I said after several moments of silence.

"Aye. I do not believe Ernaud slew Odo."

"Why not? Is there conflicting evidence?"

"Some. Ernaud's cheeks are unmarred. There is no sign that Odo fought against him if Ernaud is the guilty man. Might you have been wrong about what you found under Odo's fingernails? On the other hand, more than where the candlesticks were found is the truth that Odo and Ernaud were not friends."

"Not friends? You mean they were enemies?"

"Nay. Neither friends nor enemies. I have heard them disagree upon matters, but never to the point where one abused the other. Not within my hearing. But if one held a view of some matter, the other was certain to dissent."

"Did Peter and Odo also quarrel?"

"Nay. Both Peter and Odo seemed amenable fellows when in the company of others. And Ernaud and Peter had no animosity one for the other that I ever saw or heard."

"But Ernaud disliked Odo, they often disagreed, and the silver candlesticks were found in the toft behind Father Simon's vicarage. Does Father Simon believe his clerk slew Odo?" I asked.

"Aye, he does."

"The silver was found behind his vicarage. You said Ernaud protests innocence. What of Father Simon? Did he have some grudge against Odo?"

"Oh, nay. Father Simon has malice toward no man."

"Not even those who may have done him some evil?"

"Hmmm. Perhaps. But I've never heard him speak of any man who did him wrong."

"I am pleased that you told me of the resolution to this matter. Have you told Lord Gilbert yet? Oh, aye, you would have if Ernaud occupies his dungeon."

Father Thomas was again silent for a moment, then finally said, "The resolution of the matter. So all who've heard believe."

"And yet you do not?"

"I spoke privily to Ernaud when Father Simon brought him and the evidence to me. He protested innocence. He knew not how the stolen silver came to be in Father Simon's toft. I told him that if he confessed he could receive absolution. He would not hang. Holy Church slays no malefactor. The bishop's court would perhaps require some repugnant service of him, or an arduous pilgrimage. He knows this, and perhaps this is why he will not admit his guilt. I warned him of hell fires, but he was adamant."

"You have heard the confessions of many sinners," I said.

"All of the confessions I have heard are of sinners," the priest answered.

"Indeed. We are all sinners. You have heard many confessions. But here is a man who will not confess, even though doing so would not increase his punishment. Why do you believe this is so?"

"Because," Father Thomas said softly, "I believe Ernaud. I cannot tell why, but something within my soul says the clerk speaks true."

"Why, then, would stolen silver be found so near his abode?"

"To point to his guilt. If Ernaud did this murder he would have had wit enough to bury the loot farther from Father Simon's vicarage."

"You believe there is a felon who has slain Odo and now seeks to lay the guilt upon Ernaud?"

"Aye. Do not ask me for evidence of this. I have none."

"Why do you bring this to me?"

"I wish for you to investigate the matter. If you can allay my fears and prove Ernaud guilty I will be content. But mayhap you will find that Ernaud did not slay Odo and some other man did. I will be content then also. I will not be content if matters remain as they now are."

"Your clerk's murder is not of my bailiwick."

"True. But if Ernaud did not slay Odo, the man who did is likely of Bampton and therefore under your authority."

"And you want me to prove it so?"

"Nay. I want you to seek truth, wherever that path may lead."

In service to Lord Gilbert I have been asked often to seek felons and prove their guilt. Here was something new. I was asked to prove a man guiltless. How would I go about that? I supposed that if I found Odo's slayer and 'twas not Ernaud le Tournier I would thereby prove the clerk's innocence.

"Show me the place where Ernaud is supposed to have buried the candlesticks."

"Come," Father Thomas said.

He led me up Church View Street to Father Simon's vicarage. The three priests who serve the Church of St. Beornwald live within shouting distance of each other; Father Ralph on Church View Street, and the other two just round the corner on Landell's Lane.

Father Thomas led me behind Father Simon's vicarage and pointed out the small hole where the stolen silver was found. 'Twas no deeper and wider than my hand from wrist to fingertips, and little longer.

"The hole was so shallow that 'twas sure to be discovered when the earth was turned for planting, as 'twill soon be," Father Thomas said.

"True. But if Ernaud was the one to do the digging he would be prepared for the find. Mayhap he thought this a convenient place to temporarily hide his loot."

"Mayhap," the vicar said, "but more likely one of Father Simon's servants would prepare the soil of the toft, not Ernaud. The man who buried the candlesticks here wanted them to be found."

"To implicate Ernaud in Odo's murder?"

"Aye. Ernaud or some other of Father Simon's servants."

"But Odo had no past disagreements with any servant? Only Ernaud?"

"Just so," the priest agreed.

"There is merit to your observation," I said. "If this is so, then the theft was likely a ruse. But did the slayer, if 'twas not Ernaud, seek harm to Odo foremost, or Ernaud? Did he wish to murder Odo and lay blame on another, or did he use Odo's murder to avenge himself against Ernaud?"

"And what of the blood under Odo's fingernails?" Father Thomas said. "Odo could not have lacerated a man's cheek after his assailant stove in his skull with a candlestick."

"Aye. He saw the attack coming, but had nothing with which to defend himself but fists and fingernails.

"A poor defense against a silver club weighing near a stone," I continued. "And if he saw the blow coming and tried to defend himself, then the blow that struck the right side of his head was likely delivered by some left-handed man. What of Ernaud's hands and wrists? Is there any sign of these being raked by Odo's fingernails?"

"Nay. When I saw that his cheeks bore no marks I inspected hands and arms, thinking perhaps Odo reached out for Ernaud's arm as he saw the blow coming. There is no sign of injury to either of Ernaud's arms. And Ernaud is right-handed."

"And yet the silver condemns him," I said. "Mayhap I was wrong about dried blood under Odo's fingernails. I have been wrong before."

"What, then, did you see under Odo's fingernails," the priest said, "if 'twas not dried blood? Dirt?"

"That is unlikely," I replied. "Is it not the custom that those who stand watch at the Easter Sepulchre must bathe before they accept the duty?"

"It is."

"There is no earthen floor in St. Beornwald's Church where a man might scrape up soil under his nails, and what I saw under Odo's fingernails had not the consistency of earth. Nay. 'Twas dried blood I saw there. I am sure of it. I did not construe wrongly."

"Will you seek to prove Ernaud innocent?"

"To do so I will need to find some other man guilty."

"Indeed. Is that not the nature of truth, rightly dividing right from wrong, truth from falsehood, innocence from guilt?"

"There are men who wish truth to remain obscure," I said.

"Aye. And such men are usually wicked, false, and guilty."

"To that I will agree. Truth remains always true. 'Tis men's perception of it that changes, not truth itself."

"So will you seek to alter men's perception of the truth regarding Ernaud's presumed guilt for Odo's death?"

"I will visit the castle and speak to Ernaud. Then I will give you my answer."

"That will suffice," Father Thomas said, before bidding me good day.

CHAPTER 4

$\mathcal{B}$ampton Castle's dungeon is a foul place. 'Tis below the level of the castle yard, with only a narrow slit well above the level of a standing man's head to allow air and light into the place. But not much air, and even less light. A stone wall separates the dungeon from the castle cesspit, and when the builders constructed this wall they were not particular about the fit of the masonry in a place where gentlefolk were unlikely to take notice.

So the wall between cesspit and dungeon leaks. I knew this, having visited the reeking place in the past. I had no wish to spend time where my nostrils would be assailed, so called upon Sir Henry Hering, Lord Gilbert's marshal of Bampton Castle, to bring Ernaud to me in the hall.

I suppose it is good for a dungeon to be an evil place. The knowledge that it is so may persuade men to avoid the misdemeanors and felonies that would see them incarcerated. And if not, the stinking cell might convince any who do find themselves locked away, in the future, to shun the deeds that brought them to the dungeon.

The stench of leaking cesspit arrived with Ernaud. His robe was thick with the odor and I hoped the smell would dissipate when the clerk was returned to the cell, before grooms set up tables for Lord Gilbert's supper.

The marshal stood back as Ernaud approached me. Likely Sir Henry had told Ernaud who it was that wished to speak to him, and knowing that, the clerk could guess why. Or could he? Ernaud would, like other folk, think my duties to be limited to the collection of fees, rents, fines, and the apprehension of malefactors in Bampton and collecting evidence of their guilt. That I had been urged to prove him innocent of Odo Fuller's death would not occur to him. So I would not mention this. Not at first. Mayhap a frightened man would tell me more than one who was less concerned for his future. Even if in his conversation he did not realize what knowledge I sought, or why.

Ernaud faced ecclesiastical judgment and, if found guilty in a bishop's court, a punishment prescribed by the church. So he did not fear a hangman's noose. Until, that is, he learned who it was that waited for him in the hall. A bailiff has naught to do with a bishop's court. A man arrested by a bailiff, even a cleric, might find himself before the King's Eyre and soon after upon a scaffold. I saw this understanding in the clerk's eyes and pale features.

I pointed to the bench upon which I sat and said, "Be seated." I noticed that Ernaud's hands trembled as he did so.

In past interrogations I have found it useful to stand over a culprit while the miscreant I wished to question was seated. Even the most miserable rogues will lose confidence when an irascible bailiff stands over them and asks onerous questions. But Ernaud's situation was different. If Father Thomas was correct – and I was willing to believe he was – the clerk did not need to be intimidated. To be falsely charged with murder would be daunting enough.

"Why did you bury the candlesticks where they might easily be discovered?" I began.

"I did not do so," Ernaud cried. "Look, see my face, my hands, my arms. I have no scratches upon me. I heard you say that you found blood under Odo's fingernails and that he must have injured the one who slew him."

As he spoke he turned his face from one side to the other so that I might see clearly that his visage was unmarred. He then drew up his sleeves past his elbows and offered his hands and arms for my inspection. Which, of course, he would not have done had they borne any scratches deep enough to leave traces of blood under Odo's fingernails.

"Did you assail Odo in company with another who now bears wounds from Odo's fingernails?"

"Have you found another man in Bampton or the Weald who hides his face?" Ernaud asked. "That will be the man who did this murder and hid the silver in Father Simon's toft so as to cause my arrest."

"Who hates you so much he would part with two silver candlesticks so that you will be charged with murder?"

Ernaud's face told of his bewilderment. "I know of no such enemies," he finally said, nearly in a whisper. "The Lord Christ said we are to live at peace with all men, and so I try to do."

"I have heard that you and Odo often disagreed."

"Cannot two men disagree without becoming adversaries? 'Tis true Odo and I often saw matters differently, but I never thought myself in danger from him, nor did he, I warrant, believe himself in peril from me."

"What was the subject of your most recent disagreement with Odo?"

Ernaud looked away, as if he found the beams supporting the roof of Lord Gilbert's hall suddenly enthralling. I waited.

"Odo charged me with being a Donatist."

"Are you?"

"No more than he was."

"Odo was a Donatist?"

"He would not admit so."

"Of course not," I said. "Even Master Wycliffe abjures the term."

"Aye. But of all the masters at Oxford he comes closest to the tenet."

"He does, I grant you that. What of Father Simon? Have you discussed the issue with him?"

"What? And lose my position? And if the archdeacon discovered my thoughts I might lose more than that."

"Aye, so you might. Why do you feel so free to discuss the matter with me?"

"All men hereabouts know that you studied under Master Wycliffe and likely share his opinions. None hold that against you," he hastily added. "So I feel free to mention the matter."

Here was a shock. I had no idea men so easily could read my mind. Do my thoughts speak even though no words escape my lips? Evidently. Bishops and archdeacons loathe any doctrine that might question their authority and reduce their power. And they loathe men who hold such doctrines. When a bishop despises a man, the fellow should look to his safety. Best not to draw the attention of a bishop. I resolved to be more circumspect in my conversation. Am I a coward? Possibly. What is of greater service to the Lord Christ: a hero dead or a cautious man alive? What is of greater value to Kate and Bessie and John? I know what Kate would answer. Donatists have a telling argument, but I will not be caught out saying so.

I had not extracted Ernaud from the dungeon to discuss theology, although it seemed theology might have to do with Odo's murder. Were the stolen candlesticks a ruse to cover some other reason for the felony? The thought had been nagging at the back of my mind since Father Thomas mentioned the possibility. But how to prove it so? How to prove it not so, for that matter?

"If you did not slay Odo, nor bury the silver in Father Simon's toft, who did? Surely if you are innocent of these felonies you have been considering who might be guilty."

"I have," Ernaud said. "Especially because where the stolen candlesticks were found must mean you and the vicars were to presume me or one of Father Simon's servants guilty. What other intention must the felon have? Were the murder done for gain the fellow would be now in Oxford selling the silver to fatten his purse."

"Aye. Either the rogue has no need of money, or he hates you enough that he will forego gain in order to send you to the bishop's court. Of course, the silver cresset has not been found. Perhaps that has been carried off and sold. Are you sure you cannot think of any man who so despises you?"

The clerk shook his head slowly. "In a dungeon," he said, "a man has much time to consider the events that put him there. Some man would rather see me before the bishop's court than have the coins from selling two silver candlesticks."

"But you cannot guess who this might be?"

Again Ernaud shook his head. "Nay, I can think of no man I have harmed."

I motioned to the marshal to approach and told him to return Ernaud to the dungeon.

"You do not believe me, then?"

"Whether I do or not, so long as the vicars accuse you 'tis the dungeon for you... until the bishop can be told of the accusation against you and send men to take you to him. As for me, I believe Father Thomas may be correct. Mayhap you did not slay Odo. But mayhap you did."

* * *

Upon my return to Galen House I found Kate and Adela preparing our supper. As 'twas a fast day the meal was a charlet of cod with maslin loaves. Adela shared the meal, then set off for her home in the Weald. I had said nothing of Odo Fuller's murder or of Ernaud le Tournier while the lass was present, thinking that whatever she heard would be bandied about Bampton and the Weald before the sun set next day.

I poured another dose of hound's-tongue and oil of lavender into John's ear, then Kate took him and Bessie to their beds. I was pleased to see that the lad no longer clutched at his ear when he sneezed. Indeed, he sneezed but once while we were at our meal, and this may have been due to a crumb up his nostril.

On warm evenings I am fond of hauling a bench to the rear wall of Galen House, where Kate and I may discuss matters facing the setting sun. But the fifth day of April is seldom warm enough to enjoy an evening in fresh air. Instead I set the bench before the hearth (when Galen House was rebuilt after Sir Simon Trillowe burned it, I had a brick fireplace installed), stirred the embers and placed two more sticks upon the smoldering blaze.

"John is improved," Kate said as she sat beside me. "And Bessie also."

"What of you? You took only a small portion of cod for your supper." I touched her forehead. "And you are yet feverish."

"Oddly enough, I feel chilled," she said, "even though I know I have yet the ague. The warmth of the fire is pleasing."

46

"As is your presence beside me," I said. "When I first laid eyes on you in your father's shop in Oxford I did not imagine that such a beauty would deign to wed such as me. How is it you were able to look past my overlarge nose and slender form?"

Kate rested her head upon my shoulder. She did not reply, but here was answer enough.

Kate knew that I had gone to the castle that day, and knew why. She asked what I had learned. "Does Father Simon's clerk yet proclaim innocence?"

"He does."

"Do you believe him?"

"I can see no reason for him to slay Odo. Perhaps some fit of passion, but that does not match with the manner of Odo's death, I think."

"That does not tell me you believe him guiltless."

"He spoke freely of the disagreements he had with Odo," I said. "A man wishing to deflect an accusation of murder would surely try to cause me to believe he had never quarreled with Odo."

"The stolen candlesticks being so easily discovered seems suspicious," Kate replied.

"So Father Thomas believes. I asked Ernaud if there was a man who hated him so much that he would slay Odo and then devise a way to make him seem guilty of the felony. He claims ignorance of any such foe. He said as far as he knows he has wronged no man. He can think of no reason that he should be so treated."

"What will become of Ernaud?" Kate asked.

"The Bishop of Exeter has been told of Odo's death and that Ernaud is charged. He will likely send an archdeacon and servants to take Ernaud to Exeter. There he will stand before the bishop's court."

"And if found guilty?"

"The church hangs no man. Likely he will be required to take an arduous pilgrimage, then if he does not perish upon the journey will be assigned to live out his days as a lay brother in some Scottish monastery where the cold will attack his bones, and he will subsist upon coarse bread and water."

"'Likely, you said. What is unlikely?"

"The bishop's court might turn him over to the king for punishment. Since the time of Becket that is unlikely, but had Odo friends in high places or was he of a powerful family such a thing might happen."

"Odo was but a clerk," Kate observed.

"Aye, his family was in the woolen trade."

"So Ernaud will not hang?"

"Probably not."

My Kate sat silently, gazing into the dying embers. I thought she was near to sleep, but her silence was of another sort.

"What if 'twas not hatred that provoked some man to slay Odo and lay the blame for the murder at Ernaud's feet. What if there was some other cause?"

"What other cause might there be? What have you in mind?"

"Fear, mayhap?"

"Fear of Ernaud?" I could not help but smile. "The clerk is a small man who spends his days going about his duties with ink-stained fingers between church and vicarage, and seldom ventures farther away from either place than the tithe barn. Who would fear him?"

"You misunderstand," Kate said. "I do not mean that some man fears Ernaud might attack him as Odo was attacked. It may be that some man fears what Ernaud has seen, or knows."

"If so, Ernaud does not know what it is he knows, else he would have spoken of it."

"Are you sure? It may be that he is ignorant of the reason some man fears him, or it may be that he does not want you or any other to know of it."

"If some man fears Ernaud, why slay Odo... unless he feared Odo also," I said.

"If a man slew both Odo and Ernaud, the bishop would not rest until he discovered who had done the evil," Kate said. "The felon would likely be caught. But by making it appear that Ernaud did the murder, the real felon, if Ernaud is indeed innocent, might escape the penalty due his villainy.

"And both Odo and Ernaud would vanish from Bampton," Kate said, "along with what it is they might know that struck fear into some man's heart.

"What of Peter Bouchard?" Kate continued. "Do you suppose he is in danger? Mayhap he also knows what Ernaud and Odo knew. Perhaps all three clerks of the Church of St. Beornwald knew a thing dangerous to them."

"If such knowledge is the cause of all this wickedness," I said. "But perhaps our imaginations are inflamed, sending me off on some foolish chase, making a muddle of what is a simple matter."

"Perhaps," Kate said. "But will you speak to Peter? If he knows a thing dangerous to him he must be warned."

"Indeed," I agreed. I began to think my Kate had begun the unraveling of a knotty mystery. "I will seek Peter tomorrow."

That night, in my bed, considering what I might say to Peter Bouchard, it occurred to me that he might also be suspect in Odo's death. Ernaud's supposed guilt left Peter the only clerk serving the vicars of St. Beornwald's Church. Would there be some advantage to Peter because of this? None that I could see. Indeed, as the single clerk serving three vicars his duties would increase. Most men would find that objectionable.

* * *

I heard the dawn Angelus ring and knew where I would find Peter Bouchard. I leaped from my bed, dressed quickly, and clattered down the stairs. Kate sat up in bed sleepily, rubbed her eyes, and watched me depart.

Father Ralph conducted the Angelus devotional this day and Peter assisted him. I waited in the nave until the rite was concluded. Ten others attended the devotional. Most of them had accumulated many years and now sought to win the favor of the Lord Christ since they were assured of meeting Him soon.

The worshipers departed the church slowly when Father Ralph concluded the liturgy. Of course, most of the aged congregants did everything slowly. As will I one day. Creaking knees and aching backs cannot be persuaded to move in haste.

I waited in the porch for the priest and clerk, who followed the last of the worshipers from the church. It seemed to me that Peter held back. This is no sign of guilt. Most men are reluctant to meet their bailiff. We who occupy such posts are not popular for what our duties require of us; collecting the lord's rents and fines and such. Although Peter is assessed of none of these.

"Ah, Sir Hugh," Father Ralph spoke. "The mystery is solved and Ernaud will soon be off to the bishop's court. Never would I have thought he would slay another." The priest clucked his tongue. "But he and Odo were at times disputatious. And I suppose silver may tempt any man."

Peter looked at his feet while Father Ralph spoke. He seemed to want no part of the conversation. He stepped back when the priest spoke.

"You seldom attend the dawn Angelus," Father Ralph said. "I am pleased to see your new piety. May the Lord Christ reward you."

"Indeed. I wish it may be so. But I admit that I am come here for another reason." I pointed to the stone benches that lined the porch. "May we sit?"

Clerk and priest looked to each other, exchanged puzzled glances, then swept aside their robes and sat. I took the bench opposite.

"How may I serve you?" Father Ralph said.

"Two clerks are no longer serving the priests of St. Beornwald's Church," I began. "One of these is dead, the other charged with his murder."

The priest rolled his eyes as if to say, Why do you speak of what is already known and waste my time? I would break my fast.

"You and Father Simon believe Ernaud le Tournier the felon who slew Odo. Do you know that Father Thomas does not share your certainty?"

"Aye. He's spoken of his doubts."

"And you believe he is mistaken?"

"The evidence is plain."

"Mayhap too plain," I said. "Father Thomas has asked me to look into the matter."

"What is there to look into? Ernaud and Odo were not friendly, and the stolen silver was found behind Father Simon's vicarage. Who else would have put it there?"

"Who indeed."

"Do you find Father Thomas's doubt credible?" Father Ralph asked.

"Credible? I do not find his doubt incredible."

I turned to Peter. "If Father Thomas is correct, and Ernaud did not slay Odo, then it may be that some man wishes to remove the clerks of St. Beornwald's Church, and if so he has but one remaining."

Peter stiffened at this. Here, I decided, was a new thought to trouble this young man.

'Twas a new thought to the vicar as well, it seemed. "You believe Peter in danger?"

"If Ernaud did not slay Odo, and the stolen candlesticks were not the root of the felony, then the death of Odo and the discovery of the silver remains a mystery. 'Til it is solved it would be well for Peter to be cautious."

Of one thing I could be certain: Peter's cheeks bore no trace of recent scratches. And at the moment I considered this, he folded his arms across his chest. The movement drew the sleeves of his robe toward his elbows. No abrasions marked his hands or wrists. For several days I had kept an eye open for the marks of fingernails drawn across skin and had seen no man with such disfigurement.

"We thank you for your concern," Father Ralph said.

"Aye," the clerk agreed.

Both stood to depart the porch and I saw Peter glance in both directions as he left and entered the churchyard. This seemed the behavior of a worried man. If so, it meant he had no knowledge of Odo's death nor of Ernaud's guilt or innocence. Probably.

CHAPTER 5

Two days later, upon a Saturday, the archdeacon arrived, his white robes mud-spattered. He rode a mule as a mark of humility. In my experience, there are few men less humble than archdeacons. Six men accompanied him: four to assist in escorting Ernaud to Exeter, and two younger men assigned to replace Odo and Ernaud as clerks to Father Thomas and Father Simon. If the clerks were worried about supplanting a slain man and his accused slayer they gave no sign.

Ernaud would soon be away from Bampton. If I thought of more questions to ask him I would need to follow them to Exeter. Fortunately, in the next days I could think of nothing new to ask of the clerk, so was spared a journey.

Some man, if Father Thomas was correct, hated or feared Odo and Ernaud enough to murder the one and fix the guilt upon the other. Which was it: hate or fear? If Ernaud did not slay Odo the solution must be one or the other. But the silver cresset bowl was yet missing. Would a man give up the value of two candlesticks in order to lay the blame for theft and murder upon another, yet keep the cresset?

Father Thomas's new clerk was a lad named William Walle, and the clerk assigned to Father Simon was Alan Hillyng. I debated whether or not they should be cautioned, as I had done with Peter Bouchard, and decided not. What enemies could men newly arrived in Bampton have? Or who would fear them enough to see them silenced? The youthful scholars would be apprehensive enough in their new positions without me adding to their uncertainty.

After a dinner of stockfish and barley loaves there came a rapping upon the door of Galen House. Adela ran to open it, and a moment later reported that Father Thomas wished to speak to me. I knew what he had to say. He had called upon me and spoken much the same words for the past four days.

My hall at Galen House should not be dignified with such a term. 'Tis hardly more than a bay. Nevertheless this room is where I entertain guests and see the Bampton residents who need my services to repair a wound or some injury.

"Good day, Father. How may I serve you?" The question was rhetorical. I was sure I would have learned the answer even had I not raised the question.

"Ernaud is on his way to the bishop's court. You have been unable to prove his innocence. The man is not culpable, I am sure of it. What now can be done?"

"Why are you so certain he did not slay Odo? Odo was your clerk. Seems to me you, above all, would wish justice done."

"Aye, so I do. I have told you why I believe Ernaud did not do this murder. And justice does not mean presuming guilt where none is only to be able then to claim a felony recompensed. If so, we might simply haul a man off the street, hang him, and consider a murder avenged. One life for another. What matter guilt or innocence?"

"I see your point, and I understand what you have in the past said about the reasons you have for believing Ernaud innocent of the felony. Have you new thoughts on the matter?"

"Ernaud never showed himself to be a man of guile before. And if he was he would have chosen a better place to hide the candlesticks."

"Aye," I said. "I give you that."

"And we know he bore no marks of a struggle. 'Twas you who said whoso attacked Odo was scratched when Odo resisted."

"This also is true," I replied.

"And if a man wished to remove both Odo and Ernaud from Bampton without slaying both, how better to do so than arrange that one is thought guilty of slaying the other?"

"I admit to the same thought."

"Then what are you doing about it?"

"What are you doing about it?" I rejoined. "'Tis your obligation to keep order in the church, among its servants and within the bishop's lands."

"You refuse to see justice done because the man ill-used is not of Lord Gilbert's manor? What if the real culprit is Lord Gilbert's man?"

"I do not refuse justice. But seeing it done seems to me more your obligation than mine. If the felon who has done these evils is of Bampton Manor I will take action against him."

"How will you do that if you take no action to discover if 'tis so? You will seek justice if the felon is of your bailiwick but will do nothing to discover if he is. We vicars of the Church of St. Beornwald must first prove some man's guilt? If we can do so your aid will not be needed."

Against my will I saw and agreed with the priest's argument. How would I know if Odo's murderer was of Lord Gilbert's manor or of the bishop's lands until I found him and proved his guilt?

I fear I am becoming obdurate as I grow older. Or is it that I am becoming so with more experience of malefactors? Likely both. And experience has taught me that discovering felons and miscreants may often entail disagreeable circumstances, even though when the conclusion of such a matter is clear a sense of satisfaction replaces discontent.

"This is true," I said, "and will be the more difficult because Father Ralph and Father Simon do not share your view. They will be of no assistance in seeking a man they do not believe exists."

"So if you will not help I must seek aid for Ernaud alone." The priest sighed. "I am not shrewd enough to do so. I cannot think even where to begin, questions to ask, nor to whom such queries should be addressed. I have devoted my life to seeking the good in men, not the wickedness."

"Such is often the case when some felony has occurred," I said. "Many roads lead from Bampton. If I desire to travel to London, only one will take me there without many detours. If I was new to the village I might travel the wrong road and never reach my destination, or arrive in London only after many wrong turns and misdirection. To find the correct road I must ask some man who knows the way."

"Hah. All men of Bampton could tell you the road by which to reach London. But how many know of who may have slain Odo?"

"Most analogies eventually break down." I shrugged. "But you take my point. We must seek the proper road."

"We? Then you will seek the truth of Odo's death?"

I had said the word without considering its import. 'Twas unintentional. Or was it? Did I really wish to shirk the obligation that all men have to seek truth? Indeed, although I resisted the thought, I had already been considering how I might ferret out the truth of Odo's murder. Mayhap my tongue knows my mind better than I know myself.

"Aye," I agreed. "I will."

"Excellent. How will you begin?"

"How do I know? I have only now agreed to the business."

"Oh... aye... you need to think on it. I see."

I had already considered the matter after speaking to Ernaud. In theory, of course. If Ernaud had not buried the silver candlesticks behind Father Simon's vicarage, was there a way to discover who had, or at least prove that Ernaud had not done so?

"I would like to see the place where the candlesticks were buried again," I said.

I told Kate what I was about, then walked with the priest to Father Simon's vicarage. Father Thomas rapped upon the vicarage door, and when the new clerk opened told him to inform his master of what we were doing. We knew 'twould be best to tell the fellow who it was prowling about behind his abode.

The hole made to receive the buried silver had been filled, but 'twas clear from the fresh-turned earth where it had been dug. Father Simon, followed by his clerk, appeared as I examined the place.

"What do you seek?" he asked. Then, with a chuckle, "Has Father Thomas enlisted you in his fantasy?"

"Was it you who discovered the buried candlesticks?" I asked.

"Aye. Saw the new-turned dirt and thought it strange, as neither Ernaud nor my servant Henry had plied a spade yet to plant vegetables. Nearly time to do so, though," the priest said and glanced to Alan.

A small shed leaned against the rear of the vicarage. This structure was divided, the larger section a hen house, the smaller closed with a locked door. I looked to it and said, "Have you a spade or hoe?"

"Aye."

"Did you examine them when you found the buried silver?"

"Nay. To what purpose?"

"To learn if the soil upon their surfaces was moist or dry," I replied.

I asked Father Simon to unlock the shed. He rolled his eyes, entered the vicarage, and a moment later returned with a large iron key. I shortly discovered why the shed was locked. Father Simon's spade was of iron fixed to an oaken shaft, although the hoe was of wood and of little value.

Father Simon opened the shed door wide and stepped back, offering me entrance. The interior was dark, but my eyes soon became accustomed to the gloom and I saw the spade among debris that the priest had allowed to accumulate.

I withdrew the spade from the shed into the light and examined it. The blade was lightly rusted as if it had not been recently used. Would a man use a wooden hoe to gouge out a hole when an iron spade was at hand? I thought not, but withdrew the hoe from the shed to examine it also.

The tool was old. Age had begun to rot the blade, and where it was not decayed it was badly worn. A hole had been drilled through the crosspiece for the shaft, and the two pieces fixed together with a wooden pin.

I took the hoe to the softened earth that filled the hole where the silver was found and began to ply it against the soil. I thought I knew what would happen. It did. The decayed pin crumbled and the hoe pulled apart.

All this time the vicars and the new clerk had watched wordlessly. Now Father Simon spoke.

"You have broken my hoe."

"And learned an important thing in so doing," I replied.

"What can a broken hoe tell you?"

"The earth here is soft where it has filled the place you found the stolen silver. If the hoe would break with so little effort, how could it have been used to dig into undisturbed soil?"

"Why use it at all when an iron spade was at hand?" Father Thomas said.

"Why indeed," Father Simon said. "Clearly Ernaud would use the spade to dig his hole. He knew where it was kept."

"But he did not use it," I said. I picked up the spade and held it forth. "See where rust clings to the spade? Had it been recently used the corrosion would have been scoured away."

Father Simon pursed his lips. He did not, I was sure, want to believe this conclusion but could think of no objection. So he said nothing. For a moment.

"Mayhap," he finally said, "Ernaud used a tool belonging to some other."

"He might have done," I said, "but why would he do so? He might be seen carrying a spade on the street. He knew you had implements in the shed. Did he know where the key was kept?"

"Aye, he did. This key and the key to the tithe barn hang from a nail in the kitchen."

"So," Father Thomas concluded, "he buried stolen candlesticks where they were sure to be found, and used someone else's spade to dig the hole. Am I the only vicar of St. Beornwald's Church to see how improbable this is?"

"If Ernaud did not do so," Father Simon said, "who did, and why do such a thing? It makes no sense."

"It makes no sense to us," I said, "because we are ignorant of the felon's purpose. If we can discover the reason some man did this we may then know the felon's name."

"Can you discover a man's intent before you learn his identity?" Father Thomas asked. "Is it not better to discover the felon and then descry his cause?"

"To learn the why of a thing will not always lead to the who," I replied. "But occasionally."

Father Simon pulled at his chin, then spoke. "I cannot see the why of burying valuable silver here, where it would soon be discovered."

"It was intended that it be discovered," Father Thomas said. "'Tis as I told you some days past, but you would not hearken to me."

Father Simon replaced his valuable spade in the shed and locked the door. This door was flimsy and I thought the vicar fortunate that no man had forced it open and taken the tool. Mayhap the proximity of his fowl made the shed safe. A man attempting to force the shed door in the night would stir the roosting hens and set them to clucking.

"Are you now convinced that my suspicion has merit?" Father Thomas asked me.

"Aye. His guilt is too convenient. Now, upon closer examination of the spade he supposedly used, 'tis not palpable."

"What will you do?"

"I must think on it," I said, "and I think better with a full stomach. So I will return to Galen House and enjoy my supper."

As it was a fast day the meal was a simple pottage of peas and beans flavored only with leeks. When the meal was done, Adela put Bessie and John to bed, then bade us good eve and set off for her home in the Weald.

"The maid has been strangely silent this day," Kate said when Adela was away. "She is normally talkative. I learn daily of events in the Weald. But today, since Father Thomas called after dinner, she has been as mute as an anchorite."

"I wonder what his appearance did to silence her," I said. "Perhaps it would be useful to know."

* * *

'Tis a custom for Kate and me that we do not break our fast upon Sunday before attending mass. So next day I had only a

59

cup of ale before Adela arrived and we set out for the church. John is not a happy child. Kate says his teeth are beginning to appear and he is cross. So instead of coming into mass with me she sat with the babe in the porch, allowing him to gnaw upon her finger. Father Thomas spoke the homily and sent the pax board through the congregation. I could not help but think that among those who kissed the pax board there was likely a murderer. Each day, nay, each hour that passed I became more convinced that Ernaud le Tournier was the victim of a grave injustice. But what to do about it?

Lord Gilbert desires that I keep him informed of matters, so after a dinner of capon in gauncelye I set off for Bampton Castle. I have found it useful to speak of perplexing events to others. Doing so will sometimes bring new thoughts to my mind, and Lord Gilbert is an astute man. Often, when I have sought malefactors among his tenants and villeins, he has made useful suggestions as to how I might best proceed to ferret out the wrongdoer.

Spring rains had made Shill Brook run high and swift. I stopped upon the bridge to gaze into the stream. The effect is trance-like, as peering into a dancing blaze. Which was it, hate or fear, that caused some man to slay Odo Fuller and artfully turn suspicion toward Ernaud le Tournier? Or greed? The cresset bowl was yet missing.

Perhaps hate for the one and fear for the other? But which was which? I surely could not go about the village asking folk if they hated or feared Ernaud or Odo. Such a scheme would be an unprofitable use of time. What man would truthfully tell a bailiff that he hated some other? Especially if the man was now resting in the churchyard. What if I asked men of Bampton if they had a neighbor who disliked or feared Odo or Ernaud?

Would a man know his neighbor's thoughts? He might. But if a man hated or feared another enough to slay him would he tell some other man of it? Only if he trusted the man. And a man so dependable might be unwilling to tell me what he knew of a felonious friend.

I shook myself free of the flowing stream and walked to the castle. 'Twould soon be time to resume archery practice, the organizing of which is a duty Lord Gilbert has placed upon me. The king requires that all commons of the realm be skilled in the use of a bow, and to sweeten the command Lord Gilbert provides six pence each Sunday for those whose arrows fly most true to the butts.

I found my employer in his solar, entertaining visitors. A knight of Sussex, his lady and grooms had arrived two days before Easter. I did not know the purpose of the visit. Lord Gilbert does not confide in me about such matters.

"Ah, Hugh, what news? That felonious clerk is away to the bishop's court. You are no longer required to deal with him."

"I wish it was so," I said.

One of Lord Gilbert's eyebrows lifted. "Oh?" he said.

"There is conjecture that the clerk Ernaud did not slay Odo."

"Conjecture? But is there evidence?"

"Some," I replied, and laid out the reasons for believing Ernaud falsely accused. Lord Gilbert's visitor listened intently, as did he.

"Hmmm. What you have said is interesting, but I'd not call it evidence, either of guilt or innocence. What was your word... conjecture? Aye, that's the proper word. What do you intend?"

"I am becoming convinced," I said, "that if Ernaud is found guilty of murder in the bishop's court an injustice will be done."

"I know you well, Hugh. You will not countenance an injustice within your bailiwick, even though 'tis the bishop's men who are most involved in the mischief. I am pleased to be informed of this. When you have the truth of the business seek me and tell me of it. Nay, seek me whenever you learn of anything that might shed light upon this dark matter."

I promised to do so and bowed my way from the solar. How many days would pass, I wondered, until I could call again upon Lord Gilbert and share some ray of light illuminating the circumstance of Odo Fuller's death? I feared many days, even weeks, might follow, for I could devise no way to begin an investigation that would either prove Ernaud's guilt or absolve him.

CHAPTER 6

$\mathfrak{K}$ate usually sends Adela home early on Sunday, after the lass takes dinner with us. So it was that as I approached the bridge over Shill Brook on the way back from the castle I saw her turn from Bridge Street and hurry to her home in the Weald. Why such haste? I wondered. At the thought, Adela turned to glance my way over her shoulder. She looked away quickly and continued to the hovel that was her home.

When I returned to Galen House I found my Kate sitting upon a bench in the kitchen, her back against the wall. She was nearly asleep, her head drooping to a shoulder. John dozed in her lap, and Bessie played at her feet with the doll her grandfather had made. Here was a pleasant scene of domestic content until I realized that Kate's somnolence was in part due to illness. I was loathe to wake her, but feared that John might slip from her grasp and tumble to the flags. When Galen House was built I had ordered the kitchen floor be made of flat stones. Too often rushes ignite from stray embers spit from hearthstones and fireplaces, and burn a dwelling to ashes. I would not have this happen to Galen House. But neither would I have John fall to the stones. I sat beside Kate and she twitched to wakefulness.

"Ah... I did not hear your return," she said softly. The embers upon the hearth provided some warmth to the room, so I could not tell if her reddened cheeks were due to heat or to the fever. I touched her forehead.

"You must go to our bed and rest," I said, "while John has his nap. Else your head will fall so askew you will break your neck and John will fall to the flags."

"Aye," Kate smiled. "I will do so. What does Lord Gilbert say about the business of Odo and Ernaud?"

"He agrees that I should look into the question of Ernaud's guilt. By the way, I saw Adela going to the Weald as I neared the bridge. She seemed hurried, and cast a curious glance my way as she neared her home. You said yesterday that she has become mute. Is she yet silent?"

"Aye. She is not the lass she was even two days past."

"Does her work suffer?"

"Nay. She does as well as ever, but wordlessly now, whereas in the past she seldom stopped her prattle."

I was silent, considering this change in our servant. Kate noticed, and spoke.

"You think Adela's silence may have to do with Odo Fuller's death? Or with Ernaud being charged with the felony? 'Twas after Father Thomas came here to speak to you about this yesterday that she fell silent."

"I cannot see what she would have to do with these matters, but it does seem a coincidence that her nature is so out of joint at the same time as these events."

"I have heard you say that bailiffs and sheriffs and constables and such do not believe in coincidences," Kate said.

"True. Tomorrow, when Adela arrives, question her about her melancholy. Mayhap she will confide in you. For now, come with me. I intend to put you to bed."

I took Kate's hand and led her to the stairs. By the time we reached the top she was wheezing and short of breath. I feared her lungs were filled with fluid. If so, she should not recline but rather stay upright. But she must also rest. She is not a horse that she might sleep while standing erect.

From my chest I withdrew cloaks, cotehardies, chauces, kirtles, all the clothing I could find. These I piled at the head of our bed, then placed both pillows atop the heap.

"What are you about?" Kate asked.

"You must rest with your chest raised. I fear your lungs are filling. If so, 'twould be wrong to lay flat. Put John into his cradle and go to bed."

She did so. I watched until she was settled and comfortable, then returned to the kitchen. Bessie was yet playing with her doll, but the little lass is observant.

"Will Ma get well soon?"

"Aye," I replied. "Soon." I said a prayer that it would be so, but my words did not reflect my worry.

Neither bailiffs nor surgeons can plan their days. What I intend to do is often displaced by what I must do. So it was this day. Shortly after I put Kate to bed I heard a pounding upon Galen House door. I opened to two men: Philip Barnabie and his aged father, John. The older man's face was twisted in pain and before the son spoke I knew John's ailment. He held his right wrist in his left hand.

I bade the two men enter and asked how I might serve them. 'Twas but a convention. When folk approach Galen House it is sometimes that they wish chat with the bailiff, sometimes with the surgeon. John Barnabie's face told me that it was as surgeon that my services were required.

"Me father fell from the ladder this morning," Philip said.

"He sleeps in the loft?" I asked.

"Aye. Lost 'is grip and tumbled to the floor."

Why was it, I wondered, that the old and infirm were required to sleep in lofts and solars, to which access was usually gained by a ladder, when younger folk in a household could more easily and safely ascend to such places?

"This happened this morning?"

"Aye."

"And you only bring him to me now?"

"Thought maybe 'twasn't serious – only a bruise, like."

What Philip thought, more likely, was that he could avoid the expense of taking his injured father to the surgeon if the old man could be convinced to live with the misery of a broken wrist that would heal improperly.

I sat the old fellow upon the bench in my hall and examined the wrist. It was already purpled and swollen, but no shattered bone had penetrated the skin.

"I can set the break," I said to Philip, "but the remedy would have been easier had you brought him to me when the accident happened. See how the wrist is swollen. Tight splints

65

are needed, but the pressure against the swollen flesh will cause your father suffering."

This prediction did not seem to cause Philip any great sorrow. 'Twas not his wrist that would ache for the next fortnight or more.

I keep a supply of reeds in my instruments chest for such times as this. From the chest I selected five good reeds, and vials of crushed hemp seeds and flakes of dried lettuce sap. The seeds and sap flakes I added to a cup of ale and stirred the liquid well. I gave John the potion and he drank it eagerly.

Past experience with this mixture has been salutary. It will not end a man's pain – I know of nothing save death that will – but it does reduce it. I told the men that I would wait an hour for the combination to take effect, then put the fractured bones aright. Bessie, her doll under her arm, stood in the kitchen doorway and watched.

While the hemp and lettuce took effect I ripped strips from an old kirtle, then from the garment's remains fashioned a sling. Bessie asked what I was about and I explained. Philip and his father also listened.

When I thought enough time had passed – John was slumped against the wall and his son was required to push against the old fellow's shoulder to prevent him tumbling to the thresh – I took the fractured wrist in one hand and gently pressed against the broken bones until I felt them align. John grimaced and gritted his teeth, but did not cry out.

I placed the reeds around the wrist and forearm and instructed Philip how to hold them in place. I then tied the linen strips about the reeds and wrist as tightly as I could. John inhaled sharply, but held his arm stationary, as I had instructed him to do.

I bound the reeds to John's wrist with four linen strips, then fashioned the remains of the kirtle into a sling.

"In a week or so the swelling in your wrist will subside," I said. "If the reeds I have tied to your wrist become loose you must return so that I can tighten them."

The old fellow nodded understanding, and stood unsteadily. The hemp seeds and lettuce sap will enfeeble even a strong young man for two or three hours if a large enough dose is given. John was neither strong nor young. I told Philip to take care as he walked his father home.

"How much will you have for this?" Philip asked.

"Four pence."

"Pay you when harvest is done," he said.

By September John's wrist will be healed and Philip will forget his debt. For four pence I will not trouble myself to remind him.

Kate slept through the afternoon. Twice I crept quietly up the stairs to listen to her breathing. The first time I found John waking, playing with his toes, so took him from his crib so he did not rouse his mother. The second time I visited our chamber I thought Kate's raspy breathing was somewhat reduced in volume.

I was quiet, but not quiet enough. As I bent close to listen to Kate's breathing she opened her eyes.

"What?" she muttered.

"Your lungs are not so raucous as before, I think."

Kate gave a weak smile and said, "Will you then allow me to rise, or must I play the invalid awhile yet?"

"If you remain abed I must see to our supper."

"Then I must leave this bed if you and Bessie are to have a decent meal," Kate said, and swung her feet to the floor. When she stood I thought I saw her tremble, but perhaps 'twas my imagination. Nevertheless I went before her as she descended the stairs, to break a fall if she lost her balance.

I watched Kate carefully for any sign of frailty as she went about preparing a supper of cabbage with marrow. I was relieved to see her bustle about with no sign of weakness and when we sat at table for the meal she ate an ample portion. Perhaps, I thought, if my mind was free of worry for Kate I would be better able to discover if Ernaud le Tournier was innocent of Odo Fuller's murder.

* * *

Adela arrived Monday morning at the second hour, a welcome help-meet for Kate, who though over the worst of her affliction, was not back to rude health. Her duty this day, Kate said, would be to set our largest cauldron in the toft upon an iron trivit, kindle a blaze beneath it, fill the vat with water, and when 'twas hot, wash our linen clothing. The process would take most of the day and Kate would oversee the work. "Adela puts too much lye in the water, and not enough soapwort," Kate said.

"If Adela is as morose as she has been the past few days," I said quietly to Kate, "seek the reason. Likely 'twill be nothing to do with Odo or Ernaud, but mayhap it will. More likely she wishes for the attention of some lad in the Weald and he has spurned her."

With my household duly occupied, I was free to go about Lord Gilbert's business. Plowing for the season was nearly completed, but I and Bampton's reeve, John Prudhomme, went about this day observing the preparation of Lord Gilbert's demesne land for planting. Plowmen will turn the soil of their own strips deeply, to expose the roots of weeds, but may shirk when at week work. 'Twas my duty to see they did not. Another reason folk look upon their bailiff with distaste.

Philip Barnabie was one of the plowmen turning the soil of Lord Gilbert's field near to Cowleys Corner. He saw me approach when he and the goad man turned the oxen at the end of a furrow. He knew why I was there and tugged a forelock.

"How does your father this morning?" I asked.

"Tolerable."

"Did he sleep well?"

"Nay. Couldn't climb the ladder to the loft, so I made 'im a pallet on rushes. Tossed an' turned all night. Couldn't sleep meself."

"I'm not surprised. You should have brought him to me sooner. His pain would still have been great, but not as severe as it now is. I will bring some herbs tonight that will ease his hurt and allow you both to rest. Even when his wrist heals you should find a place for him to sleep upon the floor. He is much too frail to crawl up to your loft ever again."

Philip did not reply, and turned back to the plow handles. The goad man prodded the beasts into motion. Philip's son followed behind, breaking clods with his bare feet. I saw that they had turned a reasonable furrow without my presence, so were likely to continue even if I was elsewhere.

A bailiff spends much of his day watching other men work. When villeins and tenants labor upon their own land no oversight is required, but when they must plow, plant, and harvest Lord Gilbert's demesne it is useful to be seen examining their efforts. Lord Gilbert is a fair master, and as his overseer my reputation is reasonable. So most men of Bampton Manor do their work without complaint. Most men. And few have abandoned Bampton to rent from some other lord. The Statute of Laborers forbids this, but if a lord has lost many villeins and tenants to plague he may violate the statute and reduce rents upon his lands so as to attract laborers from other lords.

Two years past Bampton lost a tenant in such a manner. The fellow was prosperous, with a plump wife and three healthy children. He owned an ox, which in the spring he yoked with others' beasts to plow each other's fields. He also owned a cart. One morning in February it was reported that tenant, wife, children, ox, and cart were missing. The fellow had departed the town in the night, after the beadle had made his last rounds. I might have organized some of Lord Gilbert's grooms and chased after the man, but to what purpose? An unwilling tenant will not be profitable to his lord, and will likely seek a better situation again as soon as he may.

I returned to Galen House for my dinner. Kate heard me enter and spoke as soon as I passed the door. "You must speak to Adela. I have found the cause of her melancholy... events in the Weald."

The lass was in the toft, stirring the vat of hot water and clothing with a pole. Her face was red from exertion and the heat of steaming water and the blaze – now reduced to embers

– beneath the pot. The day was cool, so perhaps the warm work was not unwelcome.

Adela lifted her eyes from her toil and saw me approach.

"Leave your work," I said, "and come with me. Your mistress says you know of matters in the Weald which distress you."

Adela rested the stave in the cauldron and followed me silently to the hall. As we passed through the kitchen Bessie made to follow, but Kate grasped her shoulder in a manner that told the child she was to remain where she was.

I motioned to a bench and told Adela to sit. "We have noticed," I began, "that for the past days you have been subdued. I wondered if you were no longer happy in your work here, or if mayhap one of your parents was ill. Or a brother or sister. Your mistress has told me that you revealed to her the cause of your dolor and I should ask you about it."

"I do not want to bring trouble to some man's door," Adela said.

"The cause of your melancholy will bring trouble to some man if I learn of it?"

The lass nodded her head. "'Tis why I have not known what I should do. I know a thing I would rather not know."

"Tell me of it and shift the burden to me."

"Well... a fortnight past, when John an' then Bessie took ill, I was late returning to the Weald, helpin' Lady Katherine with the babes."

"I remember. You did your mistress good service. 'Twas dark when you went to your home. Did Henry encounter you on your way?"

"The beadle? Nay. Made my way past Shill Brook without 'im takin' notice, keepin' to the shadows, like."

"What happened, then, when you arrived home? Something untoward must have occurred or we would not be having this conversation."

"'Twas an hour when most honest folk be in their beds," Adela continued, "an' I didn't want to be seen by folk what's not honest."

"Indeed. So you kept to the shadows even as you neared your home?"

"Aye, so I did. Reckon that's why 'e didn't see me."

"Who?"

"Don't know. Dark, wasn't it!"

"Something tells me you have guessed who this person might have been. Is that so?"

"Aye," she said softly. "'E wore black, an' the garment was like a robe, or a lady's cotehardie."

"You believe you saw a priest in the Weald at night? Mayhap he was going to offer solace to some parishioner in need."

"Don't think 'twas one of the Fathers I saw."

"A clerk, then?"

"Aye."

"Why think you so?"

"Even in the dark I could see the man was thin."

"The vicars of St. Beornwald's Church eat well. No man would describe any of the three as thin."

"Did you follow this dark form?"

"Didn't need to."

"Why not?"

"'E disappeared behind the house across the road from me own."

"Still in the shadows?"

"Aye. 'Twas a dark night, moon just risin', so all was in shadow."

"Just so. Whose house is that? The Weald is not my bailiwick."

"Reynold Wyle an' 'is wife lives there."

"Maude?"

"Aye. That be 'er name."

"Why would some youth wearing a dark robe hide behind Reynold's house?"

"'As a daughter, 'asn't 'e?" Adela said. "Near to my age. Rosamond."

"You believe some youth – one of the clerks to the priests of St. Beornwald's Church, mayhap – went there to meet the lass?"

"Don't believe it so. Seen it. Curious, I was. Thought, who would be creepin' about behind Reynold's 'ouse when the door opened, quiet like, an' Rosamond crept out."

"You saw her?"

"Well, I saw someone. Who else would it 'ave been? She's their only daughter. Three boys besides 'er."

"Who else indeed. What then?"

"Don't know. She went toward where I'd last seen the dark lad an' after that I seen nothin' more. Didn't 'ear anything either, so went quiet-like to me own 'ouse an' sought me bed."

"And this dark encounter a fortnight past has made you morose? Why now?"

"Rosamond was found out."

"You are sure of this? How do you know?"

"Heard Reynold shoutin' at 'er. Most folk of the Weald likely did."

"When was this?"

"Maunday Thursday. Said 'e'd slay 'im did 'e ever see 'im anywhere near again."

"Who? Did he name the lad?"

"Nay, not that I heard."

"But a few days later a clerk of St. Beornwald's Church is slain, and a few days after that another clerk is accused of the murder. You believe Reynold is involved in this?"

"Didn't want to cause 'im or Rosamond trouble. Didn't know what to do. An' then folk be sayin' that Ernaud slew Odo, but I'm thinkin' mayhap not."

"And the uncertainty has been heavy upon you, no doubt."

"It 'as, sir."

"You may return to your work. Leave this matter to me."

Adela departed the hall through the kitchen and a moment later Kate appeared. "What think you?" she said. "Did Odo dally with Rosamond, and Reynold learned of it and slew him?"

"Why would Reynold slay two if one was secretly meeting his daughter in the night?"

"I have thought on this since Adela told me," Kate said. "Mayhap 'twas Ernaud who met with Rosamond in the night and Odo learned of it. If Father Simon knew what his clerk had done, Ernaud would surely lose his post. If Odo threatened to tell Father Simon of the secret meeting, Ernaud might slay him to silence him."

"Hmmm. Then why would Ernaud make his guilt plain by burying the candlesticks in Father Simon's toft?" I said.

"Mayhap Reynold knew only that a clerk was dallying with his daughter but did not know which one. He could be rid of both by slaying Odo and creating proof that Ernaud did the murder."

"What then of Peter?" I said. "If your guess is true he may be in some danger."

"Or mayhap Reynold knew of some reason Peter could not be the lad he sought. How would he know that?" Kate said. "You must solve some part of this mystery," she laughed. "I cannot do all your work for you."

After a dinner of hen in bruit I set out for the Weald and Reynold Wyle's house. Reynold, Maude said, was planting peas in a field near to Cowleys Corner.

He was not alone. Many of Lord Gilbert's tenants were at work in neighboring strips. A lad of twelve years or so accompanied Reynold, the child poking holes in the furrows with a dibble stick, and his father then dropping in the seed. So intent were the two upon their work that I was within five paces before they noticed me.

The uninvited approach of a bailiff brings no joy to most men. Even if the man is in the employ of some other master. The Bishop of Exeter is lord of the Weald. I have no authority there. Nevertheless, when Reynold lifted his eyes from his labor they appraised me beneath scowling brows.

"I give you good day," I said, and as if to confirm my opinion Reynold glanced to the sky.

The man tugged a forelock and replied. "So 'tis. What does Lord Gilbert's bailiff want with me?"

"A few words... privily. Send your lad on. Tell him you will catch him up shortly."

Reynold did so, and when the lad was twenty or so paces along in the furrow he spoke again. "What 'ave you to say to me my lad is not to 'ear?"

"Some days ago, Maunday Thursday, folk in the Weald heard you threaten to slay a man."

"Who says so?"

"Never mind who told me. You were heard bawling out the threat. And I know why you did so. Your daughter attracted the attention of a suitor you dislike. Is this not so?"

"A father's got a right to protect 'is lass."

"Indeed. From whom does your Rosamond need protection?"

"No concern of yours."

"You are wrong. A man was slain the day after you were heard breathing out threats. Rosamond was meeting some lad in the night and you discovered this. Was it Odo Fuller she saw?"

"The clerk?" Reynold said incredulously. "Why would a clerk seek out a lass in the night?"

I thought the answer obvious. "For the same reason any young man would do so."

"Hah. 'Twas no clerk I caught with Rosamond behind the shed."

"Who, then?"

Reynold did not reply.

"You will not say?"

"'Tis a matter for we of the Weald. Not of your bailiwick."

"Tell me the lad's name and I will know if this is so."

"'Tis so. You believe that because Odo was slain and I threatened to do harm to the man who was sneaking kisses from my lass that he was the lad Rosamond was sweet on? Ernaud did the murder, so all do say. 'Twas not Odo dallying with Rosamond... nor Ernaud, if that's the way your thoughts turn."

"Of course you would say so," I replied. "If it was Odo, or even Ernaud, who caused your wrath and you admitted it, I as well as others might think you the felon who did away with Odo."

"Hah. I know that Ernaud is thought guilty of Odo's murder because silver candlesticks were taken from the church when Odo was slain, and found buried behind Father Simon's vicarage. If I had slain Odo and stolen silver candlesticks, do you think I'd bury 'em? Why would a man steal if he did not intend to profit from the theft?"

"Why indeed. Perhaps there is more than one way to profit from theft. Mayhap to cast guilt upon another," I said. "If you will not tell me who it was you caught with Rosamond, I am left with you as a suspect in Odo's murder."

"Why should you care? 'Tis not your bailiwick."

"Aye, as you have said. But what happens in Bampton is, and I will seek out felons and miscreants no matter where they reside or where they do evil or whom they serve. 'Tis my obligation to Lord Gilbert."

I have a reputation in Bampton of that of a hound on the chase, unwilling to give up pursuit 'til the quarry is run to ground. I will take to my grave scars acquired due to my obduracy in pursuing malefactors who unsettled the peace of Lord Gilbert's estate. Mayhap Reynold considered this. He was silent for a moment, then when he did speak said a name so softly I had to ask him to repeat it.

"Roger Folewye," Reynold said softly. 'Twas clear he did not want his son to hear the name, although the lad had progressed so far down the furrow that he had likely heard nothing of the conversation.

William Folewye is one of the most prosperous of the bishop's tenants in the Weald. Roger is the man's son. The family holds nearly three yardlands of the bishop, and William hires laborers at planting and harvest. Adela's father is one of these. Why would Reynold be displeased that the son of a well-off neighbor was interested in his daughter? It seemed to me he would approve of such a match. I asked this of him.

"Because he's pledged to another," the man replied with venom in his voice.

"I've not heard the banns read," I said.

"You will soon enough."

"And if I speak to Roger or his father he will confirm this accusation?"

"Don't know. I didn't go to William. Don't pay to anger a rich man by denouncing 'is son as a rake and a scoundrel."

"You spoke to Roger, then?"

"Aye. He'll not be visiting in the night again. Foolish lass. Believed 'is promises."

During this conversation I had examined Reynold's face, and what I could see of his hands and arms, for scratches that might have been made by fingernails. There were none. No man of Bampton or the Weald seemed to bear such marks, and if any man did they would soon be healed. I began to doubt that what I had seen under Odo's nails was dried blood. What else it might have been I could not guess.

Adela had said the man she saw in the night wore a long, dark garment. In the night any dark-hued clothing might appear black, and there are men who don long cotehardies. But not many. Lads, especially, like to wear shorter tunics and cotehardies so as to show a manly leg.

Mayhap Rosamond had met more than one swain in the night, and her father had not discovered these rendezvous. When he caught the lass with Roger Folewye her father assumed her nightly dalliance had ended. Was it so? Did Adela see Roger creep behind Reynold's house, or some other lad, yet undiscovered? I could ask Rosamond, but I would be unlikely to receive a truthful answer if she had met some lad other than Roger Folewye.

Or did Rosamond meet some older man in the night? A man more likely to don a long cotehardie. Too many questions. Too few answers. And did discovering who might wear a long cotehardie while meeting a maid have anything to do with Odo Fuller's death?

I bade Reynold good day. The man turned from me, reached into his sack, and began dropping peas into the holes his son had poked into the soil.

* * *

Adela had finished the laundry when I returned to Galen House, and had stretched clothing upon bushes to dry. I found her entertaining Bessie and John while Kate was occupied preparing our supper.

"What have you learned?" Kate asked, and brushed a lock of hair from her cheek with the back of her hand. I was pleased to see that even though she was working over the embers in our fireplace, where a kettle of pottage was bubbling, she did not appear flushed. Her cheeks were not reddened.

"The lad Rosamond stole out to meet was of the Weald," I said. "He is pledged to another, ergo the surreptitious meeting."

"But Adela said the man she saw in the night wore a robe, as priests and clerks do."

"Mayhap the maid stole out at different times to see two men," I said. "Her father caught her with Roger Folewye. This does not mean she might not have others sniffing about. Or perhaps Roger wore that night a long cotehardie for the chill. Nights of late have been cold."

"So you believe that what Adela saw and heard has nothing to do with Odo's death?"

"Aye. When Adela heard Reynold threaten to slay a man if he caught Rosamond with him 'twas Roger Folewye who caused his wrath, not Odo. Nor Ernaud or Peter, either."

"So Reynold did say," Kate said with arched eyebrows. "And you believe him?"

"I had to press the man to get Roger's name from him."

"He spoke reluctantly? Why so?"

"William Folewye is the most prosperous of the bishop's tenants in the Weald. Reynold said he feared angering such a man."

"So he did not go to William to complain of the son?"

"He said nay. Spoke firmly to Roger, he said."

"I can imagine. Eight or so years from now, when lads begin to notice Bessie, you will be much the same."

"Aye," I agreed. Bessie takes after her mother. My Kate is slender and shapely, with hair the color of an oak leaf in autumn. And her nose is of reasonable size. If Bessie resembled me I would have less to concern me.

CHAPTER 7

The sky had grown dark with low clouds that threatened rain. Kate and I hurried to the toft and with Adela gathered the clean clothes from the shrubs where they had been placed to dry. As we hurried about the business I asked Adela if she was sure of what she had seen that evening when she returned home late. Did the dark swain really wear a long robe as would a clerk or priest?

"Oh, aye, sir," she replied.

"How can you be sure if the night was dark?"

"The moon was just risin'. 'Twasn't full yet, but near so an' gave enough light to cast shadows. I see somethin' movin' an' hid meself. The man I saw didn't see me, I think. He come past John Blythe's house an' I seen 'im clear. John whitewashed 'is 'ouse last year so the moon lit it up right well. Seen the fellow hurry past an' against the white of John's house saw what 'e wore."

"Reynold told me 'twas Roger Folewye he caught in dalliance with Rosamond. You've no doubt 'twas a priest's robe or a long cotehardie?"

"Nay, sir. Sure of it as I'm sure of the sun risin' tomorrow."

"So you believe you may have seen Odo or Ernaud that night?"

"Aye. The man I saw was comin' from Bridge Street into the Weald. Roger lives toward the end of the Weald. Seems like, was it him I seen, 'e'd 'ave been comin' to Rosamond's house from the other direction."

"Just so," I said.

Did Reynold Wyle know of two men attracted to his daughter, or even three? Did he frighten one away, then slay another? Was he cunning enough to then deflect suspicion to a third man? Or did he turn suspicion to a man who had nothing to do with his lass? More questions. Still no answers.

* * *

Next morn, after a maslin loaf and ale, I set out for the castle. I had come near to Bridge Street when I heard my name called. I turned to see Father Thomas approaching, hurrying past Galen House. Likely he had intended to seek me there when he saw me near the end of Church View Street. I waited for him to overtake me.

"I give you good day, Sir Hugh."

"And to you. How may I serve you?"

"Bartram has sliced his arm with a blade. You must come with needle and thread and stitch the wound."

Bartram Thrupp was Father Thomas's cook and therefore a man who used knives in the preparation of his master's dinner. Would a man slash his arm in the process of making a meal? I turned back to Galen House and as I did asked the cause of the wound.

"Said his blade caught in a joint as he was separating a leg of ham from the carcass. When he tried to wrest it free, his hand slipped and the knife slashed his arm."

The priest halted at the door to Galen House while I collected silk thread and a fine needle. Moments later we entered the vicarage and found the cook, pale and seated upon a bench in his kitchen, clutching a bloody linen cloth to his left arm.

Bartram looked up as I entered his domain. "Clumsy of me," he said, and glanced to his arm. On a table behind him I saw a knife and the side of pork he had been disjointing.

I told Father Thomas I would need a cup of wine and a clean cloth. While he tapped a small butt I unwrapped the cook's arm. The cut was just above the wrist of his left arm, and quite deep. Although it had bled enough to soak the linen cloth, the flow had now nearly ceased.

Father Thomas appeared with wine, which will aid in the mending of such a cut, although no man knows why. Some have tried ale as a less costly substitute, but results have not been so salutary.

Bartram winced as the wine flowed around the laceration, and again when I began to sew the edges of his wound together.

The gash was longer than my longest finger, so I closed it with eight stitches. Bartram's sleeve would hide the scar, but with more sutures a healed scar is less obvious.

Whenever I close such a wound I am required to explain that I follow the practice of Henry de Mondeville, who discovered while dealing with wounded soldiers of the French king that wounds left open, with no salve or bandage, bathed only with wine, healed most readily. Most folk whom I have patched together are troubled that I do not apply a salve of crushed cowslip leaves or oil of bay leaves. So it was with Bartram. I explained to him that his sleeve would be the only covering needed for his cut, and in a fortnight I would call to remove the stitches.

The wound was deep enough that it might interfere with Bartram's duties. Indeed, as I bade him and Father Thomas good day, the cook picked up the knife, flexed the fingers of his left hand about it gingerly, winced, then transferred the blade to his right hand and applied it to the joint to finish his work.

"What is your fee?" Father Thomas asked.

"Four pence."

The priest went to a small locked box that rested upon a table in his hall, withdrew a key from a pouch fastened to his belt, and opened the box. From it he took four silver pennies, handed them to me, then locked the chest. Why, I wondered, did he feel a need to lock his coins away? Surely at night the vicarage doors were barred, and who, in the day, would help themselves to coins from the coffer? Father Thomas is a prudent man. Perhaps he believes an unsecured chest containing coins might be a temptation. To whom? His clerk? His cook? A servant? Some uninvited visitor?

As I returned to Galen House to replace the needle and spool of silken thread I saw the holy man.

No man knew his name. He appeared upon Bampton's streets near to Martinmas and seemed to live as an anchorite. No man had ever heard him speak. His hair and beard were matted and unkempt, his face and hands unwashed. These attributes, folk of Bampton seem to believe, are the marks of piety. I have doubts, but do not voice them. Nowhere does the Scripture tell us that the Lord Christ – the most holy of all who have walked the earth – was slovenly and considered this a virtue. Indeed, He washed His disciples' dirty feet and commanded them to do likewise.

When the fellow first appeared he was seen sitting where Church View Street joins Bridge Street. He did not move from the place nor speak all that day, but sat cross-legged, often with his eyes closed and his lips moving as if in prayer. He stood – I was told, for I did not see his actions – only thrice. When children passed his place with their parents he rose, approached the children, rested a hand upon the lad's or lass's head, and seemed to mouth a silent blessing.

He was not seen again for nearly a fortnight and when he reappeared he sat again at the foot of Church View Street. Since his first appearance folk had gossiped about who he might be and whence he came. No one had answers. Or, I should say, all folk had answers. Perhaps one of these may have been accurate. Opinion had gradually unified that he was a holy man, a hermit, who had taken a vow of silence and whose blessing upon children was to be sought. If he ever again appeared.

When he did and word of his presence was spread through the village, folk brought children to him. He rested hands upon all of these, and parents thought it unseemly to seek his blessing upon their offspring without offering some compensation. He departed the village a few hours later with a sack over his shoulder in which were several loaves, a scrap of bacon, an egg, and in a pouch a collection of farthings, ha'pennies, and – who knows? – perhaps a penny or two.

If he departed that day with a supply of coins he did not spend them on a new robe or cotehardie. When he next appeared, two days after St. Stephen's Day, he wore the same tattered garment he had been clothed in before. The day was bitter cold and I suppose Father Thomas took pity on him, for when he departed that day he took with him not only a sack but an old, worn but serviceable black robe the priest had given him.

Kate had taken Bessie and John to the fellow to receive his blessing at this, his third, appearance. 'Twas shortly after that when Bessie took ill, and then John, and then Bessie again, until my Kate was stricken as well.

The hermit appeared again three days after Candlemas and as before took his place where Church View Street meets Bridge Street. Again he laid hands upon children who were brought to him and as before he said nothing. By this time folk were accustomed to his silence, and respected it. Earlier he was often asked his name and whence he came. No longer. Bampton's residents knew he would not answer, so were themselves silent in his presence.

Days in winter are short, so his fourth appearance was brief. Shortly after the ninth hour the holy man stood and silently walked west upon Bridge Street with his sack over a shoulder, crossed Shill Brook, strode past the castle upon his unshod feet, and departed the village.

But not alone. Henry followed him. The beadle told me later of what he learned. A hundred or so paces beyond Cowleys Corner, at a place where Lord Gilbert's forest verges close on the north side of the road to Black Bourton and Alvescot, the holy man left the road and entered the wood. All this time the fellow never looked back to learn if he was followed. After departing the road he made his way through the forest, stepping carelessly upon twigs so that Henry could follow by the sound of the man's progress through the darkening copse.

Henry said that when the sound of incautious footsteps ceased, he advanced more guardedly, for night was nearly upon him and he did not wish to frighten the holy man. So it was he saw, some ten or so paces before him, a derelict swineherd's hut. The holy man had evidently found the place some months earlier and decided to take up residence for the winter.

Next day Henry informed me of his discovery and in turn I told Lord Gilbert of the man's habitation in his woodland.

"He'll do no harm, I think," Lord Gilbert said. "We'll leave him be. Should he cause trouble, then will be time enough to send him away."

The holy man reappeared every week or two, taking the same place, always silent, blessing any child who passed or was brought to him, and at the close of the day leaving with gifts of food or coins or cast-off clothing. Father Simon once attempted to question the man, but had no more success than any other at prising words from him.

As I entered Galen House that Tuesday I saw the holy man take his accustomed place at the foot of Church View Street. The fellow saw me glance his way, but averted his eyes quickly. He had a haunted expression, as if he feared to look behind him, worried some apparition might be in pursuit. I had never seen him smile, but it seemed to me that his usually phlegmatic expression became one of concern whenever he saw me. Mayhap he thought I was skeptical of his blessing. Or some man told him of my office.

Kate and Adela had our dinner ready, so I consumed my portion of mortrews before continuing the interrupted journey to the castle I had begun some hours earlier.

I passed the holy man, who had, as always, attracted a covey of parents and children. The man paid me no heed, nor I him. His presence in the village was no longer a novelty. So 'tis a wonder I saw the red welt of a healing scrape across his cheek, nearly hidden by his beard.

I stopped to study the mark, and the fellow looked up from the child upon whose head his hands rested and saw me gazing at him. My scrutiny did not seem to please the man. He returned his attention to the child and I saw his lips move but, as always, no sound accompanied this.

I crossed the bridge over Shill Brook and as I did so changed my plans. I would pass the castle and Cowleys Corner and seek the place where Henry Swerd had followed the hermit into the forest. There was yet a silver cresset missing, and the holy man had a scratch upon his cheek. Did Odo Fuller put it there?

I slowed my pace when I came to the place where the wood edged the road, seeking the path Henry had followed which led to the swineherd's hut. I found an overgrown track which, I decided, must be the way to the hut, as there was no other trail that gave sign of recent use.

I found the hut a hundred or so paces into the wood. It had been constructed of coppiced poles tied together with vines, the door was of the same construction, and a roof, now mostly rotted, was made of strips of bark from oak and beech trees. A few of these bark slabs seemed new, as if the hermit had recently replaced those that had allowed rain to drip upon his head. The structure was no more than four paces long and barely two paces wide.

The holy man usually remained in Bampton 'til near dark and 'twas just past the sixth hour when I found the hut. I had plenty of time to search the place for a missing silver cresset, and even if the fellow returned early to his hideaway he had no title to the place and occupied it only because of Lord Gilbert's forbearance.

The interior of the hovel was quite dark. There were no windows. The only light in the place was that which filtered through openings between the poles forming the walls. My search of the hut was as much by feel as by sight.

I found a sleeping pallet made of cast-off tunics and cotehardies. It was soft, and a brief investigation showed it was stuffed with feathers. This bit of luxury did not comport with the ascetic image the hermit cultivated when in company of others. Were there hen houses in Bampton that had lost chickens in the past weeks? Mayhap 'twas not a fox that had taken the fowl.

In a corner of the hut I found two more threadbare tunics and a cotehardie. These were folded neatly. Beneath these was another surprise: a pair of old worn but serviceable leather shoes. Yet the fellow walked barefoot even upon frozen ground. I had seen him do so.

In another corner I found a cache of food – two stale loaves, an egg, a small sack of peas and another of oats. There was also a small bronze pot. I thought it likely that if I searched outside the hut I would find ashes where the holy man cooked his dinner. I did.

But there was no silver cresset to be found. If Odo Fuller had marred the holy man's cheek in a failed attempt to prevent theft I could not prove it. I supposed that the cresset might be buried in last year's fallen leaves somewhere near the hut, but 'twould require an army of men turning the forest floor to learn if this was so.

The hermit was new to Bampton and only rarely visited the town. If he had slain Odo how would he have known where Ernaud lived so as to cause men to suspect him of murder? I left the hut as I found it and returned to the road. The sky was gray with clouds, the forest thick. In the dim light I stumbled against a branch and felt it graze my cheek. Was the mark on the holy man's face made the same way? I entered the road and sought the castle and Lord Gilbert.

"Hmmm. So the holy man is not the pauper he seems, eh?" my employer said when I told him of my discovery.

"Near enough," I replied. "Shall I send him away? He is enjoying the charity of the manor under what could be construed as false pretense."

"He is a mendicant even though he does not live as meanly as folk believe," Lord Gilbert said. "Leave him for now. If he is truly a man of God I do not wish to antagonize him and bring holy wrath upon myself and my house. If he is a charlatan, that will likely become more evident as days pass. Then we will evict the fellow."

I told Lord Gilbert also of events in the Weald.

"Roger Folewye, eh? Don't know the lad, but I know his father. I'm not surprised to learn something villainous of him."

"Like father, like son?" I asked.

"Not always, but often enough."

"Even if the lad is a rake, I still wonder," I said, "what Kate's servant saw, or who she saw, on that night when she walked late to her home. The fellow wore priest-like garb, and approached

86

Reynold Wyle's house from Bridge Street, whereas Roger lives in the other direction."

Lord Gilbert smoothed his beard. "'Tis a puzzle," he said, "but you will ferret out the truth."

I wish I had the confidence in my wit that Lord Gilbert seems to have.

* * *

After Adela departed for her home that evening Kate and I sat before the embers on the hearth to discuss what I had learned this day.

"His blessing," Kate said with a frown, "did Bessie and John no good. One or the other or both have been ill since Candlemas."

"And you are not well," I added.

"But I improve daily."

"I agree. You consumed a goodly portion of your supper today."

"I was hungry today for the first time in a fortnight," she replied. "If I continue so you will soon have a plump wife."

"If you did not regain your appetite I might think myself in a bed filled with broomsticks, so gaunt have you become."

"You wish me to become fat?"

"Nay. Aristotle spoke true – 'moderation in all things' was his motto. A wife should be neither too lean nor too buxom."

"And a husband also."

We sat silent for a time, entranced by the glowing, flickering embers.

"Will you keep a journal of this mystery as you have in the past?" Kate said.

"Our minds work alike," I replied. "Only today I have thought to do so. But I have no parchment."

"You will need to travel to Oxford then?"

"Aye. And for another reason. The silver candlesticks that went missing when Odo was slain have been found, but not the cresset. I have thought to visit the jewelers and goldsmiths in Oxford to learn if such an object has been offered to them."

"When will you go? Will you travel with Arthur? I do not like for you to be upon the road alone."

"I will visit the castle tomorrow and seek Arthur. We will travel to Oxford on Thursday, and return Friday."

* * *

Next day I found Arthur mucking out Lord Gilbert's stables. He was not alone at the work. Two other grooms and a carter assisted him. One of these was Uctred, and when he heard that I desired companionship for a journey to Oxford he insisted that I include him. I told Arthur to have three palfreys ready on the morrow, then left them to complete their work. The dung and straw that filled the cart would be taken to a fallow field and spread there.

That afternoon I visited Father Ralph to learn what I could of the missing cresset. It was, I learned, a gift from his father upon his ordination, and therefore worth more to him than its weight in silver.

"About as large as my two hands encircled," he said. "With thorns worked into the lip to represent the thorns which circled the Lord Christ's head. In the bottom of the bowl the silversmith engraved the letter 'R.'"

"As the cresset has not been found in Bampton, tomorrow I will travel to Oxford," I said, "to seek it among the goldsmiths there."

"It was unlike any other I have ever seen," the priest said. "If you see it you will know it immediately."

This was surely true. Most cressets are ceramic, or even wooden. A silver cresset is an oddity in itself. One embellished as Father Ralph described would be instantly recognized.

* * *

Kate's rooster woke me at dawn Thursday. After a maslin loaf and a cup of ale I kissed my Kate and set off for the castle. I met Adela walking to Galen House as I crossed Shill Brook.

'Tis sixteen miles, thereabouts, from Bampton to Oxford. With fresh, rested horses the journey can be completed in three hours. So it was that Arthur, Uctred, and I passed Osney Abbey and crossed Bookbinders' Bridge at the fourth hour. We left our beasts at a stable just off the High Street to be fed and watered, ate a dinner of roasted capon and barley loaves at an inn behind All Saints' Church, then set about our business.

Since plague has taken so many scholars, demand for parchment is reduced, and likewise the price. I purchased three gatherings at a stationer's shop off Broad Street for but eighteen pence. With this need cared for 'twas time to seek the town's goldsmiths.

I found the stolen cresset in the second shop I visited, on Northgate Street, near to St. Michael's at the Northgate. 'Twas the goldsmith from whom I had purchased Kate's emerald wedding ring who had it, although the proprietor did not remember me for my custom. A goldsmith sells many rings, whereas a husband buys but one. If he is fortunate.

The goldsmith had in his shop a shelf upon which numerous items were displayed. There were spoons and forks of silver, several silver cups, three gold rings, one of these set with a ruby. There were also two small silver candlesticks and Father Ralph's cresset. I knew it immediately.

The shop owner noticed my interest in the cresset and, rubbing his hands together with an ingratiating smile, proceeded to persuade me of the quality of the piece. He saw Arthur and Uctred, assumed they were my servants, and set a price accordingly.

"Only three shillings and six pence," he said, concluding his remarks.

"There is the letter 'R' worked into the cresset," I said. "My name is Hugh."

"Ah... those are similar in shape. I can work the silver so that 'R' will become 'H'."

"How did you come by this object?" I asked.

"Uh...'twas the possession of a wealthy burgher of Witney. When he died his widow removed to Oxford and, needing funds, offered it to me."

"You lie," I said.

"What?" The fellow bristled. He would have set upon me with his fists, I believe, but for Arthur standing close behind me, his thick arms folded across a burly chest. When Arthur accompanies me I am bold to speak an objectionable truth to those who dislike candor. I don't see myself as a coward, but there are degrees of courage and mine is greater when Arthur and Uctred are my companions.

"This cresset is the possession of a priest of the Church of St. Beornwald, in Bampton. Father Ralph, hence the 'R'. 'Twas stolen from the church at Easter, and a clerk was slain in the taking. Now, I ask again, how did you acquire this cresset?"

"I have told you. A woman offered it to me. Told me what I have told you."

"How much did you pay her for it?"

The goldsmith hesitated. "Two shillings."

"A bargain, for you. Now you demand three and six for it. What was this woman's name? Where is her domicile?"

"Don't know, do I? She didn't say an' I didn't ask."

"Describe her. How old was she? What was the color of her hair? What was her garb? Tall or short?"

The goldsmith pulled at his beard. "Tallish, she was. Near as tall as me. Buxom. Dark hair, what I could see of it under her wimple. Not young, but her face didn't have the wrinkles of old age. Near to forty years, I'd say. Wore a green cotehardie, as I recall."

"If she calls here again learn her name and where she may be found. Regardless of who she might be or how much you paid for the cresset it is stolen and must be returned."

"Who are you to say so?" the goldsmith demanded.

"I am Sir Hugh de Singleton, bailiff to Lord Gilbert Talbot at his manor of Bampton."

I saw the man's lip curl when he heard that I was a bailiff. Most of my cohorts in similar villages are known to be avaricious schemers, ready to cheat all, including their employers. But there is a way to know if a bailiff is honest. Ask him. If he says yes, he probably is not.

"Do not sell or dispose of this cresset until the rightful owner calls for it. I will not require that you release it to me now. I will tell Father Ralph where he may find it."

"An' what if I do sell it?"

"No doubt Father Ralph will seek a lawyer. And Sir Roger de Elmerugg is a friend to Lord Gilbert. I am sure that he and Lord Gilbert would be displeased to learn that you deal in stolen silver."

Sir Roger is Sheriff of Oxford, and to help recoup the cost of purchasing his position from King Edward would be delighted to levy a handsome fine upon a goldsmith who trafficked in stolen goods. The goldsmith knew this also, but I reminded him before leaving his shop.

I wondered at the time if I should demand possession of the cresset. But without evidence that what I said was true I thought the goldsmith would protest and mayhap set the sheriff's serjeants after me. I thought 'twould be best if Father Ralph called for his cresset.

"You think 'e told the truth?" Arthur said when we set off down Northgate Street.

"Mayhap. If so, the woman is in league with whoever slew Odo. She'd not travel from Bampton to Oxford alone, either, that's for sure. If she's not of Oxford. And I doubt a woman dealt the blow which sent Odo to the Lord Christ. A matron might deliver a blow that would knock a man senseless, but could a woman cave in a man's skull?"

"I've known some what could," Uctred said, "was they much vexed."

"Aye," Arthur agreed.

"Why would a woman be angry enough with Odo to dent his head?" I said.

Neither man replied. I likewise had no answer to that question. Nay, 'twas a man – I believed – that did the murder in the Church of St. Beornwald, but he was likely assisted in turning the stolen cresset into coins. Perhaps a woman was involved in the matter after all . . .

I had found Father Ralph's stolen cresset and purchased three gatherings of parchment. I had no more business in Oxford, so led Arthur and Uctred to the stable, retrieved our palfreys, paid the bill, and set off for Eynsham and the abbey where we would spend the night.

We splashed across the Thames at Swinford as the light faded. The abbey is less than a mile from the ford, but the porter had already closed the gate and I was required to pound upon the planks and shout before his assistant admitted us.

The porter's assistant and a lay brother led our beasts to the abbey stables, and the guest master was summoned. He led us to the guest chamber and promised a supper would be provided. Two novices soon appeared with barley loaves, a pea and bean pottage, and ale. The lads had no sooner set our meal upon a table than the bell rang to call them to vespers. We were about to take to our beds when one of the novices returned with a message that Abbot Gerleys wished for me to visit his chamber in the morning, after matins.

The abbot holds his position in part because some years past, while investigating the death of an abbey novice, I discovered a heresy within the abbey, and learned that the prior, whom it was assumed would soon replace the aged, ailing abbot, was the secret leader of the heretical monks. The prior was sent to an abbey in Scotland, and when Abbot Thurstan died Brother Gerleys, the novice master, was chosen to replace him. I have often wondered whether or not Abbot Gerleys is pleased with this elevation. 'Tis surely an honor that other men see him suited to govern them, but his conversation often leads me to believe that he considers the office more an onerous duty than an achievement. Plato said that those who seek power are unfit to hold it. Abbot Gerleys would meet with the philosopher's approval.

* * *

Monks do not break their fast but for a cup of ale, but they do not send guests on their way with empty stomachs. Immediately after matins a novice brought wheaten loaves and ale to the guest chamber. When I had consumed my loaf I set off for the abbot's chamber, advising Arthur and Uctred that I would soon return and we would be off for Bampton.

The monk who serves as Abbot Gerleys' clerk knows me well, and when he saw me approach announced my appearance through the abbot's open door.

"Tell Sir Hugh to enter," I heard in reply.

Abbot Gerleys' eyes are weak, mayhap due to much study. I found him with a glass in his hand, to enlarge the letters of the book open upon his desk.

"Come in, Sir Hugh...come in. What has brought you to St. Mary's Abbey? Most often when you seek hospitality you have been to Oxford about some puzzling matter. What is it this time which brings you here?"

I told the abbot of Odo, Ernaud, the buried candlesticks, the silver cresset, and the nocturnal prowler in the Weald. He listened intently, his chin resting upon a fist.

"How could a woman obtain a cresset stolen from the church?" Abbot Gerleys said when I had completed the tale.

"She is surely an associate of the felon who slew the clerk and stole the cresset," I said, "if she truly exists."

"You believe the goldsmith might have spoken falsely?"

"Aye. He might have. Although I cannot see how he thought he might benefit by dissembling."

"The wife, perhaps, of the murderer?"

"Could be. If so, Ernaud is exonerated."

"Seems to me he is absolved already. The clerk could not have given the cresset to some woman while passing his days in Lord Gilbert's dungeon."

"Aye, although if the woman knew where it was hid she might retrieve it without his presence."

"Would Ernaud seek out a woman to aid his evil?" Abbot Gerleys said. "She would not travel alone to Oxford to sell the cresset, and it could not be sold in Bampton. The woman would need a man to accompany her on the road to Oxford. Why not simply find some man to transport the cresset to Oxford?"

"Indeed. Mayhap," I said, "some man did, but did not want his face recognized or remembered, so sought a woman of Oxford to offer the cresset to the goldsmith."

"Hmmm. Possible. Perhaps even likely. What about the clerk, Ernaud?"

"I must send word of the discovery to Exeter before the bishop's court decides some penalty which may not be undone."

"You were asked to prove a man innocent rather than guilty. Seems to me you have done so. Will you now seek the true felon?"

"Aye. I have unearthed evidence that makes Ernaud an unlikely felon, but he cannot be proven innocent until the guilty man is named."

"Or guilty woman," the abbot said.

"Aye. Improbable at it seems this possibility must not be rejected."

CHAPTER 8

Abbot Gerleys bade me good day and I returned to the guest chamber to collect Arthur, who had put the delay in our departure to good use: I found him snoring upon his pallet. He, Uctred, and I then went to the abbey stables. Lay brothers saddled our mounts and by the fourth hour we saw the spire of St. Beornwald's Church above the forest east of Bushy Row.

The first matter was to speak to Father Thomas and tell him what I had learned, then to tell Father Ralph that I had found his cresset. I dismounted at Church View Street, sent Arthur and Uctred on to the castle with the palfreys, and walked directly to Father Thomas's vicarage.

"A woman?" the priest said incredulously as I told, for the second time that day, of what I had learned in Oxford.

"If the goldsmith spoke true," I cautioned.

"You have doubts?"

"Bailiffs and serjeants and constables always have doubts," I replied.

"What do you intend?"

"Your new clerk must return to Exeter with a message. I will write to the bishop, and you and Father Ralph and Father Simon must sign the letter. It seems clear that Ernaud did not slay Odo, as he could not have had possession of the cresset. I believe the bishop will agree and will release him."

"*Should* release him," Father Thomas said.

"You believe he will not?"

"Do you know Bishop Brantyngham?"

"Nay."

"If you did you would understand my doubt."

"The lad will reach Exeter sooner if he is mounted. I will ask the castle marshalsea to have a palfrey ready tomorrow morning. Meanwhile collect Father Ralph and Father Simon. I will seek my dinner, then this afternoon tell them what I have told you."

I stopped at Galen House to tell my Kate that I had returned, told her that I must seek the marshalsea, but would return anon for my dinner.

Lord Gilbert's groom of the stables promised that a palfrey would be ready next morning. When I returned to Galen House I found a dinner of stewed herrings awaiting me. 'Twas good to be home, sitting quietly by my hearth, watching Bessie play with her doll and listening to John gurgle happily.

An hour later I met with the three vicars of St. Beornwald's Church, along with their clerks. We assembled in Father Thomas's vicarage, his cook bringing cups of ale to lubricate our conversation. I repeated to the other priests and the three clerks what I had earlier told Father Thomas.

"So my cresset is in an Oxford goldsmith's shop!" Father Simon exclaimed.

"Aye, it is. The shop is on Northgate Street, near to St. Michael's at the Northgate. I told the proprietor that the cresset was stolen and he must not sell it. He was to expect you, or someone you send, to call for it."

I expected William to object to being sent with a message to the bishop. He did not. The young are often ready for new experiences. As I spoke, it came to me that one lad alone upon the road might not be safe. I said that perhaps two should travel – William and Alan should both make the journey.

Father Simon objected. "A clerk alone on the road is safe enough. All men know such men have nothing worth stealing. And Alan is needed here."

"William will have a horse," Father Thomas said, "and a purse of coins to pay for food and an inn if he cannot find an abbey to keep him overnight as he travels. Such things are worth stealing."

Whether or not Alan was essential to Father Simon in his duties I could not say. But 'tis true enough that poor clerics are generally safe upon the roads. They have little to plunder. Nevertheless I should have agreed with Father Thomas.

Next morning I accompanied William to the castle and made sure that he had my letter, signed also by the priests of

St. Beornwald's Church, folded securely in his pouch, then saw him seated upon one of Lord Gilbert's palfreys.

The lad did not mount the beast gracefully. He was, I later learned, reared in Cirencester, the son of a minor burgher of the town, and thus had small experience of equestrian pursuits.

He set off well enough, grinning as he clucked the palfrey to a trot. I hoped he would not continue at that pace, or the beast would tire before he reached Faringdon. I saw the lad slow his mount to a walk as he neared Cowleys Corner and disappeared. I was relieved. The journey to Exeter would take four days, I thought. And four days to return. I would know in eight days of Bishop Brantyngham's response to my discoveries. Mayhap by that time I would know more.

* * *

I awoke next morning to the ringing of the Angelus Bell but turned my face to the pillow. John announced his desire to break his fast, so Kate arose and took the babe from his cradle. Kate was thus awake and heard the pounding upon the door of Galen House.

I had drifted back to the arms of Morpheus when my wife shook me awake. "'Tis Arthur," she said, "with news from the castle. Lord Gilbert asks for your presence, and to make haste."

When a peer of the realm requires a lowly knight to make haste, the knight does so. I pulled on chauces and cotehardie, and tumbled down the stairs. I found Arthur waiting in the doorway, cap in hand.

"What news?" I asked.

"The beast what the clerk William set off on yesterday, it come back."

"Come back?" I said stupidly. Well, I was newly and abruptly awakened.

"Aye. Alone. No rider. Porter seen it in the forecourt when 'e lowered the drawbridge."

My first thought was that William had toppled from the palfrey, or the beast had shied from some fright and thrown the clerk. We would need to assemble a party of searchers and find

97

the fellow. Mayhap he lay injured in the road, or was even now limping back to Bampton. Not so.

"Sir Henry says there's blood upon the beast's saddle."

Was William thrown from the horse and injured, but then managed to climb again to the saddle before tumbling once more to the road? Whatever the situation, he must be found and his injuries dealt with.

I told my Kate of the matter that had brought Arthur to our door, advised her that I was not likely to see the search for William completed before time for mass, swallowed a cup of ale, and hurried to the castle. I did not linger at Shill Brook to study the flow.

Lord Gilbert, Sir Henry, Sir Jaket – one of Lord Gilbert's household knights – and a dozen or so grooms and valets surrounded the palfrey as Arthur and I came into view of the castle gatehouse.

Lesser folk moved aside when I approached, and Lord Gilbert said, "Some mischief has befallen the clerk you sent to Exeter. Look – here are drops of blood."

My employer looked to the rear of the saddle. Four dark circles stained the brown leather. One of these was smeared, as if William had smudged it while sliding from the beast. Did he dismount, or did he unwillingly fall from the palfrey?

I thought it strange that the blood was on the rear of the saddle. A man who falls from his beast will not likely smite the ground upon his back so as to leave bloodstains upon the rear of his saddle if he remounts. More probable, he would bleed upon the fore part of the saddle, the pommel.

"Has Father Thomas been told?" I asked.

"Aye, I sent Uctred to tell him," Lord Gilbert said.

At that moment I saw the priest come round the curtain wall, his robe flapping about his bony ankles in his haste. Uctred followed, his ankles as bony as the priest's, but no robe to mask them.

"Did any man see the beast return?" I asked the marshal.

"Nay. 'Twas not here when the drawbridge was raised

last night, but it was at dawn when Bartholomew lowered the drawbridge and raised the portcullis."

"Then the clerk may have been as much as half a day's journey when some mishap befell him," Lord Gilbert said.

No man likes to contradict his employer, so I was tactful. I pointed out that the palfrey might have stood patiently for some time after William toppled from the saddle.

"Oh, aye," Lord Gilbert said, and raised an eyebrow.

"Mishap?" Father Thomas said. "Or was he set upon?"

"What had he to steal," Lord Gilbert said, "but for my palfrey, and here the beast is?"

"Whatever the case, we must seek him straightaway," I said. "He may lie injured or wounded, and need help."

"I wonder," Sir Jaket said, "whether some traveler has not already found him and taken him somewhere for care."

"Mayhap we will learn that this is so," I replied. "But remember the Lord Christ spoke of the man who was set upon by robbers. Most who came upon him passed by and ignored his need."

"Horses will speed the search," Lord Gilbert said. "Sir Henry, prepare four... no, six palfreys."

The marshal turned and trotted under the gatehouse toward the stables. Three grooms attached to the marshalsea followed, not needing to be told their duty.

We others remained at the drawbridge, exchanging opinions and predictions of what the search for William would disclose. We were all wrong.

Sir Henry and the grooms did not linger at their work and they soon appeared leading six horses.

"You," Lord Gilbert said to me, "will take charge of the search. I will go, along with Sir Henry and Sir Jaket. Who else shall accompany us?"

I caught a glimpse of Arthur at that moment. There was pleading in his eyes. The man objects to being left behind when excitement may be in the offing. Not that finding a man who has fallen from his horse is likely to be dramatic, but if the clerk was discovered to be the victim of felons Arthur would be displeased to miss their capture. I chose him and Uctred, who also seemed pleased with the decision. Father Thomas wished also to participate in the search, but I told him to await our return at the castle.

I told the searchers that we would seek the missing clerk in three groups. Lord Gilbert and Sir Henry would ride the middle of the road. Sir Jaket and Uctred would examine the sinister verge, while Arthur and I would study the dexter side of the road. I thought it possible that an injured man might crawl from the road to the grass of the verge.

"Watch for hoofprints that seem unusual," I said, "as if a beast stood in one place for some time. Or any sign that violence may have happened. There was blood upon the saddle William used. Mayhap some drops have fallen to the road."

* * *

'Twas as the distant bell of St. Beornwald's Church announced time for the mass that Lord Gilbert drew back on the reins of his ambler and shouted, "Hold! What is this?" We had just passed Cowleys Corner, upon the road to Clanfield.

I rode a few paces behind Lord Gilbert and he was peering at the road to his left, so I did not at first see what had caught his attention. He flung a leg over the pommel and leapt to the road. He then placed hands upon his knees and bent to examine the dirt. I also dropped from my saddle, hurried behind Lord Gilbert's mount, and immediately saw what had caught his attention. A stain nearly as large as the butt end of a wine cask darkened the dirt.

"What is this?" Lord Gilbert asked again when I joined him. "Blood?"

"I fear it so," I replied. "And if it is, the injured man is in peril of his life. A great flow of blood has made this stain."

The others of our party, hearing these words, began to cast their eyes about, seeking a wounded man or a corpse.

"You believe a man so wounded will travel far seeking aid?" Sir Jaket asked.

"Nay. And this," I said, pointing to the bloody dirt, "was not caused by a fall from a horse. A blade has opened a large cut. On some man."

"Some man?" Lord Gilbert said. "You think it may be someone other than the clerk who has spilled his blood here?"

"'Tis likely William who was attacked here, but 'til we find him we'll not know of a certainty."

"Who would attack a lowly clerk?" Sir Henry said.

"First things first," I replied. "We must find William and, if he lives, treat his wounds. Mayhap he has crawled off somewhere near. I doubt he could go far, and it is unlikely his assailant would go to the trouble of carrying him away."

"Aye," Lord Gilbert agreed. "To what purpose?"

"Odd," Sir Jaket said, "that we saw no sign of him while on the way from the castle. I'd think he would try to return there."

"Just so," I agreed. "Mayhap he crawled into the weeds seeking to avoid his attacker, and there perished. A dead man cannot call for aid nor hear men pass him by. We should return to the castle, walking, and prowl the weeds and bushes alongside the road."

"Look there," Arthur said, and pointed behind us.

'Twas the holy man. He had appeared perhaps a hundred paces from where we stood surrounding the stain in the road. I realized then that the place where William had been wounded was near to the track I had followed through the wood to the hermit's hut.

The holy man saw our faces turn to him. He stopped and beckoned with a finger that we should follow. He did not speak.

The six of us led our beasts to the opening in the wood where the holy man had appeared. When he saw that we obeyed his gesture he turned and disappeared into the wood.

I charged Uctred to remain with the horses and five of us followed the fellow. 'Twas easy enough to do. The few low-growing bushes in the wood had not yet come to full leaf so as to obstruct vision along the forest floor, and the hermit made no effort to walk noiselessly over leaves and twigs. I was only five or so paces behind him when the ancient swineherd's hut came into view.

The door of the hut was constructed of broken branches tied together with interlacing vines. Other vines formed hinges, and a stick placed through a loop of vines held the door closed. All this I had seen before. The holy man removed the stick, dragged the door open, then stood aside and pointed to the dim interior. All this time he said nothing, nor did any of our party direct a question to him. His silent reputation was known to those of the castle, and even Lord Gilbert respected the choice.

I was closest to the hut, so plunged ahead. I thought I knew what I might find there, and I did. William Walle lay upon the holy man's feather-stuffed bed. One of the tattered old cotehardies the hermit had been given covered the clerk.

I knelt over the prone figure and listened for the sound of breathing while I watched his chest. The sound, and the rise and fall of the clerk's chest, were nearly imperceptible, but the lad was alive.

I drew the cotehardie from William and sought the cut that had caused him to bleed so profusely. 'Twas not visible until I turned him to his side. There I found a small gash in his robe in the center of a large stiffened patch of dried blood. It appeared to me that someone had plunged a dagger into William's back as he rode from Cowleys Corner.

I stooped to leave the hut's low door and told Sir Henry what was needed. "Take Arthur and return to the castle. Find a pallet. William is within, and lives, but mayhap not for long if his wounds are not dealt with. We will take him to Galen House where I may see if his life can be saved."

The marshal did not protest at being assigned groom's work, but motioned to Arthur, and the two of them trotted off noisily toward the road, the snapping of fallen twigs and branches under their feet marking their progress and soon growing faint.

Even though the holy man never spoke I thought he might respond to questions that could be answered yes or no with a shake or nod of the head.

"Did you find this man injured, and bring him here?"

The hermit nodded.

"Yesterday?"

He shook his head.

"This morning?"

A nod.

"He has been stabbed," I said, but before I could complete the question the holy man shook his head vigorously.

Then, before I could speak again, he ducked into the hut. A moment later he reappeared with the broken halves of an arrow in his hand. These he offered to me.

"Shot with an arrow, by heavens," Lord Gilbert exclaimed.

In the darkness of the hut, intent as I was upon the clerk, I had not noticed the broken arrow. The half that included the arrowhead was bloodied its entire length, the feathered half was unstained. I knew the likely cause.

"Did you break the arrow to remove it?" I asked the hermit.

He nodded.

How could this be? If the arrow was broken so it could be removed, the iron point must have been withdrawn from the front of William's body. I crawled again into the hut. This time I raised the clerk's robe until I could view his abdomen. There I saw the slash and hole in his flesh the arrow had made as it penetrated from William's back to issue from his belly.

The arrow had stopped within the clerk's gut, not traveling far enough to leave a cut in the front of his robe. And while this exit wound had bled, the flow was small compared to what had gushed from William's back.

The holy man had known what to do with such a wound. An arrow cannot be withdrawn by wrenching it back through the passage it made as it entered the body. Well, I suppose it could be, but the barbs on the head will do more harm to the wounded man as it is extracted than when the arrow first entered his body. Only if the barbs are compressed, bent back to the shaft with pliers, can an arrow be withdrawn whence it came. The holy man had no such tool, so he had broken the arrow and drawn the pointed half completely through William's body.

'Twas too dark in the hut for a complete examination of the wound, but I thought it fatal. Indeed, I wondered that he yet lived. The arrow had entered the right side of his back, below the ribs, near to his waist. Within that part of a man's body are many vital organs, which when so abused are likely to fail and lead to death. Nevertheless I resolved to move William to Galen House as rapidly as possible and see what might be done to save him. If he survived the transfer.

A living man might be able to tell me something of his assailant. I surmised that whoso wished to slay William knew the reason for his journey. He was not, I was sure, attacked by some robber. What man would attack the clerk so near to Bampton and the castle? A man who dared not be away from his duties long, so he could not lay in wait for William many miles from the town? Who would want the clerk's mission to fail but the man who wished Ernaud to be found guilty of Odo Fuller's murder?

I know little of archery. Lord Gilbert and Sir Jaket, on the other hand, know a great deal about bows and arrows. While I examined William's wounds I heard them speaking outside the hut but paid little attention to their conversation. When I had completed this second and more thorough inspection of the wounds I left the hut and saw Lord Gilbert and the knight examining the arrow.

"Here is a strange weapon," Lord Gilbert said to me.

"How so?" I replied.

"Look at the shaft. 'Tis snapped in two, but that's not what you need to see. Even in one piece it would be as crooked as a pardoner's promises."

He sighted down each shaft, then handed them to me. He spoke true. An arrow so warped as this would not fly true.

"And see the arrowhead. 'Tis not iron. No smith made the thing. What do you suppose it is?"

I studied the point. Again Lord Gilbert was correct. The arrowhead was crudely formed. From impressions in the metal I thought it might have been hammered to its present shape. Iron could not be pounded so unless red hot, and 'twas clear no skilled smith would have done such clumsy work. Pewter might be hammered thin and filed to a sharp edge without the use of a forge. And the gray color indicated pewter rather than iron.

"This," I said to Lord Gilbert and Sir Jaket, "is a spoon. Some man has fashioned a rough point for his arrow. See where the hammer blows have dimpled the pewter."

"See the fletching," Sir Jaket said and handed the rear half of the arrow to me. I scoffed at the unskilled application of feathers. They were fastened to the shaft with black thread for whipping. No glue had been applied.

"These are chicken feathers," I said.

"Aye," Sir Jaket agreed. "No goose produced them. And see how two come from a dexter wing and one from a sinister. Whoso created this did not know, or care, that all the fletching must come from the same wing, else the arrow will not spin true in flight."

"You said the arrow did not pass through the clerk's body," Lord Gilbert said.

"Aye. This point entered his back but opened only a prick on his belly."

"Hmmm. No arrow so warped will be accurate at a great distance. But from a close distance a bow of reasonable power should send a shaft completely through a man. The arrow would enter his back and continue on its path."

"What, then?" I said. "Was this arrow sent to its target from no great distance, from a weak bow?"

"Either from a weak bow," Sir Jaket said, "or a bow drawn by a weak man."

As the knight delivered this opinion I heard Sir Henry and Arthur return, stumbling through the wood and tripping over roots in their haste. Arthur carried under his arm two poles. A heavy hempen canvas was wrapped about them.

Arthur and I spread the pallet upon the forest floor, then entered the hut and gently drew William out into the light and laid him upon the canvas. He gasped twice, but did not open his eyes, nor did he try to speak. But I saw his chest continue to rise and fall, so we had not slain him by moving him to the pallet.

All this time the holy man stood watching, listening. I turned to him.

"Did this wounded man come to you for help?" I asked.

He shook his head.

"You found him?"

He nodded.

"Why will the fellow not speak?" Lord Gilbert thundered. "Have you taken a vow?" he asked the hermit.

The holy man shook his head.

"Then speak! Tell us what you know, what you saw, what you heard."

Barons like Lord Gilbert are accustomed to obedience. But the holy man simply stared at him, unblinking. Finally, slowly, the fellow opened his mouth. But not to speak. Where his tongue should have been was a small, tattered lump of tissue. It was hideous to behold. Lord Gilbert stepped back in revulsion.

"No wonder the man will not speak," Sir Jaket said softly. "He cannot."

"What has happened to this man?" Lord Gilbert asked me, as if I would know.

I did not know, but had a suspicion. I turned to the holy man and said, "Did some man tear your tongue from your mouth?"

He nodded, his head downcast and his eyes upon the pallet and William.

"How long ago did you find this man?" I asked. "An hour past?"

He shook his head.

"Less than an hour?"

He nodded.

"Were you on your way to seek help when you came upon us in the road?" I said.

Again he nodded.

"Sir Henry," I said, "go, and send Uctred here while you see to the horses for a moment."

When Uctred arrived I told him and Arthur to carry William to Galen House. "Be as gentle as you can," I urged, "but make haste. I will ride ahead to prepare."

Arthur and Uctred lifted the pallet and carefully moved through the wood to the road.

"We will learn little more here," I said. Then, to the holy man I asked, "Do you read or write?"

He shook his head. This was to be expected, but was unfortunate. Had he done so I might have interrogated the fellow more completely.

I tucked the halves of the broken arrow under my arm, then addressed the hermit. "If you think of some information I have not asked about, which might lead to the felon who has done this wickedness, come to me."

The fellow nodded his head. We left him standing before the hut, watching solemnly as we set off for the road and our palfreys.

Arthur and Uctred had got to the road before us with their burden, but we soon passed them. I left my palfrey at the castle for Sir Henry to deal with, and hurried afoot to Galen House to make ready for my patient.

Kate and Adela had returned home from mass and were at work in the kitchen, preparing our dinner.

Kate said later that she did not expect such an early return and was startled when she heard the door crash open and my hurried footsteps in the hall.

I hastily told Kate and Adela of William's wound, then ran up the stairs to my instruments chest to select the scalpel, needle, silken thread, and herbs that I might need. Until his death some months past, Kate's father had occupied a room on the ground floor of Galen House. His bed was yet there, a wooden frame with a feather-filled mattress supported by entwined hempen ropes.

When I returned to the ground floor I told Adela to hasten to Father Thomas's vicarage. She must tell the priest that William was found, but near to death. "Tell him," I said, "to hurry to Galen House with wine with which I might cleanse the clerk's wounds. But tell him also that he should be prepared to observe Extreme Unction."

Adela scurried off as Arthur and Uctred appeared at the corner of Church View Street and Bridge Street. They walked swiftly but were heedful of my request to jar their burden as little as possible. I held the door open for them and directed them to the room ready for William.

"Set the pallet upon the mattress," I said. "We'll not try to lift him from it to the bed. Just draw out the poles and set them aside."

Uctred did so while Arthur bent over one side of the bed and I the other.

"He alive?" Arthur asked. "We did like you said... tried to keep 'im steady-like."

"He lives," I said. "See his chest rise and fall."

The door to Galen House remained open and through it came Father Thomas and Adela. The priest found me bending over William, considering what must be done. "Dead?" he asked when he saw the clerk.

"Nay, but near so. He is not yet to the gates of pearl, but he can see them not far off."

"Here is the wine," the priest said, and held out a flask. With my scalpel I cut away William's robe, kirtle, and braes. Then, with Arthur's help, I turned the clerk to his side and washed the wound in his back with a scrap of linen soaked in the wine. I had thought to stitch the wound closed immediately, but decided not to do so. An arrow, even with a broad point, does not make a large entry wound. Perhaps it might be best to allow the cut to drain for a few days. The clerk was not losing more blood through the laceration.

I turned William to his back to address the smaller wound in his gut. As I did so he caught his breath, then released it in a great sigh. Moving him had caused a pain that penetrated to his senseless mind.

"Shall I perform Extreme Unction now," Father Thomas asked, "or should I wait?"

It is not good to perform the sacrament while there is a chance a man might recover from his illness or wounds. If he lives he must fast perpetually, go barefoot, and never again lay with his wife. But I thought William near death, and he had no wife nor was he likely to ever have one. I nodded to the priest.

William was incapable of answering the seven interrogations. Father Thomas said the paternoster over him, then gently opened the clerk's mouth and placed a fragment of the host upon his tongue. This act seemed to bring William out of his unconsciousness somewhat. His eyelids flickered, his mouth closed over the bread, and I saw him clench and unclench a fist.

Then he opened his mouth and tried to speak. Three times the clerk tried to form some word, but he failed. And then his breathing stopped. 'Twas as if this effort to speak had consumed what spark of life remained within him.

"I have lost two clerks," Father Thomas said, and made the sign of the cross over William's corpse. We others in the chamber crossed ourselves as well.

"I will send Peter to sound the passing bell," Father Thomas said, "then send him and Alan to take William's corpse to my vicarage. Who has done this murder?"

Father Thomas had seen William's wounds and knew they were the result of a felony. I explained briefly what I had seen and heard that morning.

"'Tis as I thought," the priest said. "Here is more evidence that Ernaud is no felon. Surely the man who slew Odo and laid the evil at Ernaud's feet is the same who put an arrow into William's back."

"I agree. Here is the arrow."

I had propped the broken shafts next to the door to the chamber. I picked them up and handed them to the priest. I said nothing, awaiting his judgment.

Father Thomas is no archer, but readily discerned the crude nature of what he held. "No arrowsmith made this," he said. "'Tis a travesty that such rubbish can end a man's life."

I did not ask the priest if a wounded man would prefer receiving his death stroke from a cunningly made weapon rather than some vulgar dagger or arrow. But I thought it.

The priest took a last, lingering glance at the corpse, then departed Galen House. "Return to the castle," I said to Arthur and Uctred, "and tell Lord Gilbert of this regrettable death."

Shortly after they departed I heard the doleful sound of the bell of St. Beornwald's Church announcing to the village that a man was dead. Soon after that Peter and Alan arrived to carry William's corpse to Father Thomas's vicarage. The poles Arthur and Uctred had used were replaced in the pallet and the two clerks set off with their burden.

Kate approached as I watched Peter and Alan depart. "Will you take some dinner?" she asked. "There is pomme dorryse and wheaten bread with parsley butter."

This is a favorite meal of mine – come to think on it, there are few meals which are not among my favorites – but this day I had little appetite. Kate urged me to consume a reasonable portion, and to please her I did so. I did not need an unhappy wife added to my other vexations.

From her kitchen Kate had heard my conversation with Father Thomas, so combined with what I had earlier told her she knew of the morning's discoveries. When dinner was past and Adela sent home for the day she spoke of what she had heard.

"If the same man slew both Odo and William he did not plan either murder," she said. "I heard you and Father Thomas speak of the arrow."

"You likely speak true," I replied. "The man did not take a weapon to the church, but rather used what was at hand. As for the arrow, he did plan far enough in advance to slay William that he had time to fashion a crude arrow. Such a thing might be done in an hour, mayhap less."

"But not a bow," Kate said.

"Nay, not a bow. 'Tis Lord Gilbert's belief that the felon was near to William when he loosed the arrow. A shaft so crooked would not fly true any distance. Yet, if this is so it is odd that the arrow barely penetrated William's body."

"Why is this odd?" Kate asked.

"Because an arrow discharged at close range should have passed through William's body and continued on its path. Unless 'twas a crudely made bow fashioned in a few moments, or a worthy bow drawn by someone of little strength."

"A woman, perchance?"

"I had not considered that. Why would a woman slay two clerks and shift blame to a third?"

"Why indeed?" Kate said. "'Tis not that I wish to complicate my husband's life, but such a thing may be, even if it seems unlikely."

"Unlikely... aye, I can agree with that. But possible."

My wife had just doubled the number of suspects for two murders. For this I must thank her. Someday.

CHAPTER 9

William had resided in Bampton so briefly that few inhabitants knew him. So Father Thomas decided against a wake. Those who might have attended would have done so only for the ale and carousing.

On Monday morning when the church bell rang to tell the village that William's funeral was about to begin fewer than a dozen men assembled behind the priests and catafalque, and no women were hired to wail out pretended sorrow. 'Twas a quiet funeral. I would prefer the same when my time comes to rest in St. Beornwald's churchyard. Although if Kate survives me and hires a legion of Bampton matrons to screech behind my corpse on the way to the church the din will not trouble me.

When William's funeral was done I saw Father Ralph speaking to Peter and Alan. When the conversation was finished the clerks set off down Church View Street and disappeared around the corner at Bridge Street. Father Thomas saw me watching and spoke.

"They are off to Oxford," he said. "Father Ralph wishes to have his cresset returned and has sent the clerks with a signed letter to fetch it. How much did the goldsmith pay for it?"

I told him.

"The fellow will not be pleased to part with it."

"Nay. But next time he purchases such a thing mayhap he will be more heedful of the object's origin.

"Bishop Brantyngham must be told that Ernaud cannot be guilty of caving in Odo's head," I said. "But this time we must send more than one man, and those sent must be able to defend themselves."

"You think the man who slew William would attack another?"

"Aye, if he knows why the man is upon the road."

"How did the villain know what William's mission was about?"

"I've puzzled over that," I replied. "If the felon learned of William's errand he'll likely learn of who else might be sent. Mayhap the villain is close to you or Father Ralph or Father Simon."

"One man slew William?"

"Likely."

"Why do you think so?"

"Two or more men would likely have first unhorsed William upon the road, and then pierced him with daggers. A man alone might not be certain he could overcome William, so lay in wait for him to pass, then sent that crude arrow into his back."

"Who will you send to Exeter?"

"Sir Jaket and his page, if he will accept the commission. I will seek him at the castle later today."

After a dinner of pease pottage with bacon I first sought John Fletcher. I took the broken arrow with me. John was at work in his toft, hoeing weeds from his cabbages. I greeted the fellow, explained my visit, and held the two halves of the fatal shaft out for him to inspect. He studied the arrow and chuckled.

"This slew Father Thomas's new clerk?" he asked.

"It did."

"'Tis a wonder it would fly true enough to strike its target," he scoffed.

"I know you did not make such a thing," I said, "but have you seen work such as this before? A point hammered from what seems to have once been a pewter spoon, and a shaft fletched with chicken feathers?"

"Nay. A man would be embarrassed, I think, to make such a thing and allow me to see it."

"Do you know of men who make their own arrows rather than buying from you?"

"Aye, there be some. But them as do so do better work than this. They purchase arrowheads from the smith, an' either own a goose or two, or pluck a few feathers after curfew."

"Hah. If a man hears his goose squawk in the night it may be that some man needs feathers for his arrows?"

"Or mayhap a fox has need for a feather or two for his kits."

"Who are these men who make their own arrows?"

"None would have made this repulsive thing."

"So you have said. Nevertheless, I would like their names."

Fletcher shrugged and named five residents of Bampton and the Weald. "Thomas Derlynge, John Prothos, William Attemore, Richard Wryttle, and Reynold Wyle."

I resolved to visit Reynold Wyle on my way to the castle. I had a few questions for him, then I would seek Sir Jaket and request his help in taking a message to Bishop de Brantyngham.

I found Reynold hoeing among his onions. When he glanced in my direction I saw he wore the same frown that had creased his face when I last visited the man. Did he never change his expression? Or is my presence enough to bring a scowl to his face?

I greeted Reynold in the customary manner. The salutation did not modify his countenance. He rested upon his hoe and waited for me to state my business.

I held out the broken halves of the arrow drawn from William Walle and said, "John Fletcher has told me that you make your own arrows. Is this one of yours?"

I knew the answer would be nay, even if Reynold had made it, and was not disappointed. Wyle took the broken arrow from me, studied it, especially the bloodstained forward half, then said, "What man would claim such a wretched thing?"

"'Tis not of your making?"

"Nay," he said.

"Show me some of your own work."

Reynold did not hesitate. He returned the broken arrow to me, said "Wait here," and stalked off to his house. A moment later he returned with a clutch of arrows in his hand. When he came near he held them to me for my inspection. These arrows were of good work, nearly the equal of those John Fletcher made. The shafts were straight and true, the heads of iron and with a keen edge, and the feathers matched and were skillfully attached with frequent whippings and hide glue. 'Twas plain to see that Reynold had not made the arrow which slew William Walle. Unless he made such a crude weapon intentionally to turn suspicion from himself.

Why would he do so? Had he been untruthful about Rosamond and Roger Folewye? This was possible, because Adela had seen Rosamond's nocturnal visitor approach from Bridge Street, whereas Roger would have come to her from the opposite direction. Did Reynold know of this? And did he act upon the knowledge?

I bade Wyle good day, and set off for the castle and Sir Jaket. As I walked under the portcullis I received a pleasant surprise. A painted and enclosed wagon had moments before entered the castle yard. Half a dozen or so grooms were dismounting from their beasts, and the postilion rider was patting his runcie upon its flank. One of the grooms went to the rear of the wagon, dropped the gate, and helped a lad of perhaps ten years to descend. The child was not eager to accept assistance. In the manner of small boys he pulled away from the groom and leaped to the ground, raising puffs of dust as his feet struck earth.

The groom smiled, shrugged, and rubbed the lad's tousled head. He then turned again to the wagon to assist another occupant. 'Twas the lady Joan de Burgh. I had not seen Lady Joan since she was Lady Joan Talbot. She was Lord Gilbert's widowed sister, evidently come to Bampton with her son to visit her brother. Her husband, Sir Charles de Burgh, was lost returning from the siege of Limoges when his ship foundered in a storm crossing from France.

Many years past I had looked fondly upon Lady Joan. Lord Gilbert had seen this sentiment and guessed that the interest was mutual. He had tactfully warned me from pursuing the lady. I was not Sir Hugh at the time and therefore an inappropriate match for the sister of one of the great barons of the realm.

'Twas all for the best. I found my Kate and what could be better for a man than a wife he loves and who loves and respects him? So as I watched Lady Joan descend I remembered with pleasure the moments we had spent together, but with no thought of what might have been. What is cannot be improved.

Lord Gilbert strode from his hall to greet his sister. His son Richard and his household knights followed. Lady Joan would be popular among these bachelor knights, I thought, for she possessed her husband's lands near Banbury 'til her son was of age, and even then would enjoy half of the revenues. Perhaps Sir Jaket would not be pleased when I asked him to travel to Exeter, even though Lady Joan was older than he by perhaps six or seven years.

I watched as Lady Joan's son bowed politely to his uncle. The lad had been taught proper manners. Lord Gilbert, in response, solemnly held out a hand to shake the child's small hand in his. Lady Joan looked on with a smile.

She had not yet noticed me, or if she had, did not recognize me. I thought this might be for the best, so drifted to a corner of the castle yard where I was hidden behind grooms, valets, and maids employed in Lord Gilbert's service.

Eventually, greetings and introductions accomplished, Lord Gilbert led his sister and her entourage into the hall. Sir Jaket was among those who followed. Behind him came John Chamberlain. I called to the chamberlain and he stopped and peered about to learn who sought his attention.

"Ask Sir Jaket to attend me," I said to John. "Tell him 'tis an important matter but will not take overmuch of his time."

The chamberlain followed the party into the hall and a moment later Sir Jaket appeared. He looked to me with questions in his eyes and I set about answering them.

"If you are willing and Lord Gilbert agrees I would like for you to travel to Exeter and take to Bishop Brantyngham the message that William Walle was to deliver."

The knight offered no hesitation. "When?" he said.

"Tomorrow. And 'twould be best to travel with your squire. One man has already perished at this business. He rode alone and was not armed. Two men, armed, may cause a man who has felonious intent to reconsider his design."

"Aye. And this time we will be alert for some scoundrel who wishes us harm. How did such a rogue learn of the clerk's errand? The matter puzzles me."

"Few men knew of what William was assigned to do, and fewer yet would care, even if they knew," I said.

"The man who knew, and cared, must then be the felon who slew Odo Fuller and cast blame on Ernaud," Sir Jaket replied.

"So I believe. Already a day has been lost in sending word to the bishop. This is why I ask you to leave tomorrow. The bishop's court needs to know the truth of the matter before some decision is rendered which may be beyond recall."

"You think the bishop might turn Ernaud over to Exeter's sheriff?"

"I cannot predict what his court may do. But if so, Ernaud would likely hang. More likely the bishop will send him to Scotland to serve as a lay brother at some frozen abbey."

"Where he might wish he'd been sent to a scaffold."

"Mayhap. But most men would rather awaken of a morning cold upon their pallet than not awaken to this world at all."

From within the hall we heard a valet ring the bell that announced supper. I sent the knight to his meal after brief final instructions for what he was to say to the bishop. I told him that also I would prepare a letter to the bishop, and seal it with Lord Gilbert's seal.

My own supper could wait. I decided to visit the other men John Fletcher had named as makers of arrows for their own use. I did not expect to find arrows as inferior as the one which penetrated William Walle's back and indeed did not. Although none of the others Fletcher had named made arrows as skillfully as Reynold Wyle, their work was beyond what some man had produced to slay the clerk.

I saw Adela setting off for her home in the Weald as I approached Galen House. I raised a hand as she came near. The lass curtsied and asked what service she could do.

'Twas not yet dark upon the village streets, but I remembered that in the past week she had departed Galen House twice when the sun was nearly set.

117

"Have you seen any shadowy forms prowling about near to Reynold Wyle's house in the past few days?"

"Nay, sir."

"What do folk in the Weald say of Rosamond? Is there gossip about the lass and Roger Folewye... or any other? Rosamond is a pert lass," I continued. "I expect folk do talk of her suitors, real and imagined."

"Aye, sir, they do, but I've 'eard nothin' of Roger. Many folk 'eard Reynold shout that 'e'd slay some man if 'e saw 'im about again. Though I don't know as them what 'eard Reynold make that threat knew 'e was speakin' of Roger. An' mayhap 'e wasn't. Could be some other 'e'd learned of."

"This was his warning made on Maundy Thursday?"

"Aye."

"Have you heard of any more threats Reynold may have made?"

"Nay, sir. Matters is quiet an' peaceful in the Weald."

"If that should change tell me immediately," I said, and sent the lass upon her way.

Kate and Bessie were at a supper of fraunt hemelle when I arrived at my home. I propped the broken halves of the crude arrow in the hall and joined my wife and daughter at their meal. John lay content in his crib. Evidently he also had recently enjoyed his supper. Kate asked of the day as she spooned out a bowl of pudding and spread honeyed butter upon a thick slice of barley loaf.

I told her of the men John Fletcher had named, of sending Sir Jaket and his squire to Exeter on the morrow, and concluded by speaking of Lady Joan de Burgh's arrival to visit her brother.

"She is the lady whose husband perished crossing from France?" Kate shuddered. "That might have been you. What would I then have done?"

"Lord Gilbert promised that if I did not survive the expedition you would receive ten pounds each year."

"You believe I could survive on ten pounds?"

"'Tis a considerable sum."

"I need more. I need a husband. Ten pounds will not replace you."

I was struck momentarily dumb. I had considered my value to Kate only as a matter of how much coin would be needed to provide for her and my children had I been slain. What amount could replace Kate? King Edward's treasury would not suffice.

"Will the lady wed another?" Kate asked.

"Lord Gilbert does not confide in me upon such matters," I said. "But she is young, and Lord Gilbert keeps three bachelor knights at Bampton Castle. It could be that he has invited her for the purpose of meeting these knights."

"This is the sister whose broken wrist you treated?"

"Aye. She was with Lord Gilbert at Goodrich Castle, and fell whilst hunting when her horse refused a wall."

Kate was silent for a time, then spoke softly. "Do you ever wish Lord Gilbert had not forbidden your suit?"

How did she know that I was once fond of Lady Joan? And she, I believe, of me? How did Kate know that Lord Gilbert had admonished me when he saw that Lady Joan and I were become friends? Gossip has but a short distance to travel from the castle to Galen House.

"Never," I replied with some vehemence. My tone was not artifice. "Holy Writ tells us that all things work together for good to those who love the Lord Christ. When Lord Gilbert chastened me for my interest in his sister I was discontented. But shortly after, I saw you at your father's shop when I purchased parchment and since that day Lady Joan has seldom crossed my mind."

* * *

Next morning, about the second hour, I took a message for Bishop Brantyngham to the castle. I asked Lord Gilbert to read it and, if he approved, to seal it with his seal. He did. A short time later Sir Jaket and his page set off for Exeter.

"I am pleased to see you," Lord Gilbert said when Sir Jaket was off. "I have arranged a banquet to honor Lady Joan. You and

Lady Katherine and your Bessie must attend. Tonight, at the ninth hour."

I returned to Galen House and told Kate of the invitation. She immediately set about preparing her finest gown, of green velvet. She brushed it 'til it was spotless.

'Tis a simpler matter for a man to prepare for such an affair. I trimmed my beard and brushed my best cotehardie, of softest wool and a russet brown.

Adela would remain at Galen House to care for John. Bessie was ecstatic to learn that she would attend her first feast at the castle. Kate, on the other hand, was much perturbed that our lass had no suitable gown for the occasion. She dug out an old blue satin gown of her own that was now too snug, then she and Adela set off for Will Shillside's haberdashery. They shortly returned with a small sack of buttons, ribbons and lace.

Bessie was placed upon a kitchen bench and Kate set about measuring our daughter for her first fancy frock, pinning and tucking until the blue satin fit the girl's lithe frame. This business was beyond my competence, so I devoured a portion of barley loaf, drank a cup of ale, and left Galen House to Kate and Adela and the business of making Bessie presentable for the knights and ladies who would grace Lord Gilbert's hall.

I wondered if Sir Jaket and his squire would be unhappy that they would miss the feast. I wandered to the castle, saw Sir Henry about to enter the hall, and called out to him.

"Sir Jaket," I said, "is likely near to Faringdon by now. Was he peevish about missing Lord Gilbert's banquet?"

"Didn't seem so. Not ready to wed, he said."

Apparently Lord Gilbert's household knights had fathomed his reason for inviting his sister to visit. Whether or not this was truly Lord Gilbert's scheme, who could know? And did Lady Joan know of his plan, if it was indeed her brother's design?

I wished to keep myself busy and away from Galen House whilst Kate and Adela made Bessie's gown and did whatever else must be done to prepare a lady for a feast. So I called upon Father Thomas to learn how his cook's lacerated arm healed.

A servant answered my knock upon the vicarage door and called for the priest when I announced the reason for my visit.

"Bartram is well," Father Thomas said when I asked of his cook. "Gone to the tithe barn, but should return anon."

"Does he complain of pain in his wound, or of a discharge?" I asked.

"Nay. Well, he does speak of weakness in his arm."

"I'm not surprised. The cut was deep and some of the muscle severed. 'Twill be a month or more before such a laceration is completely healed."

I heard a door open and close. Father Thomas said, "Ah, Bartram has returned. You may see for yourself how he does."

The priest led me to his kitchen. Bartram had set a sack of peas upon a table and was turning his attention to a capon that lay dead upon another table. The cook glanced up in surprise to see me in his domain.

"Sir Hugh wishes to inspect your wound," Father Thomas explained. At those words Bartram drew up his sleeve and held his arm to me.

"Aches a bit when I must lift some weighty thing," the cook said. "Heavy pots and such."

There was some redness bordering the cut, but this was to be expected. No pus issued from the wound. Galen and other ancient physicians taught that thick, white pus draining from a cut was good – "laudable pus", they called it – while thin, watery pus was dangerous. I hold with Henry de Mondeville, who taught that no pus at all is best.

"All seems well," I said. "The stitches are holding. If you feel pain when you lift some heavy load, stop. Pain is your arm's way of telling you to cease whatever it is you are doing to cause the ache."

The cook turned to the capon and began plucking feathers from Father Thomas's dinner. I saw Bartram wince as he yanked feathers from the fowl.

"Sir Jaket Bec departed Bampton this morning, with his squire, to take word to Bishop Brantyngham that Ernaud cannot be guilty of slaying Odo," I said to Father Thomas as we left the kitchen.

"I pray that he will be in time to halt an injustice," the priest replied.

"You believe the bishop's court may act hastily?"

"Aye. Was Odo a priest or archdeacon or a cleric of some standing the bishop would deal swiftly with Ernaud. But only a clerk? I fear he will not be sympathetic to Ernaud's claim of innocence."

* * *

I decided that for such an auspicious occasion as a banquet in honor of Lord Gilbert's sister I would move my bathing barrel to the kitchen, heat water, and soak myself clean. I set all of Kate's larger pots upon the fire, stoked the blaze with more wood, and went twice with our bucket to the village well for more water. Kate saw what I was about and sent Adela and Bessie to the hall, where Adela continued the stitching of Bessie's gown.

The barrel is an old wine cask which I sawed in half, then paid a smith to reinforce with an iron band. I sealed a few leaky staves with pitch and for but a few pence had a serviceable bathing tub. 'Tis not as fine as Prince Edward's copper-lined tub, but the water within is as wet and I will emerge as clean as the prince does from his more fashionable vessel.

Whilst I soaked away the grime, Kate went to the well and returned with more water with which she filled the pots again and when I finished my bath she dismissed me from the kitchen and took over my tub. We might not be the most finely garbed of Lord Gilbert's guests, but we would likely be the cleanest and least fragrant.

Before we departed Galen House for the castle, Kate lectured Bessie upon proper behavior. The lass listened soberly, which was unlike her normally obstreperous disposition. She was old enough to understand the honor bestowed upon her, being included with her parents at such a notable occasion. Kate concluded by telling her that for this evening she was no longer

Bessie, but was henceforth Lady Elizabeth, and must deport herself as such.

I suppose this was all necessary, but I rather like my daughter's rambunctious nature, and hope that when the feast is past she will, for awhile yet, revert to being my Bessie. She will have – I hope – a lifetime to be the Lady Elizabeth.

I am prejudiced, I know, but we did make a fine sight strolling down Church View Street: me in my best russet cotehardie, and my wife and daughter in green velvet and blue satin. Kate and Adela had worked a miracle to create Bessie's gown in such a brief time. The finest tailor in Oxford could not have done better.

Three musicians plucked and tooted upon a gittern, rebec, and sackbut as we entered the hall. Sir Henry directed us to our places. We were seated at the left side of the high table. Father Simon, Father Ralph, and John Chamberlain, also. In the center, of course, were Lord Gilbert and his gangly son Richard. As for the dexter side of the table, the places were as I expected. Lady Joan and her son were placed between Sir Roger des Roches and Sir Piers Godfrey. Father Thomas was seated beyond them, and at the far end was Sir Henry Hering. Other than Charles, Bessie was the only young child present. Surely Lord Gilbert had included her in our invitation so that Lady Joan's son would not feel out of place among adults.

Valets and grooms, squires and pages, and other lesser folk sat upon benches at tables that lined the hall perpendicular to the high table. When all were seated Lord Gilbert's chaplain stood to bless the meal, the musicians began to play again, and a team of valets began to serve.

The first remove was roasted venison with parsley bread and honeyed butter. The second remove was a boar's head, with fruit and salmon pie, pears in compost, and lemon rice with almonds. The third remove was pork in egurdouce and apple moise. The subtlety was a cunning gingerbread castle in the shape of Lord Gilbert's hall. The void was baked apples and pears in cinnamon. Valets served hypocras to conclude the meal. I could drink but little, so filled was my stomach.

There was a matter I should have noticed, but was enjoying the meal too much. Kate, however, saw, and when we left the castle she spoke quietly.

"Did you observe young Charles?"

"Lady Joan's son? Nay. What would I have seen had I done so?"

"I will tell you later," she said. 'Twas nearly dark, but I thought I saw her wink.

John was abed when we returned to Galen House. Kate sent Adela home and packed Bessie off to her bed. As she tucked the lass in I heard my daughter ask her mother, "Was I a lady?"

"You were indeed. But tomorrow you may be Bessie again."

"Good," the child said. "'Tis a bother to be a lady."

I had nearly forgotten that there was something Kate wanted to tell me. When she came down the stairs she reminded me.

"I did not want Bessie to hear, although she knows of what I speak, I suspect."

"You know and Bessie knows? Why am I the only one ignorant?"

"Because you are a man."

"There are things that a little lass knows that her father does not?"

"Indeed. Many things. She learns more every day."

"And these things are beyond my comprehension?"

"Most likely. But as she grows older you will find opportunity to address matters 'til now hidden to you."

"You speak in riddles."

"Ah, but you are a bailiff. You should be able to work out my meaning."

"So then I am a dolt, but you have me in ignorance."

"The lad Charles looked up from his dinner often. To smile at Bessie. You did not notice?"

"Nay. My attention was given to the roasted venison. How is it that you saw this?"

"I was observing Lady Joan, to see if she favored Sir Roger or Sir Piers."

124

"Did she?"

"Nay. I think Sir Piers made a valiant effort to be charming, but he was gently rebuffed."

"Gently?"

"An attractive lady with wealth and lands learns how to deflect attention she does not desire."

"Bessie," I said, changing the subject back, "was the only child, other than Charles and Richard, at the feast. No doubt she was included so Charles would not be self-conscious. Richard is much older."

"Likely. He did seem rather shy about being caught out."

"Caught out doing what?" I said, still perplexed at my wife's meaning.

"He became red in the face when he knew that I saw him smiling at Bessie."

"Did she smile in return?"

"Aye."

"Our lass takes after you, so no doubt she will receive many smiles from lads. But she is yet a child."

"She is, and for that you must be thankful. You have a few more years to learn to be more observant."

"So you think Lord Gilbert's attempt to match Lady Joan with one of his knights is a failure?" I asked.

"'Twas not the reason for her visit, so John Chamberlain did say. I heard him speaking to Father Ralph of the visit. Its purpose was to make arrangements for Charles to reside in Bampton, to serve as page to Lord Gilbert."

I should not have been surprised at the news, and indeed was not. Few lads with noble or knighted fathers remain in their natal hall until adult. Why this is the custom I cannot say. My own father did not send me away, likely because I was youngest of four sons, and not bound for a knighthood. I wish he might see how I have risen. But he and my brothers perished of plague. My oldest brother's son is now lord of the manor of Little Singleton.

"What will you do if Charles visits Galen House often?" Kate said.

"I will shoo him away."

"I believe it likely you will need to."

"Then I must get some practice at running lads off."

"You were a lad once."

"Aye. This is why I will chase them away."

"Charles will someday be a wealthy knight with a prosperous manor."

"Aye, he will. If he comes to Galen House in twelve or so years I will admit him then."

"When our Bessie is Lady Elizabeth?"

"Aye. Then. Not before."

CHAPTER 10

Wednesday morning dawned cloudy and misty. John, as is his custom, awoke with first light and demanded to break his fast. So Kate was up and about when Adela appeared at the door of Galen House. I heard Kate lift the bar to admit Adela, and moments later I heard the lass ask if I was yet abed. I was, but not for long. Adela would not have asked but that she had some matter to tell me. I hastily drew on chauces and cotehardie, ran a comb through my hair, and clattered down the stairs.

I found Adela and Kate in the kitchen, sharing a loaf. I went to the sideboard, poured myself a cup of ale from the ewer, and asked Adela what she wished of me.

"Last night I came late to my father's 'ouse because you 'ad not yet returned from the castle."

"Aye," I agreed. "'Twas near dark when we sent you home."

"I saw the man again."

"The man you saw creeping about Reynold Wyle's house?"

"Aye, sir. Him what wears a long robe."

"And did he, as before, approach the Weald from Bridge Street?"

"Aye, 'e did. Wasn't Roger Folewye, unless 'e passed by Rosamond's 'ouse in the dark, then come back."

"Unlikely," I said. "And you are sure the fellow wore a long garment, as do priests and clerks and such?"

"Aye, sir. Saw 'im clear against John's 'ouse."

"Did the fellow know he was seen?"

"Don' think so. When I knew 'e was about I 'id behind some bushes 'til 'e'd passed."

"Did you see him go past Reynold Wyle's house?"

"Nay. 'E went behind Reynold's 'ouse an' I never seen 'im again."

"Did Rosamond appear?"

"Nay. There was a cresset lit in Reynold's window. Likely 'e was not abed, so Rosamond couldn't sneak out."

"Aye... likely," I agreed.

"Who d'you think it is I been seein'?"

"I know who it was not. 'Twas neither Odo nor Ernaud."

"Mayhap then Peter Bouchard, or one of the priests?"

"Mayhap. But not likely a priest. The vicars of St. Beornwald's are too old to go about in the night seeking a lass." Probably.

Kate had listened silently to this conversation. Now she spoke. "Could it be that this nocturnal prowler has something to do with Odo's murder?"

"I cannot see what the association would be, but 'tis a great coincidence that the events, if unjoined, are happening at or near the same time. Just because I do not see a connection does not mean there is none. If I knew who Adela has been seeing I could arrest him for violating curfew, even though it's the bishop's lands he's been seen upon, and press the fellow about what he has been doing, and why. I might not discover who slew Odo, but I might learn who did not. But first I must seize him."

"How will you do that?" Kate asked.

"I will don my dark gray cotehardie and blend with the night; then seek bushes and shadows and discover who it is Adela has seen. Mayhap, if I have no success, I will confront Rosemond. Although I doubt I would get a straight answer from her."

"Will you do this alone? What if the rogue is armed?"

"Would a man wearing a priest's or clerk's robe carry a dagger?" I said. "Hmmm... I suppose he might, was he not really a priest or clerk at all."

"Indeed. You might discover it to be so and in the finding make a widow of me."

"Would your mind be eased if Arthur accompanied me?"

"Aye, it would. But how could he wait with you, then return to the castle after the drawbridge has been raised for the night?"

"I will tell him that he may sleep in the spare room. Upon the ground floor, his snores will not be too onerous, I think. We will be above, and I will close his door."

* * *

Shortly after dinner I answered a knock upon the door of Galen House and found Father Ralph. I bade him good day and asked how I might serve him.

"Alan and Peter have returned," he said.

"With your cresset?"

"Nay. They went to the goldsmith you named, but saw no silver cresset there, and the burgher said he'd never had such an item for sale."

"He lies," I said. "I saw it."

"Mayhap the clerks visited the wrong shop," the priest said.

"Not likely. My instructions were clear. 'Tis the only goldsmith's shop on Northgate Street near to St. Michael's."

"I have lost my cresset," Father Ralph said dolefully.

"I will return to Oxford and confront the fellow," I said.

"You would do this for me?"

"I would. That cresset may be a key to whoso slew Odo. If we can trace possession of the cresset back from the goldsmith's hands to another we may eventually come to a murderer. I have another matter to deal with first, but then I will seek the Oxford goldsmith and press him about his lies."

I was torn about whether to travel to Oxford immediately to seek the cresset, or to seek a nocturnal prowler in the Weald first. I decided to seek the secretive visitor before traveling to Oxford.

Arthur spent two nights in our ground floor room. I was wrong about his snores. Kate and I heard each stentorian blast, 'til we were so fatigued sleep finally overcame the din.

For two evenings Arthur and I crept into the Weald, hugging the verge and skulking from one place of concealment to another 'til we squatted behind some shrubbery across the path from Reynold Wyle's house. We saw no man. Nor did Rosamond steal from her father's house. The morning of the third day I fed Arthur a maslin loaf, provided a cup of ale, sent him back to the castle, and told him that we would end the watch. I began to wonder if Adela was seeing things in the night that were not there.

Nay. She had surely seen some man approach Reynold's house in the days before Easter. If she spoke true then, why not now? It must be that whosoever she saw three days past did not make his visits to the Weald a nightly practice. What was I to do? Wait in the dark and cold, night after night, watching for some man who may appear, but who may not?

Even if I finally succeeded in catching the fellow what would that tell me of Odo Fuller's death? Perhaps nothing, but I could not know that unless I apprehended the man. 'Twould have been an easier decision if the month was July. By the time Arthur and I gave up the watch each night near to midnight and returned to Galen House we were chilled to the bone.

Shortly after Arthur left Galen House for the castle Adela arrived for her day's labor. She knew where I had spent the last two nights but was sworn to secrecy. Most days the lass completed her work before night was near. I would not ask her to delay returning to her home so that she might see the secretive visitor should he appear again. I would do my own work, not require it of someone else.

I downed a cup of ale and a maslin loaf to break my fast. While I did I discussed matters with Kate. Adela overheard as she bustled about, following Kate's instructions, making preparations for our dinner.

"Perhaps," Kate said, "Henry has seen some man lurking about."

"The beadle has no authority in the Weald," I replied. "He would not likely seek there for curfew violators."

"But Adela said the man she saw came from Bridge Street."

This was so, although such a man prowling the streets after curfew would be careful to avoid Henry Swerd, else he might find his purse lighter next day. It would be my duty to levy the fine.

The priests of St. Beornwald's Church are responsible for keeping order upon the bishop's lands in the Weald, but to save money – and impress Bishop Brantyngham with their frugality –

they employ neither bailiff nor beadle. So a man skulking about the streets of Bampton will think himself safe from observation when he enters the Weald. Being seen by a lass like Adela would not likely enter his mind.

I set off for Catte Street and the beadle's house. I found Henry wiping his mouth upon a sleeve after emptying a cup of ale. I told him that more than once in the past weeks a man had been seen in the Weald, after curfew, and 'twas likely the fellow had come from Bridge Street.

"I've seen no man," Henry replied. His tone indicated concern that I thought him derelict in his duty.

I assured him this was not so. "All men know 'tis your obligation to walk the streets and see that all honest men are closed within their own doors. A man up to no good will simply conceal himself until you pass, then go about his nefarious business."

"You want me to hide myself near to where the Weald departs Bridge Street an' see who may be about in the night?"

"As part of your rounds you might do so. If you see some man, do not apprehend him, nor show yourself to him, but come straight to me, no matter the hour."

I heard nothing from the beadle either Saturday or Sunday morning. Meanwhile I went about Lord Gilbert's business and considered the disappearing cresset. Another visit to the goldsmith's shop was required. I would take Arthur and Peter with me – the one for brawn, the other to attest that the goldsmith was a liar. I sought both men Sunday afternoon and told them we would depart the castle Monday morning an hour past dawn.

* * *

Monday when I awoke I heard rain pelting the windows of our chamber. Oiled skin windows do not make such noise, but Kate desired glass for the windows of our chamber so that she might see out to welcome each new day.

The thought of travel to Oxford drenched by a cold rain did not appeal. If the goldsmith had disposed of the cresset, another hour, or even another day, would make small difference in its recovery.

Peter Bouchard arrived at Galen House as I had asked. I opened the door so that he might enter. He shook water from his cloak and was pleased when I told him that we would delay our departure 'til the rain eased. He should return at noon, I said, if the rain ceased.

Arthur also needed to know of the delay, for he would be at the marshalsea saddling three palfreys. The beasts should not be required to stand saddled and bridled for five hours. I might have used my rank and sent Peter to the castle to tell Arthur of the change, but thought it unseemly to abuse my position so. By the time I returned from the castle to Galen House, sodden, I had begun to rethink my decision.

I spent the next hour before the fire, drying myself, my cap, and my cotehardie. By the fourth hour the downpour had abated to a drizzle. Kate and Adela had prepared sole in cyve for our dinner, with maslin loaves, and I was wiping my lips when Peter rapped upon the door.

The rain had ended and as we walked muddy streets to the castle, I could see a few patches of blue sky in the west.

The road to Oxford was a sea of mud. I wished to reach the city before shopkeepers closed their businesses for the day, but did not wish to cover myself in mud, as would happen if we pressed our palfreys to a trot. So we crossed Bookbinders' Bridge unspattered, but barely in time to enter the Northgate Street and seek the goldsmith's shop. He was yet accepting custom, his shutters open.

I had thought to first visit the castle upon entering Oxford and there seek Sir Roger. I desired for the sheriff to assign a serjeant to attend the goldsmith with me, Peter, and Arthur, to lend the sheriff's authority to my demand that the fellow tell me what he had done with Father Ralph's cresset.

But there was no time to do this and yet seek the goldsmith before he shut his door, as there would have been had we departed Bampton as planned, an hour past dawn.

Arthur remained upon the street with the palfreys while Peter and I entered the shop. The goldsmith had a customer. The man stood with his back to the entrance. He was tall, garbed in a fine blue cotehardie. His gray chauces were of finest linen. A few white hairs mingled with the brown which escaped from under his red cap. Here, I thought, was a prosperous buyer. Another man, not so well attired, stood silently behind the gentleman.

The goldsmith looked from his customer to see who had entered his shop. The smile vanished from his face, replaced by a frown. The gentleman he served also turned to see who had so altered the goldsmith's visage. 'Twas Oxford's sheriff, Sir Roger de Elmerugg, who was doing business with the goldsmith, accompanied by one of his servants.

The sheriff recognized me. I had asked his aid in the past. He was a friend to Lord Gilbert, Third Baron Talbot. They had fought together at Poitiers and few things make men brothers as does combat.

I doffed my cap and said, "Ah, Sir Roger. You are well met."

The sheriff raised his eyebrows. "Indeed? How may I serve Lord Gilbert's bailiff?"

"Two days before Easter, as men watched over the Easter Sepulchre at the Church of St. Beornwald in Bampton, one of the watchers was slain. Two small silver candlesticks were stolen, and a silver cresset. The candlesticks have been found, as was the cresset. I found the stolen cresset here, in this shop, a week past, upon that shelf.

"The cresset belongs to a priest of the Church of St. Beornwald. I told this fellow that he had a stolen object for sale, and he was not to part with it; that men would soon come from Bampton to retrieve it. Men did. Here is Peter Bouchard, clerk to Father Ralph, to whom the cresset belongs. He and another clerk came here last week to claim the cresset. Peter, tell m'lord sheriff what you found."

"Alan and I came here to collect Father Ralph's silver and this man," he pointed to the goldsmith, "said he had no such piece and never had."

133

Sir Roger looked to the goldsmith and said, "What have you to say?"

"I... uh... mistook his meaning."

"Whose meaning? Sir Hugh's, or this clerk's?"

"Uh... both."

"How could you mistake my requirement," I said, "that you not dispose of the cresset?"

"You said I was to keep it 'til someone came from Bampton to collect it. Someone did. Said 'e was sent for it."

"You gave the cresset to another? When?"

"Uh... day before this clerk an' the other came."

"Then why," Sir Roger growled, "did you tell them you'd never had such a thing among your wares?"

"Uh, puzzled, I was. Didn't know who was truthful, did I – them or the fellow what collected it day before?"

"Describe the man who came to collect the stolen cresset," I said.

"Don't remember much about 'im. I've many customers, now that Lent an' Easter is past an' folk may wed."

"Tell Sir Hugh what you do remember," Sir Roger said. The sheriff spoke in a tone of voice which indicated clearly to the goldsmith that he must ransack his memory.

"Plump fellow. About my age, I'd say. Beard was going to gray. Bald, likely. Saw but a few wisps of hair under 'is cap."

"What did he wear?" I asked. "A scholar's gown?"

"Nay. Brown cotehardie, or mayhap black. Dark."

"His cap?"

"Gray, I think."

"Did he give his name?"

"Nay."

"And you did not ask? What did the fellow say to convince you to surrender the cresset to him?"

"Said 'e was of Bampton an' was sent to collect the silver cresset what was stolen from 'is master."

"And you gave it up with such thin evidence?" the sheriff said with skepticism in his voice.

"This fellow," he said, pointing at me, "said I must. Said someone would come to collect it. Didn't say a name I should ask."

He spoke true. I should have done, but how could I know who Father Ralph would send to retrieve his silver?

Did the goldsmith speak true, or was the cresset hidden away in his workroom, or in his quarters above the shop?

I turned to Sir Roger and spoke. "I have some doubts about this tale. I'd like to search this man's shop and rooms."

"Good idea," the sheriff agreed. "But 'tis drawing on to evening and the light will soon fail. It will be too dark to see well into hidden corners. I will close the place and post a man here for the night to see that nothing is disturbed until you have made your search. You," he said to the goldsmith, "must leave until Sir Hugh has examined your shop."

"Now?" the fellow said with dismay.

"Aye. Now. Leave everything as it now is."

"Where am I to go?"

"There is an inn across the Northgate Street. Have you a wife? Children?"

"Nay, m'lord."

"Then go there now. Thomas," the sheriff said to the servant who accompanied him, "bar the door after we leave and admit no man. I will send Warin to relieve you at midnight.

"You and your men," the sheriff said to me, "may come with me. There are empty chambers in the castle where you may spend the night. In the morning, when the light is better, perhaps at the fourth hour, you may return here and seek the cresset."

* * *

The sheriff's table provided a splendid supper. We at the high table enjoyed pottage wastrel and sops in fennel, while Sir Roger's serjeants and constables, along with Arthur and Peter, consumed a pottage thick with peas and beans. Arthur is accustomed to plain fare, as such has been his diet since he was a small boy. It is difficult to imagine Arthur ever being small, and the simple meals have not harmed his growth. Peter, on the other hand, glanced often from his bowl to ours at the high table. He dines at Father Ralph's table, so has developed a more refined palate.

As I am now Sir Hugh my chamber for the night was fitted with glass windows, and embroidered hangings depicting a hunt covered two stone walls. If they warmed the room I cannot say, but silk seems warmer than stone whether it is or not.

I slept well. The mattress was stuffed with feathers and Arthur was in a distant chamber with Peter. How well the clerk rested I can only guess.

To break our fast Sir Roger's table served wheaten loaves to gentlemen, maslin loaves to others. The ale was fresh brewed. As the sheriff did not plan to visit the goldsmith's shop 'til the fourth hour I set off from the castle to the stationer's shop where I had purchased parchment upon which to record this tale. I decided 'twas likely I would need another gathering, as the solution to Odo Fuller's murder seemed yet far off.

Near to the fourth hour Sir Roger, three of his serjeants, Arthur, Peter, and I approached the Northgate and the goldsmith's shop. I was surprised that Oxford's sheriff would take such an interest in the matter. I attribute this to his friendship with Lord Gilbert. We saw the goldsmith pacing before his business, impatient to open to trade. Or was he troubled about what I might find when I searched his shop and rooms above?

The sheriff banged upon the shop door with the pommel of his dagger and shouted for Warin to unbar it. The man did so, but not immediately. He rubbed an eye with a fist as he swung the door open. The serjeant had been commanded to keep watch from midnight and, I suspect, as dawn peeped through the cracks in the goldsmith's shutters he had succumbed to the gentle persuasion of Morpheus.

"We will divide our numbers," Sir Roger said. "Send your man and the clerk to the rooms above, with one of my serjeants. I will examine the shop with another of my men. You and Warin examine the goldsmith's workroom."

The sheriff's scheme seemed good. I walked through the shop to the door at the rear, which led to the room where the goldsmith plied his craft. Upon a table I saw several items in the process of creation: three silver plates, a gold ring prepared for a jewel, and a collection of spoons and forks of both silver and pewter. A small chest rested upon another table. It was not locked. I opened it and found within two silver ingots, each slightly larger than my middle finger. Several windows, two of glass, lighted the workshop. No doubt the goldsmith required light for the skillful working of his craft. The light illuminated no silver cresset in any corner.

At the back of the workroom was a door that opened to the rear of the structure. I unbarred it and stepped through. Three paces from the door was a kiln, now cold, where the goldsmith might smelt the metals he used to craft his wares. Might he also melt a cresset into two small ingots? There was no way to know. The goldsmith peered through the door as I poked at the ashes with a handy scoop. I found no cresset, only cold ashes.

Warin and I returned to the shop at the same time as Arthur, Peter, and the serjeant who had accompanied them to the upper floor. Arthur saw me, shrugged, and raised his hands palms up. "No silver cresset," he said. "'E's got one of fired clay – as who would not? – but none of silver."

"Him bein' a goldsmith," Peter added, "you'd think he'd 'ave 'is best for himself."

"Rather sell an' have the coins," Arthur said.

"No silver cresset, then?" Sir Roger said when we had assembled. "You think he spoke true… that some man came for it before this fellow –" he nodded toward Peter – "and the other clerk?"

"If so," I replied, "the man somehow knew that Father Ralph's cresset was in Oxford, at this shop."

"And how would he know that," the sheriff concluded my thought, "unless he was involved in the theft, or somehow learned that the cresset was here."

"Or the goldsmith speaks falsely," I said, "and the cresset is hidden away someplace where seekers would not think to look."

"Aye. To be brought out and sold some months in the future, when you've given up the search."

"Mayhap the fellow who came for the cresset, if he exists, did not leave Oxford with it," I thought aloud. "If he is from Bampton he cannot return there with it or it will sooner or later be identified. If the goldsmith spoke true, and some man he did not know claimed the cresset in Father Ralph's name, the fellow might have simply taken it to some other silversmith or goldsmith and offered it for sale again."

"Hmmm. Sly work," Sir Roger said, "to sell the same object twice. There will be time before dinner to seek other goldsmiths to learn if this may be so."

The sheriff divided our party again and sent us, two by two, to the four other gold- and silversmiths who sought custom in Oxford. We were instructed to return to the castle after seeking the cresset in these other shops, where we would discuss matters and have our dinner.

Sir Roger assigned me and Arthur to visit a burgher who did business upon Southgate Street. When we asked of silver cressets the proprietor scoffed. "Who would want such a thing? The flame would darken the silver immediately. The man who owned such a cresset would need to employ a servant to polish it every day, else it would tarnish like a lump of charcoal. Bronze cressets, mayhap, but not silver."

'Twas near to noon when Arthur and I returned to the castle. No silver cresset had been discovered in Oxford. If it was yet in the town, I decided, it was likely in the form of two small ingots in a goldsmith's workroom.

The dinner this day for we at the sheriff's high table was eels in bruit and sole in cyve. Arthur and Peter contented themselves with beans yfryed and wheaten loaves. The ale was fresh, as one might expect at a sheriff's table.

When the meal was complete I thanked Sir Roger for his hospitality, bade him good day, and with Peter and Arthur sought the stable where our palfreys were quartered. The roads had dried somewhat, so we arrived three hours later in Bampton unspattered. And unsuccessful.

As we rode from Oxford my mind had wandered to William Walle's death. Was he trying to say the name of the man who sent an arrow into him when his breath stopped? What else? Like Odo, it seemed sure that William knew the man who slew him.

The sun broke through scattered clouds as we neared Bampton. The warmth upon my face was pleasant, and spring flowers decorated the verge: yellow cowslips and celandine, bluebells, and white wood sorrel. The passing scene was nearly enough to drive thoughts of murder and death from my mind. Nearly.

Where Church View Street joins Bridge Street Peter and I dismounted. Arthur continued to the castle with our palfreys while Peter and I went to Father Ralph's vicarage to tell him the unwelcome news that his missing cresset would remain missing awhile yet.

"I should have seized it when I first found it," I said.

"You did well to find it at all," the priest replied. "I had given it up for lost."

"I found it once. Mayhap I will find it again."

"You have a thought as to where you might seek it?"

"If it has not been melted down to an ingot and cast into a plate or cup or some such thing, it will be in the hall of some knight or prosperous burgher. If a man of the commons has it he will sell it to provide himself with the coins to purchase something more practical."

"Aye," the priest agreed. "The flame from my silver cresset gave no more light than that from a cresset of baked clay."

CHAPTER 11

My supper was a simple pottage of peas and beans flavored with leeks and slivers of bacon. The sun, which had broken through clouds while I returned to Bampton, now shone from a cloudless sky. The west wall of Galen House was warmed enough that I drew a bench to the toft and sat in the slanting sun with Kate while Adela took Bessie and John to their beds.

"What is your opinion?" Kate asked when I had told her of the failed journey to retrieve Father Ralph's cresset. "Did some man truly call at the goldsmith's shop and collect the cresset, claiming to be about Father Ralph's business?"

"I'd like to think not so."

"Why?"

"Because if that happened the fellow was from Bampton, or doing the work of a man from here."

"Because how else would he know the shop where the cresset would be found?" Kate said.

"Aye. And how would some man not of this place know that I had found the cresset anywhere, and that some man in Father Ralph's employ was to retrieve it?

"Did Adela speak of seeing a man prowling the Weald after dark when I traveled to Oxford?"

"Nay. But you may ask her. I hear her footsteps on the stairs."

"Nay, sir," Adela replied when I asked of men skulking about the Weald. "Not seen any man, but mayhap there be someone."

"Why do you say so?"

"Night before last I 'eard Thomas 'opton's dog barkin' in the night."

"You believe the creature heard some man near his master's house?"

"Aye."

"When was this? Just after nightfall, or later?"

"Early. The sky was not yet dark over Cowleys Corner."

"Does the hound bark often?"

"Nay, sir. Hardly hear 'im from one day to the next."

I dismissed Adela to go to her home, then spoke to Kate. "Has Henry Swerd sought me?"

"Nay."

"Then if any man was adventuring in the night Henry did not see or hear him. Or the fellow has limited his nocturnal perambulation in the Weald."

"I've been thinking of what, or who, Adela might have seen," Kate said. "The man came from Bridge Street, she said, and wore a robe, as would a priest or a clerk. Or mayhap 'twas a long cotehardie. The holy man wears such a garment."

"So he does, and is emaciated so might cast the slender shadow of a callow youth. But what would set him wandering through the village and the Weald after dark?"

"Ask him... No, of course you cannot."

"I could. But I'd not receive an answer."

"I wonder," Kate said, "that he does not try to speak, even though he has no tongue. Surely he could form some words, enough to be understood."

"Don't know about that. I've never tried to talk without a tongue. Perhaps it can be done, perhaps not."

"Or," Kate said thoughtfully, "he finds it convenient to be silent."

"Aye. Folk will not ask of his opinions or of other matters. If men know nothing of his past or his thoughts he cannot find himself in trouble for either."

The sun sank below Lord Gilbert's forest to the west and the chill drove us in and to our bed. I lay awake wondering if Kate had hit upon some useful thought regarding who it might be Adela had seen in the night, and if the idea might have something to do with Odo Fuller's death. Could it be that the holy man entered the church in the night and attacked Odo? The fellow is so cadaverous I would think it unlikely he could deal a blow strong enough to crack a man's skull. And if he did so, how did he get Father Ralph's cresset into some woman's

141

hands who would then sell it in Oxford? If a woman did so and the goldsmith spoke true.

* * *

Next day after dinner I sought Henry Swerd at his home on Catte Street and asked him of his rounds when he traveled the village enforcing curfew.

"Start 'ere, at me 'ouse," he said. "Then go to the High Street an' east to Bushy Row. Up Bushy Row to Landell's Lane, then down Church View, past Galen House, to Bridge Street. Walk past the castle, then return to Broad Street an' Landells Lane again, then 'ome."

"You follow this route each night, never changing your path?"

"Aye, most nights."

"Tonight reverse your normal route."

"You think the fellow I was s'posed to watch for knows where I go an' when I goes there, so 'e knows how to avoid me?"

"Possibly. And when you travel Mill Street to the castle, hide yourself in some bushes for a short time, where the path to the Weald joins Bridge Street, and watch for any man approaching from the castle."

"From the castle?"

"From the direction of the castle, I should say."

* * *

Thursday morning, after I broke my fast, I set off for one of Lord Gilbert's demesne fields where men were at boon work, casting barley seed upon the new-plowed soil. The seed must be sown at a rate of four bushels per acre for best harvest, but I did not need to tell the sowers this. Their experience at planting and harvest was greater than my own.

Three lads followed those who cast the seed, tossing clods at birds who would scoop up the seed if they could. I've seen youths do this work for many years, but never have I seen a lad hit a crow or jackdaw or any other feathered thief. How was it,

142

I wondered, that boys who lobbed dirt at birds with such small result would grow to become men who could fling an arrow into a target at two hundred paces?

I had no sooner arrived at the barley field than from behind me I heard Henry call my name.

"Lady Katherine said I might find you here," he said, gasping between words. The beadle is not young, and enjoys a hearty meal. "Did as you asked an' hid meself in the bushes where the path from the Weald joins Bridge Street an' Mill Street."

"And you saw some man?"

"Aye. As you said, 'e was comin' from the castle."

"From the castle, or from that direction?"

"Well... didn't see 'im leave the castle forecourt, so I s'pose 'e might've come from somewhere else."

"Who was it you saw?"

"Don't know. Walked out in front of 'im an' told 'im to halt where 'e was."

"But he did not?" I guessed.

"Nay. Took to 'is heels."

"Where did he go?"

Henry shrugged. "Disappeared into the night."

"Did he run to the castle, or past it?"

"Past, I think. The night had turned cloudy, so moon an' stars gave little light."

The beadle was not constructed so as to be able to run down a fleeing curfew violator. I did not bother to ask if he chased the man. He'd not likely have caught him if he had. Henry would not even overtake Arthur if the two were in a footrace.

Would the fellow who prowled Bampton and the Weald in the night continue to do so now that he had been seen? He had been seen previously, by Adela, but according to the lass, he did not know it to be so. However, he did know that the beadle saw him. He might now give up his evening visits to the village. If he did I might never identify the man nor know if he had aught to do with Odo Fuller's murder.

If the man had come from beyond the castle when Henry saw him, then mayhap Kate was correct – the night visitor was the holy man. How to know this if Henry had frightened him from some usual pattern? And would the frail fellow be capable of outrunning any man, even Henry Swerd?

I told the beadle to vary his patrol in the coming days so that anyone wishing to avoid him as night fell would find his presence unpredictable. He nodded understanding and agreed to do so.

I left the barley field and sought the castle. A few days past I had conscripted Arthur to watch with me for a curfew violator. I intended to assign him the duty again. But not this night, nor the next. The man Henry saw would perhaps be too frightened of discovery to appear again so soon after being seen. If he appeared again ever.

I found Arthur, informed him of the beadle's encounter, and told him that we would watch the road to Cowleys Corner on Saturday evening, and if no man appeared, then we would keep watch for two more nights. As before he would sleep at Galen House.

"Who else but the holy man would approach from beyond the castle?" Kate said as she ladled out a bowl of lombard stew for my dinner.

"None other that I know of," I replied.

"Then it must have been him that Henry saw."

"Unless it was some man of Bampton or the Weald who first walked west, beyond the castle, while Henry was elsewhere, so he was not at first seen."

"Why would some man do that? What is there beyond the castle but Cowleys Corner?"

"No man's house," I said. "But why would the hermit be up and about in the night?"

"I know," Kate said ruefully, "and he cannot be asked the question."

"Or any other."

"What of Odo's murder? And the silver cresset?" she asked. "Have you any new thoughts regarding the matter?"

"Many. But most of them I soon discard as being useless in discovering the felon."

"Do you believe that finding the man Adela and Henry have seen might lead to the guilty man?"

"It might. Even if the fellow did not do the murder he might have seen the slayer in the night."

"And himself been undiscovered?"

"Aye. So far as I know only Adela and Henry have seen the man. No one else has told Henry of seeing someone skulking about the village after curfew."

"Have you considered what William tried to say while on his deathbed?" Kate asked.

"I think on it often. With no result."

"Mayhap he was not trying to name his slayer, but something else."

"What else?"

Kate shrugged, then laughed. "You are the bailiff. 'Tis your duty to unravel this mystery."

I had hoped when I traveled to Oxford to retrieve Father Ralph's cresset that the object might leave a trail of possession leading to the felon who slew Odo Fuller. Might the cresset leave a trail even if it was not found? Even if it now existed only as small ingots in a goldsmith's workroom?

The goldsmith said that a widow from Witney had offered the cresset to him. What part of this claim was true? According to the goldsmith the woman had once resided in Witney but now made her home in Oxford. The woman was neither old nor young. If I traveled to Witney might I discover a woman whose wealthy husband had recently died? A woman who then departed the town for Oxford? Witney is not far, only five or so miles. I could travel there, seek information, and return the same day.

But first I would seek some man who walked Bampton's streets after curfew. Although the puzzle of Odo's murder and the curious night walker often intruded upon my thoughts I spent most of the next two days upon Lord Gilbert's business.

This, for the most part, involved watching other men at work – tenants mostly, and the few villeins yet tied to Lord Gilbert's lands, as they labored upon their lord's demesne.

Saturday, after dinner, I called at Father Thomas's vicarage to inspect Bartram's wounded arm. I was pleased with what I found. The slash was mending well with but a slight redness coloring the skin where my sutures penetrated the flesh. I might have cut the silken threads away this day, but a man uses his arms regularly, and such stretching and lifting may cause a closed wound to reopen if the sutures are removed too soon. I told the cook that I would return soon to remove the stitches. He nodded, and returned to his work.

Father Thomas had observed this inspection. As he walked with me to his door he said, "Bartram will be pleased to be whole again. In the days after he did himself the injury he often complained that he could do little with that arm. Couldn't lift a ewer of ale, he said."

"Does he yet complain of weakness?" I asked.

"Nay. Not for the past week. Carries on as before."

"This is good. If the cut had been so deep as to sever a tendon he might never again lift a ewer, or any other object, without pain."

"You believe that a danger?"

"Nay. No more. I believe the cut was not so deep as that, and if he no longer complains then 'twas but the muscle which was severed, and that is healing and will continue to do so."

Mayhap Father Thomas was worried that he would not get his money's worth from a cook who might not have use of both arms.

* * *

I did not want us to be seen, so Arthur and I did not leave Galen House that evening until the only light was from the western sky, pale above the forest beyond the castle. I worried that by waiting, the man I sought might already have traveled Mill Street and be away. The Lord Christ has told men they must

146

not worry. But I find worry helpful. I have worried about many harmful things and they did not come to pass.

I stationed Arthur in the shrubbery where Henry had waited three days past, where the path to the Weald leaves Mill Street. I walked silently past the castle, which was shrouded in darkness but for a glow from a garderobe window, where Lord Gilbert requires that a cresset remain lit through the night.

'Twas too dark where the road to Cowleys Corner entered the wood to see the path that led to the holy man's hut. I had to guess the distance. When I thought I had walked far enough beyond the castle, I sat upon a rotting stump on the south side of the road and waited.

My eyes were as accustomed to the night as they were ever likely to be, yet I could see nothing beyond the pale course of the road. Likewise I heard nothing. The forest was silent. Even predators and prey made no sound, and I struggled to remain awake.

I chose to keep watch at this place not because I thought 'twas the hermit whom Adela and Henry had seen, but because if Henry saw well enough in the dark that he knew the man he had seen came from beyond the castle, I wished to be at a place where I could seize the fellow if, as on that night, he took to his heels when he was challenged.

Arthur challenged no man that night, nor did any man walk or run past the castle toward my stump. My joints were stiff with cold when I gave up the quest and left my post. Arthur heard my footsteps and challenged me, as I had instructed, when I came near. 'Twas too dark for him to see who approached.

We did not linger at the bridge nor tarry on Church View Street. The warm beds that awaited us lent wings to our heels.

We followed the same scheme the next evening, with the same result, even to chattering teeth as we gave up the watch near to midnight. Once again I was ready to give up seeking some man who occasionally walked the streets at night. Especially if Monday was as frosty as Saturday and Sunday had been.

It was, but success can make a man forget his discomfort. I had been seated on the stump for perhaps an hour Monday evening when I heard a twig snap. The sound seemed to come from the north side of the road, and was distant. I could barely hear it, but faint as the cracking was I knew its source. Some man or large beast walked nearby.

But not in the road. Broken clouds hid some of the sky, but what stars were visible gave enough light that I could have seen a shadowy form upon the road. Had the moon risen a traveler would have been plainly visible, but the waning moon would not rise for another two hours or so.

I held my breath, the better to hear if another twig broke, and to be as silent as possible so as not to alarm my quarry, whoever or whatever it was.

'Twas the holy man whose form appeared at the north verge of the road. I was not sure of his identity when I first saw the man, but he materialized from the path that led into the wood to his hut. Who else would it be?

The fellow did not know he was being watched. He made no effort to conceal himself but walked with a firm stride toward the village. I followed, about thirty paces behind. Only when he came near the castle did the hermit slow his pace and cautiously tread the grass of the verge.

Would Arthur see or hear the holy man approach? His steps upon the new spring grass were silent. The fellow was near to the path to the Weald when Arthur sprang up from his hiding place and seized him. Rather than shout for the man to halt, Arthur had waited 'til the scrawny fellow was but two paces from him, then leaped to him and caught him in his arms. The holy man cried out, but little good it did him. No man was awake and nearby to hear, and protests would do him no good against Arthur's brawn.

I broke into a run. The hermit heard and turned his head to see who else was about in the night. Even in the dim starlight he recognized me, I believe, for he ceased his howling.

"You are in violation of curfew," I said. "You must come with me. There is much I need to learn from you, for I know this is not the first time you have been upon the streets of Bampton and the Weald in the night."

Arthur kept a firm hand upon the holy man's arm but it seemed unnecessary. He came willingly to Church View Street and thence to Galen House.

I lit a candle, set it upon our table, and motioned for the hermit to seat himself upon a bench. Arthur, unsure, I believe, that the man would not try to flee, sat close beside him. I took a place on another bench opposite the two and rested my elbows upon the table.

"You have often been seen upon the streets after curfew. Are you alone in this? Do you see other men about?"

I had misspoken by asking two questions. If one was answered with a nod and the other with a shake of the head, the holy man would have a wry neck. I rephrased my question. "Do you sometimes see other men about the streets after curfew?"

He nodded.

"The same man?"

This time the hermit shook his head.

"You have seen two or more men prowling about in the night?"

A nod in reply.

"Did you recognize any man?"

This time a nay.

Of course not. The holy man was new to the village and when he saw others it was dark. And likely he did not wish to be seen by those he saw.

I had never undertaken a more difficult interrogation. The hermit was not uncooperative, but I was required to guess the questions which, followed only by his yea or nay responses, took me toward the information I desired. To write here every question I asked that night, and the holy man's responses, would require me to travel again to Oxford and purchase another gathering of parchment. I will, therefore, write only a summary of what I learned.

The man could not speak – or would not – because many years past, whilst on pilgrimage in Spain, he had lost his way and entered the territory of Granada, which was not yet freed from Mussulmen. The men who captured him resented the reconquista and that they were slowly being driven from the Iberian lands they had conquered from Christians five hundred years past. His captors demanded that he acknowledge Mohammed as Allah's true prophet. When he refused they tore his tongue from his mouth for insulting their prophet, and enslaved him.

For three years he was starved and beaten until he managed to escape his captors. Nearly a year later he found passage on a ship bound from Bordeaux to Portsmouth and returned to the land of his birth. He had tried to attach himself to a monastery as a lay brother, but due to his disfigurement the two abbeys he had approached would not have him. For five years he had lived upon the alms of monasteries and village churches and the charity of folk who honored his ascetic way of life, seeking shelter where he might.

Dawn was beginning to lighten the eastern sky when I concluded the interrogation. I never did learn from the hermit why he prowled Bampton streets after curfew, but I did learn that he had seen men sneaking about in the Weald, and twice saw a man furtively slinking from one thicket to another along the Witney road.

It seemed likely to me the man, or men, he had seen in the Weald were drawn there by Rosamond Wyle. As he was slender and wore a long robe I felt sure the holy man was the man Adela had seen when she returned late from her work at Galen House. I could not guess why he saw a man along the Witney road, north of the village, unless the man was poaching Lord Gilbert's deer. And if that was so he would not be the man who put an arrow into William Walle. Such a crude projectile as slew the clerk would not bring down a deer unless the unwary creature allowed the hunter to approach within three or so paces.

The holy man did not know whether the man he saw near to the road to Witney was leaving Bampton or approaching. Because the first time he saw the fellow he seemed to be drawing near the village. When he saw the man a second time – assuming 'twas the same person – he was leaving.

I sent the holy man on his way as the sun climbed over the stubby tower of St. Andrew's Chapel a few hundred paces to the east of the village. What had I learned from this sleepless night that might tell me who had slain Odo Fuller? Could it be that some man had approached St. Beornwald's Church on Good Friday eve from the Witney road, entered the church, which he could see was ablaze with light, cracked Odo's skull, hid his corpse in the Easter Sepulchre, then made off with three items of silver? But why, then, bury two of the stolen objects where they would be found? Why not sell all of the silver to some Oxford silversmith? Indeed, why take only three objects? Why not abscond with as much silver as could be carried?

Because Ernaud le Tournier must appear to be guilty of murder and theft. How else might these questions be answered? Could the fellow the holy man saw along the Witney road be the man who did these felonies? From what the hermit answered he had seen the dark prowler only two or three hundred paces north of Landell's Lane. Another hundred paces to the south would put the man in St. Beornwald's churchyard.

I shared a maslin loaf and ale with Arthur before sending him, grainy-eyed, back to the castle. A sleepless night had provided more questions, but few answers. There was nothing where the intruder had been seen to draw a man away from the village in the night. According to the holy man he saw the dark prowler a hundred or so paces beyond the tithe barn. Beyond the tithe barn there is no habitation until Lew, two miles distant. Whoever the holy man saw must have been of Bampton, else why would he have been so far from any other habitation? So I thought. I have been wrong before.

* * *

Just as Kate was ladling out our dinner I heard a heavy thumping upon Galen House's door. I was not amused. Who would call at noon and seek me while my pottage cooled? Mayhap, I thought, some man had injured himself. Not so.

'Twas Arthur who banged upon my door. "Sir Jaket has returned," he said.

"With Ernaud?" I asked.

"Aye. The bishop released him."

I wished to learn from Sir Jaket all that had transpired, and I desired conversation with Ernaud. But I also wanted my dinner.

Curiosity won the dispute. I told Kate that I was off to the castle and would return as soon as could be.

"I will keep your dinner warm," she said.

* * *

Sir Jaket and his page are young men, younger than me. But their faces were lined with exhaustion, as was Ernaud's. His pallor, however, was due to worry for an uncertain future as much as for many miles of dust and mud having passed under the hooves of a palfrey.

The residents of Bampton Castle were at dinner in the hall when I arrived. Lord Gilbert and his knights and two of their ladies were enjoying sole in fraunt hemelle at the high table, while lesser folk consumed a porre of peas. 'Twas difficult to tell who most enjoyed their meal. I saw no one among the commons gazing at the high table with longing. Perhaps Arthur and such folk have become skilled at disguising envy.

I did not see Ernaud in the hall. He had perhaps already sought Father Simon's vicarage, a meal, and his own bed. But Sir Jaket was seated at the high table, saw me enter the hall, and nodded a greeting. I found a bench along the wall and waited 'til dinner was finished.

"Bishop Brantyngham was not much pleased to release the clerk to me," the knight said when I asked of his journey. "But the stolen cresset appearing in an Oxford shop, the murder of William Walle, and Lord Gilbert's letter finally convinced him."

"Hah. Even a bishop does not wish to offend a great baron," I said.

"Just so."

"You had several days upon the road returning from Exeter with Ernaud. Did he speak of Odo's murder?"

"Aye, little else."

"What had he to say? He was in a gaol cell for more than a fortnight. In such a place a man has much time to think."

"The clerk has a theory, I believe," Sir Jaket said.

"About Odo's murder? What did he say? I intend to ask him, but I'd like to hear your view of his opinion."

"He didn't... he made no accusation. But several times he said that when he returned to Bampton there was a man he intended to seek and deal sharply with."

"Deal sharply with? Who would that be but the felon who slew Odo and laid the blame at Ernaud's feet?"

"Who indeed. I pressed him for a name, but he would not speak it. Said he and Odo might have been wrong."

"Hmmm. He and Odo?"

"Aye, that's what he said."

What, I wondered, might the two of them have been wrong about? As Odo was dead and Ernaud accused of the felony, I believed whatever the clerks suspected was correct, not in error. Some man knew of their suspicion, but what did they suspect? And who? What two clerks guessed, a third might know of. I must speak first to Ernaud, then to Peter Bouchard. And why, I wondered, did Ernaud not voice this suspicion when I first questioned him in the castle?

I departed the castle and returned to Galen House for my dinner, intending after the meal to seek Father Simon's vicarage and have conversation with Ernaud. I should have gone straight from the castle to the vicarage. By the time I had finished my meal and walked to the vicarage, Ernaud had sought his bed. He was exhausted, Father Simon said, from the journey and his ordeal. I told the priest that I would seek Ernaud on the morrow.

CHAPTER 12

Shortly after dawn, pounding upon Galen House's door roused me from slumber. Kate had already abandoned our bed when John demanded to break his fast, so 'twas she who opened to Father Simon. I heard her greet our visitor, then she called up the stairs that Father Simon needed to speak to me. I heard the priest's voice, then Kate's again. "Urgently," she said.

I did not take time to splash water upon my face, but hastily drew on chauces and cotehardie and plunged down the stairs. The priest looked up at me as I descended and I saw the track of a tear upon his cheek. His arms were folded across his ample belly and his hands twisted the ends of his sleeves.

"Sir Hugh," he blurted, "you must come. Ernaud has been taken ill. I fear he is dead."

"We will make haste," I said, and took the priest by his elbow. As we hurried up Church View Street I asked the reason for his belief that Ernaud was dead.

"'Twas time for the morning Angelus, as Ernaud knew, but he had not left his bed. I knew he was fatigued, but when I finally entered his chamber to awaken him I could not."

"Was he breathing?"

"Nay, I think not. Or, if so, 'twas so weak I could not detect it."

Father Simon pushed open his vicarage door and I followed him up the stairs to the clerk's tiny chamber. 'Twas as the priest had said. Ernaud lay motionless under his blanket. I opened an eyelid but received no response. I rested my hand upon his open mouth but felt no movement of air. I took his hand in mine and felt it cold to the touch.

"What has happened?" the priest said. "He complained of exhaustion last evening, but a young man will not perish of fatigue... will he?"

"I've never heard of such a cause for death," I replied. "Does he rest now just as you found him? Did you seek any wounds on his body?"

"He is as I found him. When I could not rouse him I sought you. I shook his shoulders to awaken him, but when that failed I went to you."

"Then we must seek a wound. This death, I think, is not natural. There is a cause. How old was Ernaud?"

"Twenty-two years."

"Healthy young men of such an age do not die abed unless plague be present, or some other contagion... or some man's hand is against them."

"I've not heard of any pestilence in the village," Father Simon said.

"Nor have I. I see no blood staining his bedclothes, but some wounds bleed little."

The clerk had fallen to sleep wearing his robe, so exhausted was he. Father Simon and I drew aside the blanket and robe. We found no wound, not even a bruise.

"Can men enter your vicarage in the night?" I asked.

"Nay. The doors are always barred."

"Were they last night? Whose duty is it to bar them?"

"Ranulph does this."

"He is the older of your servants, is he not?"

"Aye."

"Is he sometimes forgetful of his obligation?"

"Nay. Always reliable, is Ranulph."

"Fetch him. We must ask of last evening."

Father Simon's vicarage was home to the priest, his clerk, a cook, and two servants. With Alan Hillyng the priest had two clerks – but for one day only. Alan, the cook, and the servants knew of Ernaud's death before the priest sought me, and had gathered in the vicarage kitchen while Father Simon and I examined the corpse. The priest called out to the four and moments later they entered the garret, crossing themselves as they passed through the open door.

155

Ranulph insisted that he had barred both doors before he sought his bed the previous night. Father Simon attested that the front door had been barred, for he had to lift the bar before he departed the vicarage to seek me. The cook verified that the rear door was barred when he entered the kitchen at dawn.

"What of the windows?" I said. "Are they fixed in place from within?"

"Aye," Father Simon said. "Have been since last autumn. Not warm enough to open any yet."

"How many windows are there on the ground floor?" I asked.

"Four. Shall I examine them?"

The priest did so and announced that the window of his hall could be pushed open readily. The pin that held it closed against winter storms was missing. A man could shove the skin-covered sash open from inside, or get a fingernail or two under the sash and open the window from the outside so as to enter the vicarage. Whether or not some man had done so, and climbed to Ernaud's chamber upon the first story, I could not know. It was possible. And if so, mayhap the felon had previously been alone in the vicarage hall to remove the closing pin unseen.

"Have you had guests in your hall recently?" I asked.

"How recently?" Father Simon said.

"Within the past month."

"Father Thomas and Father Ralph dined at my table the Monday before Easter."

"Was there a time when either was alone in the hall?"

"What? You think Father Thomas or Father Ralph withdrew the lock pin so the window could allow some man entry? Absurd!"

"Aye, certainly. But some man removed the pin. Unless in the autumn you forgot to secure the window."

"Nay. I'm sure I did so. And had I not, some winter blast might have blown the window open."

"Mayhap, although the window opens out, whereas a storm would press the sash closed."

"Oh... aye. But if some man entered here in the night and slew Ernaud how did he do so? Are you sure my clerk was not of a sudden taken ill in the night?"

"Nay, I'm not sure. Folk die unexpectedly. Perhaps such has happened to Ernaud."

"But you think not?" Father Simon said.

"'Tis strange that a youth would die in this manner when but a few days earlier he spoke of dealing sharply with some man."

"Ernaud said that?"

"Aye. Did he not speak to you of this? He said these words to Sir Jaket while upon the road from Exeter."

"Nay, he said nothing of the sort. Why would he wish to deal sharply with some man?"

"Because," I replied, "he had much time to think on Odo's murder in the past weeks and mayhap had thoughts of who did the felony."

"And caused others to suspect him of the slaying?"

"Aye."

"And whoever this man may be he crept into my vicarage in the night and silenced Ernaud?"

"This may be so. The clerk's death is a riddle elsewise."

There was a second small chamber under the vicarage eaves. I asked Father Simon who slept within.

"My servants, Ranulph and Geoffrey."

I turned to the men, who along with the cook had remained in Ernaud's crowded chamber, staring open-mouthed from the corpse to me to the priest. "Did either of you hear anything untoward in the night? Did some sound awaken you?"

Geoffrey shook his head, but Ranulph spoke. "Awoke to use the chamber pot. Often do. But I thought I heard Ernaud cough. That's what woke me. I think."

"You are uncertain?"

"I wake to use the chamber pot most every night, whether some man coughs or not."

157

I cast my eyes upon Ernaud's corpse again. Did Ranulph hear him cough? Did the sound mean that Ernaud was afflicted with some illness which quickly took his life?

Some years past I had investigated a murder in which the victim was smothered with his pillow. Might this have happened to Ernaud? Would he awaken and struggle to catch his breath? Surely. Would such a tussle sound like a cough in some other chamber? Mayhap.

Only one thing was certain: Ernaud was dead and the man he intended to deal sharply with was unknown, perhaps for ever.

Father Simon gave Ranulph and Geoffrey instructions for preparing Ernaud for burial. This was unnecessary. They had seen the procedure done many times. Ernaud would be washed, then sewn into a shroud, as with all men unless they possess enough wealth to rest in a coffin. But to what purpose is a coffin? The dead cannot value a wooden box more than a linen cloth.

Father Simon and I descended from the garret to the ground floor. As we did so he asked if I intended to seek a murderer, or if I was convinced some illness had come upon Ernaud.

"Would be less worrisome for you if 'twas a malady which took Ernaud's life. This I know. You have already a murderer to seek and likely do not wish for another. But for we others, if Ernaud perished of some illness then it may be that the sickness will not be content to take but one life. A contagion may afflict others. Indeed, it may already have done so."

"Aye, such is possible," I replied. "But not probable."

"You believe there is another murderer loose in Bampton?"

"Nay. There is but one felon, I think."

"You believe, if Ernaud was slain, the murderer is the same who slew Odo?"

"Aye. And for the same reason. The evidence is thin, I know, but 'tis my belief that a felon gained entrance to your vicarage last night through the unsecured window, crept up the stairs to Ernaud's chamber – and he knew in which room he would find your clerk – then smothered the youth with his pillow. The cough Ranulph heard was Ernaud struggling for breath. I cannot prove this, but I believe it so."

I stopped at Galen House to break my fast with a maslin loaf and ale, briefly told Kate of Ernaud's death, then set out for the holy man's hut. I heard the passing bell ring from the tower of St. Beornwald's Church as I departed Galen House.

I found the hermit sitting upon a rotting log before his hut. A small fire smoldered, upon which a bronze, three-footed pot rested. The holy man was cooking a pottage – oats, by the look of it – for his dinner. Likely it would also be his supper. And as many meals on the morrow as it lasted. Most folk think oats only good for horses. But not the poor.

The hermit stood when he heard and saw me approach, then raised a silent hand in greeting. He evidently held no grudge for my lengthy inquisition of but a few hours past.

I sat beside the holy man and watched as he stirred his porridge. There came a whiff of onion when he did. Either some matron had taken pity upon him and given him the onion, or during his night-time patrol of the village he had lifted it from someone's toft.

When he returned to his seat I spoke. "Did you walk the village last night?"

I saw concern flash across the man's face. He knew that his dark perambulations were a violation of curfew, and that I had authority to expel him from both hut and village. The hermit nodded affirmatively, with some trepidation in his demeanor.

"Did you see any other man upon the streets?"

Again he nodded.

"Where did you see this fellow? Can you show me?"

The holy man looked to his bubbling pot and I read his mind.

"Your pottage is nearly ready. I will not ask you to forgo your dinner. But when you have eaten come to Galen House. I will await you there."

Mass was finished and Kate and Adela had returned to Galen House when I arrived home after visiting the holy man.

Kate knew much of the tragic events of the past few hours, and I told her more while I consumed a dish of arbolettys for my dinner. Adela listened silently.

"Ernaud knew who did Odo's murder, then," Kate said.

"Or thought he knew," I replied.

"And the man who slew Odo was convinced that Ernaud knew of his felony?"

"This seems likely," I agreed.

"You told the holy man to come here when he had eaten his meal. You believe he will?"

"He seems amenable to my requests."

"But if the man he saw last night after curfew is the villain who slew Ernaud, the holy man may be in danger from the rogue if he discovers who has identified him."

"'Twas dark, so unlikely that the hermit saw the man clearly enough to recognize his face if he saw it again."

"The guilty man will not know that. What if the holy man is slain because he spoke to you? He might not be able to identify the man he saw in the night – surely not, for he will not speak – but the man who murdered Ernaud will not know this."

Kate's thought had merit. As if I had not enough to concern me, the holy man's safety must now devolve upon me. I should not have told him to seek me at Galen House. If he was not seen at my door there would be no concern that a murderer might wish to slay him. The hermit seemed always careful that he not be seen in the night by those he observed. But careful enough?

I put down my knife and spoon, rose from the table, and announced that I must seek the holy man. If he was prevented from approaching Galen House he should be safe from the suspicions of a felon.

I hurried from Galen House, passed the castle, and met the holy man as he entered the road leaving his forest path. I glanced over my shoulder to see if any man's eyes saw our meeting, so worried for the hermit's safety I had become due to Kate's observation.

160

"We will return to your hut," I said. The fellow shrugged, turned, and led the way into the wood.

The holy man's fire, upon which he had cooked his gruel, was but a few smoking embers. Nevertheless we again sat upon the decaying log facing the cooling ashes.

"Last night some man entered Father Simon's vicarage and slew his clerk. Do you know which house is Father Simon's?"

The holy man nodded.

"You saw a man after curfew last night. Was the man near to Father Simon's vicarage?"

Again he nodded.

"Was this early in the night, or late, near to dawn? Sorry, I must remember to ask one question at a time. Did you see the fellow before midnight?"

The hermit shook his head.

"Near to dawn, then?"

He nodded.

"Did you see him walk toward the vicar's house?"

He shook his head.

"Away from it, then?"

He nodded agreement.

In a series of further questions I learned that the man the hermit saw in the night was short and stout, garbed in black or some dark hue so as to blend with the night, and was last seen creeping between Father Simon's vicarage and a neighboring house. The man did not enter that house, but passed behind it and was then lost from sight.

I concluded the inquiry by asking the hermit why he chose to prowl Bampton's streets in the night in violation of curfew. I received no satisfactory response, but mayhap I had not the wit to ask the proper questions. His nocturnal wandering was proving useful to me, so I did not press the man to keep to his hut in the night. If he could be my eyes in the darkness I would consider his malfeasance a small matter. I did not wish to keep from my bed so as to observe what some folk of Bampton were doing past midnight, but it would be useful to know of these curfew-breakers and their nocturnal habits. The holy man could be my eyes and ears whilst I slept. Eyes and ears are good things, and the Lord Christ has blessed mankind with them. If one set is good, two would surely be better.

I bade the hermit good day, and returned to the village. By the time I reached Father Simon's vicarage Ernaud's corpse had been washed and sewn into a linen shroud. A coffin rested in a corner of the vicarage hall, but this was surely temporary. Ernaud would rest beneath the sod in only the shroud. His journey from vicarage to churchyard might be made in a coffin, but not beyond.

Father Simon's face was pale when I entered his vicarage. Three clerks attending the vicars of the Church of St. Beornwald had been slain, which was enough to drive the blood from any cleric's visage.

"I have been to visit the holy man," I said.

The priest raised his eyebrows. "Why so?" he asked.

"The fellow violates curfew and walks Bampton's streets in the night."

"Did you arrest him?"

"Nay. He provided useful information. A man who knows what happens when honest men are abed is valuable to a bailiff."

"What information?"

"Near to dawn he saw a man – short and stout, he said, which describes half the men of Bampton – steal away from your vicarage and disappear between the vicarage and Reginald Shirk's house."

"Why would Reginald slay Ernaud? He has always seemed a companionable fellow."

"The holy man did not see the fellow enter Reginald's house. He disappeared between your neighbor's house and the vicarage. The holy man knows not where the prowler then went."

"You believe this may be the man who entered the vicarage and slew Ernaud?"

"Likely. I intend to walk that way and see if any man left a track to follow, and where a man who traveled that way might go... what his destination might be. Will you accompany me?"

"Aye. Geoffrey and Ranulph have prepared the corpse. There is nothing to do but watch over Ernaud until his funeral, which they can do in my absence."

The path Father Simon's tenebrous visitor had followed to depart the vicarage led through his neighbor's toft, toward a clump of bushes which extended beyond the vicarage. The priest and I sought broken shoots or other signs of the track some man might have traveled through the shrubbery, but found nothing. To the south the thicket ended at Bushy Row, which may be how the lane received its name. To the north the line of bushes ended behind Father Thomas's toft, where three crab apple trees provided the priest with fruit for jellies and verjuice.

"Likely whosoever the holy man saw crept along the shadow of those bushes, then made off down Bushy Row," the priest said.

I agreed that such a supposition seemed plausible.

"Who resides upon Bushy Row who might want Odo and Ernaud dead, and William also?" Father Simon asked.

"And who also might know some woman who would sell a silver cresset in Oxford?" I added.

We scratched our heads as if the action would bring some name to mind. It did not. Six families resided upon Bushy Row. Widows were head of two of these, and one widow had adult children with whom she resided. The four other families were upstanding residents who paid their rents and tithes when due, and so far as I knew had never caused trouble in the village.

But all men have secrets. Were there secrets within the dwellings upon Bushy Row?

No women appeared next morning to wail behind the pallet upon which Ernaud's corpse was borne to the churchyard. The clerk was not of Bampton so had no female relatives to mourn his journey to the lychgate. The sexton and his assistant had dug a grave near to Odo's, and well before noon the funeral mass and burial were done.

163

Some man, I thought, as Ernaud's corpse was lifted from the coffin and lowered into the grave, was frightened. Why else add a third murder to two others? The penalty for three murders could not be greater than for two – no man can hang thrice. So if a man feared he was near to being found out as a felon he would not hesitate to slay the man he believed might give evidence against him. Did the culprit believe that I also was close on his trail? If so, he was wrong. But perhaps I should be cautious. A man who had slain three would not hesitate to do a fourth murder.

Bartram Thrupp attended Ernaud's funeral mass. When I saw him I was reminded that I had promised to remove the stitches from his lacerated arm. I spoke to the cook as we departed the churchyard and told him that I would first return to Galen House for some instruments, then call upon him at Father Thomas's vicarage.

As I cut the sutures away I saw a tear emerge from Bartram's eye. The pain of removing stitches is little more than a pin prick. The cook, I decided, must be sorrowful for Ernaud's death.

"'Tis a sad day," I said, in response to Bartram's woeful expression.

"Aye. It is that," the cook replied. "Makes a man wonder who is next. All those slain have been employed by the priests of St. Beornwald's. Mayhap I will resign my post."

"Mayhap it need not come to that," I said, and left my patient to his morose pondering.

* * *

For many days I pondered what to do until once again the stolen cresset returned to my thoughts. Perhaps I should again seek it. Discovery might tell me through whose hands the object had passed. Would it be easier to find the cresset than to discover who had entered Father Simon's vicarage to slay Ernaud? There was but one way to know, and that was to renew my effort to find the cresset. Why? Could the cresset speak? My thoughts now seem foolish to me. I resolved to seek Arthur after my dinner and require of him that he prepare two palfreys for the morrow, and again accompany me to Oxford.

I shared my plan with Father Simon, telling him I intended to seek the aid of Master John Wycliffe. The scholar might know of a man who would be willing to visit the goldsmith who had once offered Father Ralph's cresset for sale. I intended to request of such a fellow that he ask the goldsmith if the silver cresset was sold, or yet available for purchase.

Kate demanded that I consume a wedge of cheese with my loaf next morning. "You will be starved before you gain Oxford," she claimed. I yielded to her opinion. I am no fool.

I had told Arthur to have himself and the palfreys ready by the second hour.

When I reached the castle marshalsea on Tuesday morn I found three palfreys saddled and prepared for the road. Uctred stood with Arthur, awaiting me. Uctred is as gaunt and ropey as Arthur is brawny. They are unlike in appearance but their attitude toward injustice is similar. They are unwilling to see evil succeed and are ready to do what they may to see wicked men fail in their malicious schemes.

If the stolen cresset was to tell me anything of the man who stole it and slew Odo I must find the object – if it remained a cresset and was not melted to an ingot. Most likely if it yet existed it would be within Oxford's walls. It would not be in Bampton. Mayhap it was melted to the two ingots I saw in the goldsmith's workroom, and since then had been fashioned into trinkets for some lady's neck or wrists, or made into some gentleman's new wine goblet.

Our first stop in Oxford was an inn, the Fox and Hounds, where we stabled the palfreys, then shared a roasted capon and maslin loaves. From the inn I set off for Queen's College. I found Master Wycliffe in his chamber, bent over a book, pulling upon his beard as if deep in thought. Being deep in thought is customary behavior for Master Wycliffe. I doubt the scholar has ever entertained a shallow thought. Perhaps when a lad he may have done.

Master John looked up from his book, recognized me, and stood to greet me. "Are you yet employed as bailiff in Bampton?" he asked.

"Aye, and surgeon."

"Of course. Folk regularly do themselves harm, I suppose, and require your services."

"Or," I said, "they do others harm."

"Is this what brings you to my door? Do you seek assistance, or is this but a greeting?"

"You have it right. I need assistance."

The scholar pointed to a bench drawn up against a wall. "Then sit, you and your men, and tell me how I may be of service."

I did. I began with Odo Fuller's disappearance and murder, the suspicion that Ernaud le Tournier had slain him, Adela's sightings of a man prowling the Weald in the night, and the search for a stolen cresset. I told also of the death of William Walle and Ernaud, and the found and vanished cresset. Wycliffe listened intently, pulling upon his beard all the while. He seemed particularly interested when I spoke of the holy man.

"How may I be of assistance in this matter?" Master John asked when I concluded the tale. "I am not a sleuth, but a simple scholar."

A scholar, aye, I thought. But not so simple. "I wish to try the goldsmith and see if he spoke true when he claimed that a man had come for the cresset, claiming to represent Father Ralph."

"And for this you seek my aid?"

"Aye. Can you name some mature scholar, perhaps new to Oxford so he will not be well known, who might approach the goldsmith with an offer to purchase the cresset?"

"You believe the goldsmith might yet possess the thing, hidden away somewhere?"

"'Tis possible. And, if not, I'd like to eliminate the possibility."

"Andrew Gridby might serve. He came to Oxford a year past. Keeps to himself, does Andrew."

"Is he a youth?"

"Nay. Older than most new scholars."

"Can he project an image of wealth? An impecunious scholar wearing a threadbare robe would not likely be seeking an expensive silver cresset. The goldsmith would be on his guard if such a student appeared in his shop."

"Andrew's father is a knight of Sussex, and prosperous. The lad's garments speak it so."

"Is Andrew an adventurous sort?"

"Hah, most lads are, before maturity teaches caution. And what harm might come to him asking about a rare silver object?"

"Indeed. Does Andrew have a chamber at Queen's?"

"He does. On the upper story of this hall. Shall we seek him?"

We did. 'Twas as Master John had said. The scholar was old enough that a thin cloud of dark whiskers obscured his cheeks. He was of that indeterminate age when a man is too young to grow a proper beard, but too old to appear clean-shaven without the regular application of a razor. Wycliffe introduced me to the young man, and stood aside while I repeated the tale of the deaths of Odo, William, and Ernaud, then explained what I desired of him.

"But I have no interest in purchasing a silver cresset," Andrew said. "Or any other."

"The goldsmith need not know that," I replied.

"But to say so would be a lie."

"A subterfuge," I said.

"Nevertheless, you ask me to deceive a man."

"Aye," I agreed. "I do. For a good purpose. To apprehend a felon who has done three murders."

"Can a man right a wrong by doing another wrong? Nay, I'll not put my soul in peril even to find a felon."

To this declaration I had no reply. Was I placing my own soul in danger by plotting to deceive the goldsmith? I glanced to Master Wycliffe, unsure of what I might say to Andrew.

Wycliffe spoke. "Sir Hugh does not ask you to misrepresent your appearance at the goldsmith's shop. Here is what you might do. Go to the burgher and tell him that you have heard that in the past few weeks he had a silver cresset which he offered for sale.

This is true. Tell him then that you know a man who seeks such a cresset as a gift to a friend. This also is true, for Sir Hugh seeks the cresset to return it to his friend, the priest in Bampton.

"Tell the goldsmith then that you are seeking the cresset because if you find it, you believe the buyer might reward you." Wycliffe then looked to me. "Will you do so?" he asked.

"Uh... aye... six pence if we find the cresset because of your assistance."

"Nothing of what you say will be untruthful," Master John said, "if you speak as I have suggested. Will you do so and see a stolen object returned to its owner, and mayhap a murderer unmasked? Few men are given such a chance... to make straight the path of justice."

I cannot say whether 'twas Master Wycliffe's arguments or the thought of six pence that persuaded Andrew. But he agreed to do as was suggested.

"Then let us be off," I said, "and put this plan to action."

Master John wished to accompany Andrew to the Northgate and observe from the street as the youth put our plot to the test, but I objected. Wycliffe is well known in Oxford, and the goldsmith had seen me, Arthur, and Uctred but a few days past. I wanted nothing to raise the burgher's suspicions.

So I approached the goldsmith's shop no closer than the Church of St. Mary Magdalen, a hundred or so paces beyond the Northgate, and from there sent Andrew to his task. My only knowledge of what was said within the shop comes from Andrew, but it suffices.

The goldsmith was serving another patron when Andrew entered the shop. The fellow sought an emerald ring for his bride, and was particular about the design. When that was settled the two men haggled over the price. This was Andrew's explanation for the time which passed – more than an hour – before I saw him pass through the Northgate and approach where I, Master John, Arthur, and Uctred waited before the church.

The difficult bridegroom finally agreed terms with the goldsmith and departed. The burgher gave his attention to Andrew, and the scholar spoke as Master Wycliffe had suggested. A difficulty immediately arose. The goldsmith asked the name of the friend who might wish to purchase a silver cresset. The young scholar is no dolt. He quickly thought to say that he would not provide the friend's name, for then the goldsmith might seek the fellow, make a separate arrangement for the sale, and he – Andrew – would receive no reward for finding such a rare object.

The goldsmith then asked Andrew what his friend might pay for such a cresset. I had not told the youth of the price demanded when I first visited the goldsmith and discovered the cresset, but again his quick wit came to his rescue and he, after a moment's thought, suggested that, depending upon the quality of the silver and engraving, the friend might pay as much as four shillings. That caught the goldsmith's attention, was it not captured already.

Andrew said the goldsmith did not immediately reply to this bid, as if he was considering some weighty matter. He was. He finally spoke. "I believe I know where such a cresset may be found. Four shillings, you say?"

"Aye."

"Return tomorrow, perhaps with your friend. Mayhap he will be able to judge for himself the worth of the piece."

Andrew related this encounter to me as we five stood in a circle before the Church of St. Mary Magdalen. Even if I never again saw Father Ralph's cresset I now knew it existed. The goldsmith would not have told Andrew to return except that he knew where he could lay hands on it. Unless a second silver cresset existed. Unlikely.

CHAPTER 13

aster Wycliffe found lodging for me, Arthur, and Uctred in unoccupied chambers at Queen's College. Each of us was provided with a small cubicle, so neither Uctred nor I was required to deal with Arthur's resonant snores.

The next morning, Master John provided us with a ewer of stale ale, and I sent Uctred to a baker for loaves, so we four broke our fast while considering what might be done if Andrew returned to the goldsmith and the fellow produced Father Ralph's cresset.

Andrew arrived at Master John's chamber at the second hour, as he had been instructed. I described Father Ralph's cresset to him, so if he was offered the piece he might identify it.

"The lip is engraved with a circle of thorns, to honor the Lord Christ in His torment, and at the base an 'R' is inscribed, for 'Ralph', the priest whose possession it is."

"What am I to say if the goldsmith produces the cresset?"

"Ask him for the price, then whatever he requires, tell him that you will seek the friend who is the buyer and will then return."

"You intend to pay the fellow?" Wycliffe asked.

"Nay. We will seek Sir Roger and ask if he will appoint a serjeant to accompany me when I go to the goldsmith and take possession of the cresset."

Wycliffe would not hear of going about his own business when others were upon the trail of a felon. He accompanied us to the Church of St. Mary Magdalen again, whence I sent Andrew on his way. He disappeared among the throng passing through the Northgate and I prepared myself to wait.

I was surprised to see Andrew reappear only a few moments later. When he came near he lifted his hands, palms upward. I soon learned why.

"The goldsmith says he has no knowledge of a silver cresset. The only cresset such as I seek was stolen goods, he said, and

170

a representative of its owner claimed it some weeks past. He knows of no other silver cresset, and apologized for leading me to believe he did."

Master John looked to me with raised eyebrows. Was Lord Gilbert present, he would have lifted but one eyebrow.

What could have caused the goldsmith to change his testimony so abruptly? Yesterday, if Andrew understood him, he knew the whereabouts of the silver cresset he had once displayed for custom. Now he knew nothing of it; some man claiming to represent Father Ralph had taken possession of the piece.

The goldsmith had been warned. As the thought crossed my mind Master Wycliffe spoke. "Since yesterday some man has told the goldsmith of your scheme. Who knew of it?"

"When I first devised the plan, I told Father Simon of my intentions."

"No one else?"

"Only my Kate."

"Did you tell Arthur and Uctred?"

"Nay," Arthur said vehemently. "Told me only that I was to accompany 'im to Oxford. Didn't say why, so I couldn't've told anyone else of 'is plan."

"Did you tell anyone we were bound for Oxford?" I said.

"Only the groom of the marshalsea when I told 'im to have palfreys ready."

"I suppose the groom could have spoken to others," I said, "and the felon learned of it and put two and two together."

"He'd need only to visit the goldsmith and ask if any man sought a silver cresset," Master John said. "When he learned it was so he and the goldsmith would know you were somewhere in the shadows behind Andrew."

"Indeed. But the goldsmith's words yesterday cause me to believe that he either had possession of the cresset or knew who did, and knew how and where he may lay hands on it."

"Did you not search the goldsmith's shop, you and the sheriff?" Wycliffe asked.

"We did, and found nothing... but for two small silver ingots which might have been a cresset before they were melted to bars. But if this was so, why would the man have led Andrew to believe the cresset might be had? Nay, I do not believe he melted it down. 'Tis somewhere near."

"Mayhap Sir Roger would be amenable to another search?" Master John said. "When the goldsmith's shop was searched did any man open his mattress or pillow? A straw pallet or a feather pillow might hide a small cresset."

"Especially if no man thought to rest body or head upon one or the other," I said.

"Then seek Sir Roger. You have said he and Lord Gilbert Talbot are friends. Ask for another search. Pry up loose floor boards, send some man to inspect his attic with a candle."

This seemed good advice. Even if the cresset was not found, the goldsmith would know that he was suspected, and not believed. Would that be good, or ill? Would a search make a guilty man more cautious, or mayhap worried about the sheriff's attention therefore willing to confess? I have enough trouble knowing my own mind. How can I predict what another man might do under duress?

Master John and Andrew, their usefulness to me at an end, departed for Queen's College. With Arthur and Uctred I set off for the castle to beg an interview with Sir Roger.

The sheriff was busy when I arrived. A constable told me that he was engaged with a burgher of the town. Through the closed door I heard raised voices. I suspected that the burgher was not a happy man. Likely Sir Roger had imposed a fine for some infraction and the shopkeeper was protesting. I know not how much Sir Roger paid King Edward to have the post, but it was surely a sizable amount. The only way for the sheriff to recoup the investment was to be diligent in levying fines upon those who broke or skirted Oxford's ordinances.

The heavy oaken door to the sheriff's chamber was flung open and a red-faced merchant stalked from the sheriff's presence. 'Twas the goldsmith! He'd apparently been called to

Sir Roger immediately after telling Andrew he had no current knowledge of a silver cresset. The man was so furious that he took no notice of who awaited the next visit with the sheriff.

The constable left his desk, peered through the door, and announced that Sir Hugh de Singleton desired words with the sheriff.

"Send him in," came the reply.

I motioned to Arthur and Uctred that they should remain seated upon the bench – which they knew to do without my gesture, as no groom is likely to be called before the Sheriff of Oxford unless he is entangled in some malfeasance.

"You are returned to Oxford," Sir Roger said by way of greeting. "I give you good day. Is Lord Gilbert well? Do you travel here on the same business as before, or has some new matter arisen?"

"Lord Gilbert is well, and 'tis the same matter as before."

"The stolen cresset; you saw the goldsmith leave just now?"

"Aye. He was not a happy man."

"Hah, he will be even more miserable if he does not stop selling adulterated gold and silver."

"Is not all gold and silver alloyed for strength and durability?" I asked.

"Aye, so I'm told. But this fellow is dishonest about the fraction of base metals he mixes with his gold and silver. He sold a ring which he claimed was three-quarters gold, but when weighed was proven to be little more than half. Other gold- and silversmiths have suspected him. One sent a man to purchase a ring, then assayed it and complained to me yesterday of the discrepancy."

"You fined him?"

"Aye. Six shillings. And if he does the same another time, I told him, the penalty will double. But what of your business with the fellow?"

"Yesterday he told a scholar of Queen's College that he might know where a silver cresset could be found."

"Why would a Queen's scholar want such a bauble?"

"I sent him."

"Ah… to learn if the stolen cresset was really collected by some man claiming to act for the priest whose it was?"

"Just so. And yesterday he said such a piece might be available. This morning he said he was misunderstood."

"The man is not trustworthy," Sir Roger said.

"Aye, and I purchased my Kate's ring from him."

"Is she content with it?"

"Aye, as I was, but now —"

"Then keep silent. Some things may be better not known. But as for the mysterious cresset, its whereabouts is important."

"And not only because of its value, three shillings or so. If I can trace its possession back to the man who made off with it on Good Friday I will know who has slain three clerks of the Church of St. Beornwald. Probably."

"So you desire another search of the goldsmith's premises?"

"Aye. 'Tis possible, I suppose, that the cresset may be hid some other place, but my guess is that the goldsmith told Andrew to return today because he needed but a short time to retrieve the piece from its hiding place. A thing he could not do with the lad waiting whilst he went to fetch the cresset from its place of concealment."

"And before your scheme could bear fruit the goldsmith changed his story, eh?"

"He did. I believe some man knew of my plan and warned him."

"Will he not then seek to find a new and better hiding place for the cresset, if it is hidden in his shop?"

"He may, therefore I would like to make haste."

"I can spare you four constables. My serjeant will collect them. Tell them what you require. Wait in the anteroom."

Sir Roger called to the constable who kept his door and gave instructions as he had promised. The constable disappeared, and a short time later reappeared with the serjeant and four others, all garbed in the sheriff's livery. I told the men what I sought, and required of them that the search be thorough, even mentioning mattresses and pillows.

The goldsmith was yet red-faced and fuming when seven men entered his shop. That four of these wore Sir Roger's livery widened his eyes and opened his mouth. When his glance fell upon me his mouth snapped shut and his lips became thin with anger.

"You again?" he cried. "What do you want now?"

"I seek the same thing as before – a stolen cresset. The cresset you told a man yesterday you could find. Will you find the piece, or must we?"

"I told the fellow this day I have no such thing. I told you a fortnight past that a man called for it and said he would return it to the priest whose it was."

"Very well, we will discover the cresset without your aid."

I told the constables to seek the cresset on the upper story, and if 'twas not there, the attic. Arthur, Uctred, and I would overturn the goldsmith's display room and his shop.

I heard much thumping about above my head as the constables went about their search with enthusiasm and little restraint. A feather wafted down the stairs, which told me the goldsmith's pillow had been examined. The goldsmith, meanwhile, followed me about, complaining loudly all the while.

Nearly an hour later the four constables thundered down the stairs, empty-handed. Arthur, Uctred, and I had by that time finished upsetting the lower rooms, and found nothing. The goldsmith's scowl had become a smirk. This second search was also a failure and he could not disguise his triumph.

But in his supposed victory he made one mistake. I was about to take my leave of the place, defeated, when I saw the goldsmith glance to the rear door of his workroom. As he did so the smirk deepened to a grin. What could he be so pleased about? Surely not that his shop and lodging had been overturned and would require time and effort to set right.

What lay outside the goldsmith's rear door? Only the kiln. I had examined it when I searched the shop before. I turned to the door and as I did so the smile on the goldsmith's face faded like an April frost in the morning sun.

This change in the man's visage told me I was about to do a thing which caused him distress. Good. Beside the rear door was a bag of charcoal and a small iron scoop the goldsmith evidently used to shovel charcoal into his kiln. I took the scoop with me and set to work removing ashes from the kiln. I found the cresset under a foot or so of cold ashes. Sometime within the past week or so the cresset had been removed from an earlier hiding place and hidden in the kiln, for when I had searched the kiln earlier the cresset had not been within.

'Twas Father Ralph's cresset, of that I had no doubt. The initial "R" had been carefully carved away, but the circle of thorns about the rim remained. How many cressets, silver or not, would be so decorated?

"Hah," I exclaimed. "You have hidden stolen goods and lied to the sheriff about it."

"Shall we take him to Sir Roger?" one of the constables asked.

"In a moment. First I have questions."

I turned to the goldsmith and held the cresset before him. "You told me when I first saw this in your shop that a widow sold it to you. Now, tell me the truth. 'Twill go easier for you with the sheriff if I tell him that you have answered honestly."

"'Tis true," he spluttered.

"Why should I believe that, when most other things you have said are false?"

"'Tis true," he muttered again.

"Describe the woman. Thoroughly. Everything you remember. Leave nothing out."

"She was stout," he began. "Said she was a widow who had removed to Oxford... near as tall as you. Wore a green cotehardie."

"How old?"

"Mayhap forty years," he shrugged. "She had not the flush of youth nor the wrinkles of old age. Old enough to be a widow."

I thought that in asking again of the woman he claimed had sold the cresset to him the goldsmith might forget what he had first told me of her. He did not. This description matched his first portrait, which led me to believe that, about this matter at least, he spoke the truth.

"Have you seen the woman since?" I asked. "Upon the streets of Oxford?"

"Nay," he said vociferously. "Had I done so I'd've demanded return of my two shillings and returned the cresset to its rightful owner."

I had no doubt the goldsmith would have demanded the return of his payment. I did doubt the remainder of his assertion.

I dismissed the constables and told them to tell the sheriff that the stolen cresset was recovered. This they saw with their own eyes and could testify so if Sir Roger desired to fine the goldsmith for his possession of stolen goods. I felt sure he would do so, for the sheriff's expenses are great.

From the goldsmith's shop Arthur, Uctred, and I sought the Fox and Hounds and our dinner. As 'twas a fast day the inn offered stewed herrings and we ate our fill. The ale was fresh.

We collected the palfreys and set out for Bampton. I was well content; I had recovered Father Ralph's cresset, I had a full belly, and I would be with Kate, Bessie, and John before night came. My only black thoughts had to do with what I might next do to find who had sold the cresset to the goldsmith. Mayhap, if I prowled the streets of Witney, I might see a tall, buxom woman who was garbed in a green cotehardie. Mayhap she really was a widow, and if I asked I might learn of recently deceased burghers wealthy enough to purchase a stolen silver cresset. Or a wealthy burgher who might acquire stolen goods some other way.

The goldsmith said he had not seen the woman upon Oxford's streets since he purchased Father Ralph's cresset from her. Mayhap she lied, and was not a widow, nor had she taken up residence in Oxford. Did she speak true about being from Witney? If I traveled there I might learn if this was so.

When we reached Bampton I dismounted where Church View Street meets Bridge Street and sent Arthur and Uctred on to the castle while I set off afoot to Galen House. I opened the door, called out to my Kate that I had returned with the stolen cresset and would be back anon, then hastened to Father Ralph's vicarage to return the piece to him. He was much pleased.

If I was to seek a tall, buxom woman upon the streets of Witney I may as well be about it. So I told Arthur to be ready next morning with two palfreys. Witney is but five miles from Bampton. We need not spend the night there. Uctred pouted like a small boy to be left in Bampton, so I told him to make himself ready in the morning also. His countenance lifted. No doubt he'd rather travel the countryside than muck out the marshalsea.

* * *

Thursday is market day in Witney. As we approached the place we joined other folk making toward the center of town, many carrying vegetables to sell or having squawking fowl slung over their shoulders. Most of the inhabitants would be on the streets this day. A good day to seek my quarry. If such a woman existed and if she had not removed to Oxford as the goldsmith claimed. And if the goldsmith could be trusted with that part of his tale.

A baxter sold pies filled with mutton and turnips, and I purchased three. We ate as we wandered the town. I saw tall women, and I saw stout women. I even saw several women wearing green cotehardies. But I saw no woman who matched all three requirements.

The town coroner would know who of Witney had died in the past weeks. I decided to seek him.

I had heard his name mentioned a few times, but had never met the man. I entered a cobbler's shop and asked of Henry Nolly. The shoemaker directed me to a substantial house of three bays on the High Street, near the river. As most dwellings are of two bays the house was easy to find.

I rapped upon the door and a thick, heavy-bearded man opened. I asked if I greeted Henry Nolly and he nodded and replied, "Aye."

"I am Sir Hugh de Singleton, bailiff of Bampton for Lord Gilbert Talbot. May I have a moment of your time?"

178

"Surely," the fellow agreed. "Enter. How may I serve Lord Gilbert's bailiff?" As the man spoke he swept his hand across the open door in invitation.

"Will you take a cup of ale?" Nolly asked. I agreed that we would and he called out a name in a rumbling voice.

"Rohesa" was evidently a servant. A lass darted to the hall and Nolly instructed her to fetch four cups of ale. He then pointed to a chair and benches and invited us to sit. Again he asked how he might serve me. I told him.

"I seek a widow of perhaps forty years, tall and buxom. Her husband, perhaps a prosperous burgher of Witney, recently deceased. The woman is known to wear a green cotehardie and is said to have removed to Oxford."

"Hmmm. Wealthy, you say?"

"Prosperous," I replied. "Enough so that he could purchase a silver cresset."

"A silver cresset? Who would have such a thing?"

"'Twas stolen from St. Beornwald's Church of Bampton at Eastertide. It reappeared at a goldsmith's shop in Oxford. The goldsmith claims he purchased it from a widow of Witney who had moved to Oxford after her husband, a burgher of this place, died."

"We have had three deaths since Easter. One was a woman. The two men were neither burghers nor prosperous. One was a penniless bachelor, the other had a yardland of the bishop."

"Likely the woman told the goldsmith a falsehood," I said. "Do you know of a tall, buxom woman of Witney who often wears a green cotehardie and who has a living husband?"

The coroner pulled at his luxuriant beard and pursed his lips before answering. "There's Anna Pimm. She's a plump woman. Never seen 'er wear a green cotehardie. Not as I recall."

"Is her husband wealthy?"

"Nay. A smith, is Harold. Feeds 'is family but has not the coin to buy a silver cresset."

If Anna Pimm had sold Father Ralph's cresset in Oxford she might have been but an intermediary, taking the purloined silver to Oxford for the thief for a share of the profit. But why would the man who slew Odo Fuller seek a woman to do the deed? Would not the woman's husband be a wiser choice? And would a smith's wife travel alone from Witney to Oxford? Surely not.

"Where is the smith's forge?" I asked.

"You passed it as you came here," the coroner replied. "Little more than a hundred paces south."

I thanked the fellow for his time, motioned to Arthur and Uctred, and left the coroner's house to seek Anna Pimm. When I found her I understood at once that she had not traveled to Oxford to sell stolen silver.

I heard the smith banging away upon his anvil as we approached the forge. His house, which badly needed new thatching, stood beside the forge and when we came near I heard a screeching female voice.

Two children tumbled from the house, followed by the shrill howl of an angry woman. The children, lasses of about ten and twelve years, halted their flight a few paces from the door and turned as the woman I took to be their mother appeared.

She was stout, but not overly tall, and wore a threadbare brown cotehardie over her shift. A few strands of greasy hair escaped her soiled wimple. She would never be mistaken for the wife of a wealthy burgher, even if she claimed to be.

I walked on past the smith's forge, leading my palfrey, without troubling myself to stop and question the smith's wife. She was busy castigating her daughters for some dereliction. No need to trouble her more than they had apparently already done.

We had journeyed from Bampton for a purpose that now seemed a forlorn prospect. But so long as we were in the town I thought we might as well continue the search. We sauntered again through the marketplace, although by this time most folk had completed their transactions and made for home. We even walked adjoining streets. I saw no one who met the goldsmith's description. But of course the woman in question had said she now resided in Oxford.

The coroner could remember no such woman. Was there some incomplete truth in what the goldsmith had said of how he came to possess Father Ralph's cresset? Did he purchase it from a woman who spoke falsely of how she came to have it? Was she from some other place, not Witney? Was her husband yet living? Did she travel with him to Oxford, then return to her home two shillings richer?

Men, or a man, had been seen creeping about in the Weald after curfew. Three clerks to the priests of St. Beornwald's Church had been slain; one struck down with a silver candlestick, one pierced by a crude arrow, a third likely smothered as he slept. Two stolen candlesticks were buried where they were sure to be found. A stolen cresset was found in Oxford. And twice a man was seen in the night skulking near the tithe barn and the road to Witney. How might all these events be tied together? Or were they not? Was I seeking a connection where none was?

I returned to Bampton a disappointed man. Every path I followed toward what might seem a resolution to three murders ended in a swamp of confusion.

But my Kate is able to dispel gloom with a smile. Which is how she greeted me when I entered Galen House that evening. A dish of leech lombard accompanied her welcome home and went far in helping me forget the day's failure.

Adela departed for the Weald after putting Bessie to bed, and Kate joined me upon a bench before our hearth after providing John with his last meal of the day. I had told her already of some of the events in Witney, but she was not content with only the rudiments.

"The woman does not exist," she said when I concluded the tale. "Or she is of some other place."

"I am inclined to believe the goldsmith," I said.

"Why so?"

"He described the woman twice, a fortnight apart, in the same terms. Would he remember a first falsehood well enough to repeat it later?"

"Then she must be of some other place."

"Aye," I agreed, "and known to the felon who has slain three clerks."

"Would such a man know a woman who resided a great distance from Bampton?" Kate mused.

"Probably not. If the woman is not of Witney," I said, "then she may be of Eynsham or Burford or some other town not far distant."

"Will you travel to those places seeking her?"

"Mayhap. I will sleep on it. 'Twill likely be a waste, but I can see no way to discover a murderer than by finding folk through whose hands the cresset has passed. There is no other evidence. At least none which promises a successful conclusion. The arrow which slew William Walle seems unlikely to provide many clues."

CHAPTER 14

'Twas well before dawn when I was awakened from a sound sleep by Kate's elbow in my ribs. I was sore for a week. She apologized later, claiming that gentle jabs resulted only in causing me to roll to the other side of the bed and respond with a grunt.

Kate had been awakened by a gentle pounding upon the door of Galen House. When I was finally awake she whispered the fact to me and a moment later I heard the soft thumping resume. No man called my name. There was only the faint rattle of the door against the bar as the pounding was intermittently repeated.

Such disturbance of my rest is not uncommon. Folk take ill in the night and seek me and my store of herbs. Others do themselves injury in the day, neglect to seek my services out of unwillingness to pay a few pence to see a wound dealt with, then in the night, alone with their pain, send a family member to ask my aid. So I shouted down the stairs that I would open anon, drew on chauces and cotehardie, then hurried to unbar the door.

'Twas the holy man who stood before. He glanced over his shoulder to the dark street, put a finger to his lips indicating a request for silence, then with the same finger beckoned me to follow him. Somewhere behind me I felt Kate standing at the foot of the stairs.

"I must go," I said.

"Be careful, husband," came her reply.

I intended to do so.

A sliver of moon was rising in the east, granting enough light that I could see the hermit's gestures, then follow his dark, slender form north past St. Beornwald's Church. He turned occasionally to see that I followed and silently we walked to Landell's Lane, thence to the north road.

Here we stopped, and again the holy man put a finger to his lips to reinforce his request for silence.

We stood motionless where the new tithe barn cast a shadow across the road. All was dark and silent. The holy man then grasped my arm and drew me north. After ten or so paces we left the shadow of the tithe barn and here the holy man bent to peer at the pale dirt of the faintly illuminated road. I did also, but could not see anything which might pique a man's interest.

The hermit took a hesitant step, then another, and sank to his knees. I did likewise, wondering what the man saw which so intrigued him. His arm extended slowly, an index finger pointing to the dust of the road. And then I saw it – the track of a cart wheel. But why should such a mark capture his interest in the night? 'Twas well past midnight, I felt sure, but early enough that the eastern sky was not yet grey with dawn. Why should I be drawn from my bed to gaze upon this track in the dirt?

The holy man stood, took my arm again, and slowly we retraced our steps to re-enter the shadow of the tithe barn. The man never took his eyes from the road. Then, suddenly, he knelt again. I did also, assuming that there was at my feet something else the hermit wanted me to see. The cart track reappeared, nearly invisible. Indeed, had I not known it was there, after following it from the moonlit section of the road, I'd not have been able to find it even had I known to seek it.

On hands and knees the holy man scrutinized the road, slowly making his way toward the sleeping village. He stopped, turned to me, and again pointed to the road. I found the cart track, and saw what had captured his attention. The wheel marks turned from the road toward the grassy verge and the tithe barn.

Why would a man guide a cart to the door of the tithe barn? Harvest was many months in the future. Hogs had been slaughtered and their flesh smoked and salted at Michaelmas. There was no reason a man would bring a cart load of grain or pork to the tithe barn in early May. A cart would be useful only to remove corn and flesh.

The cart tracks came from the north. The priests of St. Beornwald's Church resided to the south, in the village. And their cooks and servants would need no cart to draw from the tithe barn the victuals needed for the vicars' tables. Some man, likely earlier this night, had apparently helped himself to the stored viands of the tithe barn, and the curfew-breaking holy man had seen. So I thought.

Sparse grass covered the path from the road to the tithe barn door. There was enough vegetation that, in combination with the darkness, I could see no cart tracks no matter how intently I searched. I did not need to see the tracks lead to the tithe barn door. I felt sure I knew what had happened here.

The holy man had enjoined silence, so I walked slowly, carefully, to the tithe barn door. Mayhap whoso had brought a cart to this place was yet near. But I saw no cart, nor horse either. A beast might not be necessary. Horses make noise. They stamp their feet and blow through their nostrils like an indignant archdeacon. A small cart, drawn by a man, could make the marks in the road which the hermit had pointed out. I could not question him about this – not and remain silent. Later, at Galen House, I would seek to learn what he knew and what he had seen. Certainly he had seen a thing which drew his attention to the wheel tracks in the dust. They were too faint, in the weak light of moon and stars, to arrest a man's attention by themselves.

A large iron lock secured the tithe barn door. Rivets held the lock in place, penetrating the oak of door and jamb. There was enough light that I could see the lock was unmarred. If some man had entered the tithe barn in the night, he possessed a key. A key made for this lock, I wondered? Keys and the locks they open are much alike.

Who possessed a key to this lock? The priests of St. Beornwald's, surely. Their clerks? Servants? Cooks? Likely the cooks would, else they would need to seek the priests each time they wanted corn or peas or beans or flesh from the tithe barn. And likely, was a cook busy with his work he might send a servant to the tithe barn to bring to him the needed victuals. Would a servant have a key in his possession long enough to make a copy? 'Twould not take long. Fill a bowl with mud, press the key into it, take the form to a smith and have a key made to the shape of the original. I resolved to visit Bampton's smith soon.

I know Oswald Smith well. Well enough to know that if a man paid him to make a duplicate key, and paid him again to be silent about it, I would learn nothing. Unless I paid him more.

I motioned to the holy man to follow, and together we set off for Galen House. Why did I not tell him where we were bound for? Whatever man had approached the tithe barn in the night was now well away from the place and would not hear my voice. Although the hermit could not – or would not – speak, he could hear well. Without consciously thinking about it I was participating in his silence.

We entered Galen House as a faint gray glow lightened the sky to the east behind budding oaks. My Kate had not returned to our bed, but had placed wood upon the hearth, fanned the embers to flame, and sat upon a bench awaiting my return.

I motioned to the holy man that he should sit upon the other bench, then finally the absurdity of my silence came to me. "Be seated," I said.

The process of asking questions which could be answered with a nod or a shake of the head took until the sun was well over the squat tower of St. Andrew's Chapel. But I learned much.

The holy man had, as was his unlawful practice, set off from his hut to explore Bampton and the Weald as soon as 'twas dark enough that he could do so unobserved by any other who was upon the streets after curfew. Once again I attempted to form questions, the answers to which would tell me why the fellow did this rather than sleep through the cold spring nights wrapped snug in the cast-off cotehardies and robes he had been given. Again, I failed.

I did learn that while moving from one shadow to another near to Landell's Lane he had heard the soft squeal of an ungreased wheel. He followed the faint sound to the tithe barn, where against the dark gray of the stones he saw the black aperture of an open door.

A candle flickered and he saw the outline of a man. Only one. The fellow placed a side of bacon and two sacks into his handcart, extinguished his candle, closed and locked the tithe barn door, then grasped the handles of his cart and made haste to leave the village.

The hermit had watched all this from behind a bush across the road from the barn, afraid to seek me for fear of the felon discovering him if he left the shelter of the shrubbery. A man who would steal from God's church would not hesitate to slay a man who caught him doing so.

Had Odo Fuller discovered this thievery and paid for the knowledge with his life? And what of William Walle and Ernaud le Tournier? Had they also some knowledge of the pilferage?

With a few more questions I learned that the hermit had waited until he was sure the thief was gone and had left no accomplice behind. So when he came to Galen House the rogue was long since away. Nevertheless the holy man had rapped softly on the door so as to be heard only within Galen House and a few steps from it. I could not blame the man for his caution.

Could the cart tracks be followed now that day was come? Perhaps. But if I came upon the villain I wanted more assistance than the holy man could provide. I needed Arthur.

I gave the holy man a maslin loaf and a cup of ale, and consumed the same myself. He did not eat all of his loaf, but kept back half. For his dinner, likely.

He accompanied me to the castle, where I bade him fare well and entered under the gatehouse in search of Arthur. I found him mucking out – Lord Gilbert is particular about his stables – and he was pleased to abandon the task to the two other grooms who shared the work. I told him to make two palfreys ready and as he saddled and fixed bridles upon the beasts told him what we were to do.

The cart tracks were not difficult to find in the slanting morning sun, even from horseback. We followed at a good pace until we reached the junction where the roads to Witney and Brize Norton diverged. The cart had continued on the Witney road.

We followed the track for more than two hundred paces, and while we did I thought of my unsuccessful search in Witney. Might this thief I followed reside there, and have naught to do with murders, stolen silver, or a tall, buxom woman garbed in a green cotehardie? The cart wheels suddenly departed the road at a place where to the east was a plowed field ready for planting and to the west a walled meadow where sheep grazed. The cart had left the road where a gate opened into the meadow. I dismounted and approached it, careful to avoid the nettles which grew upon the wall and sent tendrils toward the gate.

Grass here was verdant. Nothing short of a dexter would leave an impression in the turf. Certainly a handcart would not. If the enclosed meadow had been fallow, and a handcart drawn across it, the tall grass might be bent down showing where a man had traversed the field. But the sheep had grazed the vegetation nearly to the roots. No broken stems told of a cart being pulled across the meadow.

Nevertheless that was what I thought had happened. I was on the track of a cautious thief.

The gate was fixed in place with hempen cords. I opened it, told Arthur to pass through, then brought my own beast to the meadow before securing the gate closed.

"You think the thief come through this meadow?" Arthur said as I mounted my palfrey.

"He went somewhere, and with his cart. If not here, where did he go?"

Arthur shrugged. "Got to be another gate somewheres, then," he said.

The meadow was large, nearly a yardland, and the opposite side dropped toward a wood so that the wall there was not visible from where we entered the meadow. It was a matter of but a few minutes to cross to the other side of the field, scattering ewes and lambs as we did. And there, hidden in the decline, was another gate.

This gate was little used. The wood was rotted where it contacted the soil, and the cords holding it in place were frayed. I could see why it was seldom opened. Beyond the gate was a forest. From a raised perch upon the back of my palfrey I saw a faint path through the wood. 'Twas narrow, but wide enough for a man drawing a small handcart.

Forest foliage was growing thick above our heads so that after passing through the decayed gate Arthur and I were required to dismount and lead our beasts, else twigs and branches would have slapped our faces. I studied the forest floor as we traveled the path, but the leaves showed no trace of the recent passage of a handcart.

I had no thought as to where the path might lead, but learned its terminus soon enough. After a quarter-mile or so the foliage thinned and I saw a road before us. 'Twas the road to Brize Norton, and the village was not three hundred paces to the north. We had traveled from the intersection of the Witney road a little less than half a mile. 'Twas a diversion surely designed to obscure the track of a thief to any who might follow. Where the forest path entered the road I saw again the wheel marks of the handcart.

The track was easy to follow to Brize Norton, but in the village the passage of men and beasts since dawn had obliterated the wheel marks I sought. We rode on through the village, where I hoped I might recover my quarry. Not so. We traveled nearly half a mile but did not see handcart wheel tracks again.

"Too smart by 'alf," Arthur said as we turned our palfreys back to Brize Norton. "He drew a handcart into Brize Norton but not out of it, so 'e's got to be in the village."

"Probably. Mayhap we will find a tall, buxom woman in Brize Norton who often wears a green cotehardie," I said.

"Ain't a large place," Arthur said. "Woman like that should be known to all. You think 'er husband be the felon what stole corn an' flesh from the tithe barn?"

"Mayhap. And if so, 'tis likely not the first time he has done so."

"You think Odo knew of the thievery an' was slain to silence 'im?"

"Aye, I do. And the candlesticks buried so as to implicate Ernaud in Odo's death. Ernaud perhaps knew, or suspected, what the felon was about. But greed caused the felon to keep back Father Ralph's cresset."

"So 'e traveled to Oxford with 'is wife to sell it," Arthur completed the thought.

"So I believe."

"An' now we've followed the scoundrel to Brize Norton. Shouldn't take long to find 'im."

The Church of St. Britius's tower, stubby though it is, rises above the village. I directed my palfrey to it, assuming the priest would know the members of his flock. The church was vacant, but behind it was a substantial dwelling that I supposed was the vicarage. It was.

A servant answered my knock upon the vicarage door, invited me in to the hall, and trotted off to find his master. Arthur remained in the street with our palfreys.

"Lord Gilbert's bailiff? Him who mends folk who have injured themselves?" the priest said when I had introduced myself.

"Aye, I am a surgeon."

"Heard of you and the good you have done. How may I serve you? Are Bampton's vicars well?"

I had, through much repetition, become skilled at relating the events surrounding the death of three clerks using few words. Brize Norton is near enough to Bampton that the priest had heard of the murders. In a few moments the priest knew of my search for a tall, robust woman and a felon who took corn and flesh from the Bampton tithe barn and may have slain three clerks who suspected his brigandage.

"This woman has been seen wearing a green cotehardie, you say?" the priest replied when I had concluded my tale.

"So I am told. She wore such when she sold the stolen cresset to the Oxford goldsmith... so he claimed."

The priest pulled at his beard. "I know of no woman of that description in Brize Norton. A few well-fed matrons, to be sure, but none I would consider tall. Cicily Marsh has worn a green cotehardie, but she's an aged widow an' stands no higher than my shoulder."

This reply was not what I expected. I had felt sure that in Brize Norton I would finally untangle the twisted threads which tied together three murders and the theft from the bishop's tithe barn.

The unsuccessfully disguised trail of the felon and his handcart ended in Brize Norton. Was the thief also a murderer? Was the tall woman who wore a green cotehardie from some other place, but known to the villain?

Another thought occurred to me. "Is there a man in your parish who occasionally has food to sell to his neighbors... corn and bacon and such? 'Tis coming to the time of year when folk look to their barns and larders and see them near to empty. Who might sell victuals to them?"

"Gervase Redvers might. Has two yardlands, does Gervase, and employs poorer men at planting and harvest."

A man who possessed two yardlands of his lord would likely have corn and flesh to sell without sneaking into the tithe barn of a neighboring town to pilfer more.

"Is Gervase wed?"

"Oh, aye."

"Does his wife wear green?"

"Milicent wears many hues. Whatever suits her. But she is not tall, if I take your meaning."

"She wears many colors? Does Gervase spend lavishly on his wife?"

"Aye, but he's got the coin to do so. An' forgetting my station for a moment, I'll tell you Milicent is worth a man spending his money on."

"Beautiful, is she?"

"Does the sun warm a man in July? But she's neither tall nor stout, so not likely the woman you seek."

I thanked the priest for his time and thoughts, and returned to Arthur. What to do next? I had already sought my quarry in Witney, unsuccessfully. And the cart wheels did not travel far on the Witney road before ending at the meadow, then reappearing on the road to Brize Norton.

What if the thief had found some other way to travel past Brize Norton without leaving a sign in the road that he had done so? Where would he go? But for Shilton – which since plague visited the place is reduced to only a few families – the next town beyond Brize Norton is Burford. Could a man somehow get a handcart loaded with pork or peas or oats from Brize Norton to Burford and not leave any track to give himself away? Had the scoundrel devised some way to conceal his movements?

I told Arthur that we would again travel the Burford road north from Brize Norton. We would seek any attempt to hide marks made by handcart wheels, which we had done earlier without success.

We walked our beasts slowly, scrutinizing the least suggestion of cart wheels upon the dust of the road. We were halfway from Brize Norton to Burford when I noticed the oats. I had seen them for perhaps half a mile but had paid no attention.

I knelt in the road. Arthur looked on with amazement. "What's there?" he said, and also bent to inspect the road.

Every foot or so I saw an oat grain upon the road. Sometimes two or three together. Occasionally none for a few paces. But in general the corns were regular in a line upon the dust of the road. I looked behind, saw a jackdaw, and understood why some oats were missing from the row.

"Look here," I said, and between thumb and forefinger picked an oat grain from the road.

"Hmmm. Some fellow's going to arrive at 'is destination an' find the sack what's slung over 'is shoulder has torn an' cost 'im a penny or two."

"If the loss is from a sack stolen from the Bampton tithe barn," I said, "I wonder what has become of the other sack and the bacon. And the handcart, for that matter."

Arthur's only reply was to push back his cap and scratch his balding pate. This was also my opinion.

The felon may not now be in Brize Norton, I thought, but I'd wager his handcart was. Mayhap he realized that its close-spaced track gave away his passage, so decided to leave the conveyance in the village and carry his plunder to wherever was his destination. If so, this would likely mean that the pork and a sack of grain remained in Brize Norton with the handcart. He who stole from the tithe barn would not have had time in this new day to take all of his spoils upon his back to his goal, wherever that might be – if the kernels of oats I found on the Burford road had dropped from a stolen sack of grain. There was no guarantee that this was so. Perhaps both sacks and the flesh were yet within Brize Norton and this spilled grain had nothing to do with theft from the Bampton tithe barn.

If the cart used to transport stolen goods from Bampton was yet in Brize Norton it would not be in plain sight, but hidden behind some house or hedge, or drawn into a barn.

Thirty or so paces beyond where I first saw the spilled oats the kernels disappeared. Either a flock of jackdaws had descended upon the road, or the fellow who carried the oats had noticed his loss.

CHAPTER 15

I had seen a house on the main street of Brize Norton which had before it a basket raised upon a pole. An ale wife advertising fresh-brewed ale. I suddenly realized how dry I was. The house had a short hitching rail before the door, prepared for prosperous customers who might arrive mounted. I pointed to the place, directed my palfrey to the rail, and Arthur followed – a grin splitting his face.

The ale was indeed fresh, if a little watery. Bampton's ale taster would not approve. Mayhap the ale taster in Brize Norton was not so particular, or was amenable to a penny bribe.

A stained table divided two benches in the first bay. Our shadows darkened the door and attracted the attention of the ale wife. She raised her ewer, set two wooden cups upon the table, and filled them from the ewer. "Ha'penny," she said.

"Resided in Brize Norton long?" I asked between swallows.

"All me life." This looked to be forty years or so. The woman's hair was going gray under her wimple, and what had likely once been an attractive face was creased about the corners of eyes and mouth.

"You'd know most folk of the village, then?"

"Aye," she said suspiciously. Her reaction was common to such a question. Folk dislike strangers asking nosy questions about friends and neighbors.

"Who might have oats or barley to sell?" I asked.

"For your beasts?"

"Aye... for our beasts."

"'Tis a hungry time of year," the woman said. "Most folk of Brize Norton 'ave barely enough for themselves."

"Is there no man of the village who buys and sells?"

"Nay. Got to go to Burford or Witney market for that."

I had thought that if the tithe-barn thief resided in Brize

Norton he might be known to have corn to sell. If the felon did occupy a village house he kept his takings for himself.

"Who of the village owns a handcart?" I said as casually as I could.

"Handcart? You ride a beast, like a gentleman with 'is retainer. Why'd you want a handcart?"

A valid question. The ale wife seemed amiable and artless, so rather than invent some falsehood I spoke the truth. This may have been a mistake. Are there times in a man's life when he should be dishonest for the sake of truth? And justice? May a lie be a useful tool to hammer out truth? I must ask Master Wycliffe when next I see him.

"A man has done a felony in Bampton, where I am bailiff. He used a handcart to carry away his plunder. I have followed the track here, to Brize Norton."

"Folk hereabouts don't 'ave much what needs carryin' in a handcart."

"No one you know owns such a thing?"

"Didn't say that, did I?"

"What did you say?"

"Gervase 'as a handcart, I think."

"Gervase Redvers?"

"Aye. Has two yardlands of Sir John, does Gervase."

"You believe this man owns a handcart? You do not know of a certainty?"

"My Stephen worked for Gervase at harvest some years past. Had a handcart then. Stephen come 'ome one night complainin' of 'is back 'cause 'e was put to drawin' that cart filled with rye after threshin'."

"You know of no other handcarts in the village?"

"Nay. Most folks is like me, an' haven't anything what needs transport in a handcart."

"Where does Gervase reside?" I asked.

"At the end of Moat Close. Three bays an' two barns, has Gervase."

"Do folk like Gervase, or do they resent his prosperity?"

"'E's all right. Didn't get 'is coin by stealin' other men's furrows. Keeps to 'is own strips."

A prosperous man should not need to take from others. But some men, no matter their wealth, always want more. What of me? Am I satisfied with Galen House and my possessions or would I like more? I would readily accept a few more crowns and shillings. But would I steal and kill to have them? Nay. Would some men? Probably. I can understand a starving man tempted to steal and kill to provide a meal for his family, but not a rich man who simply wants more.

I was assuming Gervase – or one of his servants – guilty of theft without evidence. Except for ownership of a handcart. And that in the past. Mayhap he no longer possessed such a thing. How might I learn if he did or not? And if he did, why not use it to take the plundered grain and pork to Burford? If the oats I saw on the Burford road came from Bampton's tithe barn.

"Does your husband labor for Gervase Redvers yet?" I asked.

"Nay. Have our own strips now, what with plague takin' so many there's land to spare."

"Are there villagers who do work for Gervase at planting and harvest?"

"Aye, a few."

"Can you direct me to one of these?"

"Why?"

I drew a penny from my purse and slid it across the table. The ale wife required no further explanation.

"Richard Speight plows for Gervase. An' he'll likely help with harvest at Lammastide. Lives behind the church, does Richard."

The ale quenched my thirst but did nothing to abate my hunger. 'Twas getting on past noon and I saw no dinner in my near future, for I had seen no inn among the houses of the village.

"Have you two loaves?" I asked the ale wife. "My man and I have had no meal since we broke our fast. I will pay."

The woman stood, disappeared into her kitchen bay, and returned with two maslin loaves. "Ha'penny," she said, and dropped the loaves to the table. They bounced.

I gave the woman two farthings, handed one of the loaves to Arthur, and bade the ale wife good day.

The loaves were not fresh. The crust was as leathery as a cheap glove. Arthur and I each chewed our way from one end of our loaf to the other while we led our palfreys to the church.

A small house of a single bay stood thirty or so paces behind the church, not far from the vicarage. The roof was decayed and much in need of new thatching, and the skin stretched over the single window was torn. This was the house of a poor cotter, no doubt. Would he tell what he knew of Gervase Redvers for a coin or two? Likely. Would he be at work for Redvers, or at home, taking what would surely be a simple dinner?

I rapped upon the patched door, which then rattled upon its leather hinges. A moment later a disheveled man, his cheeks bulging with an unswallowed mouthful of food, opened the door. The man's cotehardie was threadbare, his hair and beard unkempt, and his hands and fingernails had had but a limited acquaintance with water.

The cotter said nothing. He simply stared through the open door and chewed. I finally broke the silence.

"Are you Richard Speight?" I asked.

The fellow continued to chew, then swallowed before replying with an unfriendly tone, "Oo wants ter know?"

"I am Sir Hugh de Singleton, bailiff to Lord Gilbert, Third Baron Talbot, at Bampton."

The play of emotions that flashed across the cotter's face was entertaining. When he heard the word "Sir" he bent as if to bow. Then when he heard "bailiff" his lip began to curl in distaste. At the mention of Lord Gilbert's name the incomplete bow was continued.

"Have you been employed this day by Gervase Redvers?" I asked, and from my purse took a ha'penny and held it before the man. But I did not give it to him. Not yet.

"Aye. 'Ome fer me dinner."

"And you will return?"

"Aye. Near done with plowin'. Got three acres yet."

As he spoke, the cotter glanced often to the coin. Did he expect that I would give it to him? Surely he hoped I would. Men hope for many things which will only come to pass if their behavior warrants.

"Does Gervase Redvers own a small handcart?" I asked, and moved the coin from one hand to the other. I thought this might make my intent clear. It did.

"Why you want to know such a thing?"

"I am conducting an investigation for Lord Gilbert. More than that you need not know."

"Had one," the cotter said.

"But he no longer does?"

"Oh, 'e's got it yet, but 'tis no use to 'im or any other."

"Why so?"

"Axle broke. Henry an' Roger was gatherin' rocks from a new-plowed field an' overloaded the cart."

"When did this happen?"

"Two years past, it was."

"And the cart has not been repaired?"

"Nay. Not yet. Gervase spoke of mendin' it, but it's not been done. Sits in a corner of the small barn."

"And Gervase has not purchased a replacement, or asked a servant to build a new cart?"

"Nay. Weren't all that useful, anyway. Too small. 'Course, any larger an' a man couldn't draw it, was it laden."

"Much thanks," I said, and handed the coin to the cotter.

He snatched it from my fingers as if he feared I might withdraw the offer.

Was there another handcart secreted in Brize Norton? Probably, for we had followed the tracks into the village but seen no sign of the conveyance leaving the place. Clearly Redvers' cart had not been used to steal from the tithe barn. If there was another handcart in Brize Norton I had not the wit to discover it.

Arthur and I mounted our beasts and set out for Bampton. For a moment I considered traveling north on the Burford road to the place where earlier I had seen the oats in the road. What good would such a diversion do? The man who carried the punctured sack might have discovered the loss and effected a repair. If he did not, and I was able to track the leaking oats to Burford or some nearby place, what was I likely to find? The man who stole corn from Bampton's tithe barn? Why would such a felon leave his handcart in Brize Norton and travel with a sack thrown uncomfortably over a shoulder? Such a deviation would make no sense.

Of course, if felons were sensible they would not be felons. 'Tis a good thing that we who seek out malefactors deal mainly with fools. If such rogues were wise they would be more difficult to apprehend. Sin is but foolishness writ large. And all men are sinners and therefore foolish, although not all foolishness is sin, I think.

* * *

Arthur and I stopped before Galen House. It had been a long and disappointing day. My eyes felt as if a strong wind had blown the dust of the road into them.

I dismounted, sent Arthur on to the castle with my palfrey, then pushed open the door of my home. Bessie heard the door open – I must remember to grease the hinges – and ran to greet me. Kate followed. Her greeting was more sedate but just as welcome. For a few minutes my wife and daughter dispelled the gloom which had settled upon my shoulders during the return from Brize Norton.

A pottage of peas and beans, flavored with early onions, simmered upon the hearth. Adela ladled out bowls of the glutinous porridge and after a blessing we fell to the meal.

Adela had placed a small wooden bowl before John. He showed small talent for the use of a spoon, but 'twas not for lack of enthusiasm. The greenish meal was soon encrusting his cheeks, but plenty had found his lips.

As we ate I told Kate of the day.

"So you believed investigating the trail of spilled oats in the Burford road not worth the time and effort?"

"Aye. There are many reasons a sack of oats might discharge some of its contents, and most of these will have to do with carelessness, not felony."

"The search for a handcart was not successful. You found Father Ralph's cresset, but that did not lead to a murderer."

"Not yet," I said.

"You believe the silver will yet speak to you?"

"Nay... and I wonder that I ever did. Yet when I sought the cresset it seemed the wise thing to do."

"What will you do now?"

"I have a mind to follow the path of the man seen by the hermit the night Ernaud was slain in his bed."

"Did you not already investigate that?"

"I did. But mayhap I missed some evidence. If my eyes fall a second time upon some clue I thought was innocuous I might see it in a new light."

"You will have little light, new or old, if you do the search now," Kate smiled.

"Aye. I will seek our bed and explore tomorrow."

Why is it, I wonder, that the more exhausted I am the longer it takes to find Morpheus? Kate was sighing softly for an hour or more whilst I lay abed watching through the glass of our bedchamber as clouds drifted past, obscuring and then revealing a star-filled sky.

Of course, when I finally fell to sleep I could not force myself awake even though the light of a new day streamed through the window.

* * *

The dawn Angelus Bell sounding from the tower of St. Beornwald's Church finally roused me. I lurched from bed, splashed water from a basin upon my face, and drew on my clothing. By the time I descended the stairs I was reasonably stable.

Adela had already visited the baker's wife, who brewed ale for most of the village. So the ale was fresh and the maslin loaf with which I broke my fast was but one day out of the oven and not yet gone stale.

"If you see nothing this morning which might lead you to the felon who slew three clerks, what then?" Kate asked.

"You believe nothing will come of the search? I cannot blame you. Nothing much has come of other measures I've taken to discover a murderer."

"I did not wish to belittle your efforts, husband," Kate said apologetically.

"The answer to your question is, I do not know. Perhaps some new thought will come to me. If so, 'twill likely be as unfruitful as past endeavors."

I took a last swig of ale to empty my cup, kissed Kate, and departed Galen House for Father Simon's vicarage. As I approached I saw the priest coming from the opposite direction. The Angelus devotional was completed, and he was no doubt returning to break his fast.

"I give you good day, Sir Hugh," he greeted me. "What brings you to my door?"

"I intend to walk the path the holy man indicated was taken by the man he saw in the night, when Ernaud was found dead in his bed next morn."

"We have already done this."

"Aye. To no good purpose. It may be that surveying the place again will be another waste of time, but it may be also that I will notice something out of sorts which before I did not perceive."

"I wish you good success," Father Simon said, then strode to his door and his ale and loaf. He had no desire to waste his time while his stomach growled. As my stomach was temporarily satisfied I did not hesitate to waste my time but plunged ahead between the vicarage and Reginald Shirk's house.

Again I walked to the hedge of bushes which bordered the tofts of vicarage and neighbor. Slowly, casting my eyes about, I followed the bushes to Bushy Row, as I had done some days earlier. And as before, I saw no sign that any man had traveled this way. There was not even a trace of my own previous passage.

I reversed my route and walked the line of bushes north, to Father Thomas's vicarage. The crab apple trees behind his toft were in glorious blossom, the profusion of petals just beginning to fall and tint the grass below a soft pink. I halted before the first tree to enjoy the sight, and noticed that several sprouts had grown from lower branches. Whoso had pruned the tree last autumn – or more likely the pruning had happened eighteen months past – had been overzealous with the knife, and the tree had done as trees so insulted often do. It had put forth new growth in several places. These new shoots extended straight up, smooth and unblemished, seeking the sun, some nearly as long as I am tall.

These growths should also be pruned back, and I saw that one had been. The scion had been lopped off at the base, where it had sprung from the trunk. Here, I thought, was an odd thing. One of Father Thomas's servants had known to cut this new growth back, for such a shoot would bear no fruit, but did not complete the task. He had pared away one sprout, but left the others.

I was about to turn from the tree and return, disappointed, to Galen House when an image came to mind. I remembered when I had previously seen a slender shaft which resembled the scions from the crab apple tree. I hurried home, but not to escape frustration at another failed quest.

The two halves of the crude arrow used to slay William Walle remained in the corner of my hall, where I had propped them many days past. I had thought the arrow should be retained as future evidence if I discovered the felon who had created and employed it.

Kate heard me enter and called from the kitchen, asking if I had learned anything from the morning's investigation.

"Aye," I replied. "I believe I have discovered the source of this arrow." I held the broken shaft before me as she entered our hall.

"Indeed? From whence did it come?"

"There are three crab apple trees behind Father Thomas's vicarage."

Kate looked at me blankly, uncomprehending.

"This arrow was cut from a sprout of one of those trees, so I believe. I will know if 'tis so in a few minutes."

I gave Kate a peck upon the cheek and hastened to the rear of Father Thomas's vicarage and the copse of crab apple trees. I held the broken arrow against an unpruned scion. They were the same. I then placed the butt end of the broken shaft against the base of the pruned shoot. But for the groove cut for the bowstring the match was perfect. I had discovered the source of the arrow which slew William Walle. But who made the weapon?

The crab apple trees were visible from the road before the vicarage. The slender, vertical scions were somewhat obscured by blossoms and new foliage, but were apparent to anyone passing who took time to study the trees. Any man might have cut the sprout.

The cut which removed the shoot was fresh, the tissues paler where the scion was slashed away. The arrow was cut from green wood for a particular purpose, this was clear. When I learned who had done this I would know who had slain William Walle, and had likely also slain Odo Fuller and Ernaud le Tournier.

I was so intent upon my discovery that I did not notice the rear door of the vicarage open. But as I compared arrow and scion a voice said, "What are you doing to Father Thomas's trees?" The tone was unfriendly.

'Twas Bartram Thrupp, Father Thomas's cook, who had come from the vicarage, perhaps seeking leeks or new onions from the toft to flavor the pottage he was preparing for the priest's dinner. The man knew me well. I wondered at his hostility. Mayhap he did not at first recognize me.

"Ah... Sir Hugh," he said. "How may I serve you? Thought 'twas some miscreant skulking about."

Bartram was short and rotund, as a cook who samples his creations might be. I was about to tell him of my discovery, or part of it, but then remembered that the holy man had described the man he saw in the night when Ernaud died as being short and stout. Could Bartram fit through an open window? Could he climb to it? Possibly, but 'twould be a struggle for him. A man believing himself threatened with a noose is capable of actions beyond what might be expected.

The vicars of St. Beornwald's Church needed to know that some man had a key to their tithe barn and was pilfering the bishop's victuals. And Father Thomas needed to know that the arrow which slew William Walle was surely cut from his crab apple tree. I decided that since I was near Father Thomas's vicarage I would seek him and tell of the events of this day and the previous. I left the cook to his onions, circled the vicarage to the front door, and rapped upon it.

A servant opened to me and when I told him I sought his master he bustled off, leaving me standing at the threshold. I had not long to wait. Father Thomas appeared immediately and when he saw me standing in the doorway invited me into his hall.

"You are about early this day," the priest said. "Have you news for me?"

"Aye. But not, I think, what you hope to hear. Yesterday, well before dawn, the holy man awakened me. He was about the streets after curfew and watched as a man opened the door of your tithe barn and took from it two sacks and a side of pork. These he carried off in a handcart."

The priest listened, open-mouthed. "But the door is locked," he finally said.

"Some man has a key who should not. When dawn came I went to the castle, collected Arthur, and together we followed the cart tracks to Brize Norton. There they disappeared."

"The thief is from that village?" Father Thomas said.

"So it seems. We followed the tracks to the village, but there was no sign on the road of a handcart leaving the place."

"If some man has a key to the tithe barn then 'tis likely," the priest said, "that he will return to take more of the church's goods."

"Aye. A successful thief is not likely to end his predation so long as his wickedness succeeds."

"What do you suggest be done?"

"Gather Father Ralph and Father Simon and together assemble the names of all of your clerks and servants who may have opportunity to use a key to the tithe barn. Then, of those who do not have such access, organize a watch each night for the next fortnight or so."

"Why only those who do not have a key? Here at my vicarage there is but one key. 'Tis the same with Father Ralph and Father Simon. Mine hangs by a nail near the hearth. All who serve me know where it is and what lock it opens. You think one of our clerks or servants gave the key to some felon?"

"Perhaps. Sometime not long past one of the keys was copied, so I believe."

"Who would do such a thing?"

"Oswald Smith could, and would, I think, was he offered a few pence to do so. There is another matter you must hear," I continued. "Behind your toft, near to the hen house, are three crab apple trees."

"You tell me what I already know," the priest said. "Bartram makes verjuice from the fruit."

"There is a matter involving one of the trees you do not know, I think. Come with me and see what I have discovered."

As I spoke I held the broken arrow before me. The priest had surely seen it in my hand but had said nothing about it. 'Til now.

"That is the arrow which slew William Walle, is it not?"

"It is. Come with me and I will show you its source."

Father Thomas followed me through his door, around the vicarage, to the small grove of crab apple trees. I found the severed scion and held the feathered end of the arrow to it. The priest could see that this was the source of the arrow shaft which took William Walle's life. "The man who slew William cut the missile from my tree!" the priest said indignantly.

"Aye. And see the fletching. Not goose feathers, but chicken." As I said this I glanced to Father Thomas's hen house, not twenty paces distant, where two dozen or so hens and a cock pecked at the ground.

"How can we discover what man has made himself free with my trees and hens?"

"How many spoons have you?" I asked.

The priest was taken aback by this abrupt change of subject. "Spoons? What have spoons to do with whoso slew William?"

I held the pointed end of the arrow before the priest. "This point," I said, "seems to have been hammered from a pewter spoon. 'Tis not iron. Too soft. A man would need a forge to craft an iron arrowhead. But with a hammer a man might make such a point of pewter. And though it is not so hard as iron, 'tis rigid enough to pierce flesh."

"As we have seen," Father Thomas said softly. He was silent then for a moment. "Eleven," he said. "Three of silver, for when the archdeacon may visit, and eight of pewter."

"Will you count them while I wait here?" I said.

"I will," he replied, and strode purposefully away, his cassock flapping about his ankles. He was not away long.

"One of the pewter spoons is missing," he said angrily. "There are but seven in the chest. I will call my servants together and find who has done murder."

"Nay. Do not do so. You will learn nothing. They will all protest innocence, and all but one will be speaking truth. The guilty man will then know we are close on his trail. This will make him more cautious and the harder to catch at his felony."

"Oh... aye," the priest agreed. "What do you suggest?"

"The felon we seek is likely of your household, so the less said to any of your servants the better. Send a servant to Father Ralph and Father Simon and ask that they assemble here quickly. Have him tell them the matter is urgent. Do not tell the servant why this is to be done."

206

CHAPTER 16

Father Thomas sent a servant to collect Father Ralph and Father Simon, and within half an hour we four were assembled under the blossoms of the crab apple trees. I told Father Ralph and Father Simon of the theft from the tithe barn, and gave my opinion that this was not the first time such thievery had been done. The holy man's witness bore this out.

I then showed them the crude arrow and the stub of the scion where it had been lopped free. Father Thomas then told of the missing spoon, and I showed the priests the crude arrowhead which had surely once been a spoon.

"It seems sure," I said, "that the felon we seek is of Father Thomas's household."

"You think the man who took from the tithe barn has to do with three murders?" Father Ralph said. "Or are these felonies not associated?"

"I believe they are, but have no good evidence to prove it so." To Father Ralph and Father Simon I said, "I propose that you identify two servants each whom you believe beyond reproach. With these four, and Arthur and Uctred from the castle, I will form a watch in the night before the tithe barn. You must impress upon the four you nominate that they say nothing to any man – no matter how trustworthy they believe the fellow to be – of what they are assigned to do."

"You think the thief will return?" Father Ralph said.

"What does Holy Writ say about a dog returning to its vomit?"

"Oh... aye."

This conversation took place about twenty paces from the vicarage rear door.

"When will you begin this surveillance?" Father Simon asked.

"Tonight, although I doubt the thief will return so soon. I will collect Arthur and Uctred and they will join me this night."

"If you watch tonight it will carry into Sunday morn. Would a man steal from God's storehouse on the Lord's Day?" Father Ralph said.

"The day of his crime makes no difference to a man bound for hell," Father Thomas said.

"I will create a rota for each night this week, so that Arthur, Uctred, and I and the servants you name will be able to spend two nights out of three in our own beds."

We four departed the crab apple trees with the understanding that Father Simon and Father Ralph would provide me two names each the next day.

Kate and Adela had prepared stewed herrings for our dinner. I ate my fill and was well satisfied. And not only with the meal. I felt sure that sometime in the next week, or perhaps fortnight, a man would be apprehended attempting to steal again from the tithe barn. If such a man was not caught this night, or next – and I doubted he would be, as so little time had passed since the last theft – I would call upon Oswald and demand of the smith whether he had made a copy of a key for any man in the past few months. The fellow, and his father before him, had run afoul of me some years past, and knew that at a word from me Lord Gilbert would raise his rent. That knowledge, and a penny from me to reward cooperation, might tell me much. If there was anything to be told.

Were the deaths of three clerks of St. Beornwald's Church tied to the tithe barn theft? I felt sure they were, but had no evidence to prove it. Had Odo and Ernaud learned of the thievery? Were they slain because their knowledge was suspected? If so, the murderer was surely of Father Thomas's household, but not Father Thomas himself, of that I was sure. I had known the vicar too long – and had seen too much proof of his godly character – to suspect him of such a foul deed.

Therefore, that narrowed the list of suspects to four: the cook and three servants.

Did one of the four creep from his bed early the previous morning armed with the tithe barn key and steal corn and flesh?

Not likely, for where would he find a handcart, and if he could not return before dawn Father Thomas would wonder at his absence. Were there two men at the tithe barn door in the small hours – one with a key, the other with a handcart? The holy man saw but one.

Whoso stole from the tithe barn was in league with some man of Father Thomas's household. And that man, fearing discovery, slew Odo, William, and Ernaud. He knew when I traveled to Oxford, and what I sought there. He knew when William Walle would set off for Exeter, and why. All I devised in order to find a felon the man knew about, and could therefore deflect my purpose.

I finished my meal and set off for the castle to tell Arthur and Uctred of my plan for some of their evenings. I had not reached the bridge over Shill Brook when the identity of the felon came to me.

In the days after Odo Fuller's murder I and the vicars of St. Beornwald's Church had sought a man with a scratch upon his face. When we could not find such a person we then began to seek some man who might have a deep abrasion on his arm. We were not successful. Every servant of the vicars knew what we sought, and could therefore disguise or hide such a scrape. A man might even feign slashing his arm whilst hacking away at a capon – a serious wound to hide a minor scratch. A wound deep enough that it would cause a man difficulty when he drew a bow to loose an arrow...

William Walle had attempted to speak a name with his last breath; I thought he was attempting to name his killer. He likely was, for I believe he knew the man.

I stopped at the bridge over Shill Brook to review the insight that had come to me. Did the facts I knew fit Bartram Thrupp as the murderer? Aye. Could I prove it to the King's Eyre, Oxford's sheriff, and Lord Gilbert? Nay.

If I caught a man pilfering stuff from the tithe barn I could learn from him who had provided the key that gained him entrance. Would he give me the name of his companion in crime?

He would if he thought he'd otherwise hang for three murders that another felon had done.

I found Arthur and Uctred in the castle hall, finishing their dinner. They had not consumed stewed herrings. Lord Gilbert's grooms dine upon plain fare on fast days. They are like the grooms to other nobles, I think. A lord's high table on a fast day might feature a salmon or pike in cyve sauce as one of the removes, but grooms will fill their bellies with a pottage of barley or peas and be content.

Lord Gilbert saw me enter his hall and motioned me to approach the high table. Lady Joan was yet at Bampton Castle and nodded and smiled as I came near. Her lad was busy attacking a dish of mussels in shells and paid me no heed.

"What news, Hugh?" Lord Gilbert said. "You have avoided the castle recently. Do I then assume that no murderer has been discovered?"

"Aye. But mayhap soon."

"A felon has not been found but may be identified before long?"

"I believe I know who has slain three clerks of St. Beornwald's and I think I know why."

"You believe? You think?"

"I cannot prove it yet. But I have come to collect Arthur and Uctred for a duty that may confirm my suspicion."

"What is this duty?"

I glanced around me at the occupants of the high table, and the valets who served them. "I would rather not say, m'lord."

Lord Gilbert followed my gaze. "Ah… you mistrust the folk who dine at my table to hold their tongues?"

"And those who serve. A man cannot repeat a tale he has not heard."

"Very well. I will contain my curiosity. But I will know of the scoundrel as soon as you have proof against him."

I promised my employer that this would be so, then hurried to catch Arthur and Uctred before they departed the hall. I did not tell them all. They could wait til they were within the walls of Galen House to learn their assignment where no others might hear. But Arthur knew that my requirement that he and Uctred present themselves at Galen House before dark had something to do with the unsuccessful search of the previous day.

If I was to be awake all night, I decided that I should find slumber when I might. I walked home, told Kate and Adela that I would seek my bed, and why.

The day was heavy with clouds, so no sunlight streamed through the chamber windows. I fell to sleep immediately and did not awaken until Kate gently nudged my shoulder and whispered in my ear that my supper awaited.

'Twas a simple pottage of peas and onions which bubbled upon the hearth. I ate my fill, along with a maslin loaf, then awaited the arrival of Arthur and Uctred. I had not to wait long.

The two grooms rapped upon the door of Galen House as Adela was departing for the Weald. The evening was cool, so I drew a bench before the hearth, then poured cups of ale.

While we drank I explained my belief that Bartram Thrupp had slain the three men. And I told them that unless I could catch the thief who had access to the tithe barn and force his confession I had no way to prove the cook's guilt. At least, no way I could presently devise. So this night, and every third night for the next fortnight or so, we would conceal ourselves after nightfall beneath bushes which faced the tithe barn door and watch for the appearance of a thief.

Arthur can sleep anywhere, any time. Such is the nocturnal experience of a man whose conscience does not condemn him. Uctred also. Uctred does not snore... well, not much. But we had been squatting in our hide before the tithe barn door for but a quarter of an hour when Arthur began rasping like a carpenter shaving a plank. I prodded him awake, but although he tried to escape slumber he was spluttering again half an hour later. Uctred elbowed him awake.

"This will never do," I whispered. There was little light under the shrub where we crouched, but enough for me to see that Arthur was crestfallen. "Too late for you to return to the castle,"

I said. "The drawbridge will be up and the portcullis down. But if you remain here we might as well announce to the village where we are and what we are about." Arthur has been a most valuable assistant, but now I learned the limit of his service.

"What you want me to do?" he whispered. "What if I stand against yon tree. Mayhap that'll keep me awake."

"Mayhap. Else you must return to Galen House. Your snores may be heard halfway to the Weald."

Arthur might as well have lain on the grass and snored the night through. No man approached the tithe barn that night. I did not expect that the thief would so soon after his previous depredation. Nevertheless I had hope that the matter of three murders might soon be resolved. Not this night.

As dawn approached I became reflective. I had spent many nights in the past month away from my bed seeking those who did villainy when good men were under their own roofs. Too many. But that is the nature of felons. Holy Writ says that men love darkness rather than light because their deeds are evil. Bailiffs must spend too much time dealing with men who love darkness.

I sent Arthur and Uctred back to the castle, told them we would again observe the tithe barn in three nights, and sought Galen House and the warmth of my hearth. I was stiff with cold.

'Tis a good thing that folk stand for the mass at St. Beornwald's Church else Kate would have been required to prod me awake. I admit to feeling joy when Father Simon sent the pax board through the congregation and I could leave the church for my home and bed. I did not even hesitate for my dinner. My days and nights of late had become confused. Why would they not? Confusion had become such a part of my life for the past month that I was becoming accustomed to the sentiment.

My repose was brief. My head had dented the pillow for no more than an hour when Kate woke me. Four servants from Father Ralph and Father Simon were at the door, she said.

Here were the men who had been appointed to keep watch at the tithe barn. I knew each of them by name: Randle, Maurice,

Nicholas, and Geoffrey. But I knew nothing of their character. I would have to trust the vicars' judgment that these men could be relied upon to do me honest service. And remain silent about it.

I assigned Randle and Nicholas to watch that night, Maurice and Geoffrey to do so the following night. I told them the reason for the watch, and that they should remain at their respective vicarages until dark, so they would not be seen approaching the hiding place. And they must return to the vicarages at the first sign of dawn in the eastern sky. I did not want the thief frightened away. I would tell Henry Swerd that men under my authority would be upon the streets after dark so that the beadle would not trouble them. If no felon was apprehended within a few nights the four would resume their watches every third night.

The next week passed with no nocturnal intruders seen near the tithe barn. I had not told the holy man of my scheme to apprehend a thief, so one night, near to midnight, he rapped upon the door of Galen House and when I opened to him he made sign that he had seen men near the tithe barn. I asked him how many, and when he raised two fingers I told him of Maurice and Geoffrey and their hiding place. When I asked if the men he had seen were concealed behind a bush before the tithe barn, he nodded. I thanked the hermit for his observation and told him the watchers were in my employ.

Midway through the second week of nightly observation of the tithe barn no man had been seen near the place after curfew. I was sorely disappointed and began to fear that my scheme had been discovered.

Kate saw my frustration and knew the reason. I had explained to her that I thought Bartram Thrupp the felon who had slain the three clerks, and how I intended to identify his accomplice in wickedness.

"Is Father Thomas's cook of Bampton?" she asked.

"Don't know. Why do you ask?"

"If the cook is of some near village he may yet have friends there who steal from the tithe barn with his aid. Or family," she added.

"I will ask Father Thomas," I said.

"You believe your plan to catch a thief was found out?" Kate continued.

"Either that or the rogue has become cautious. 'Tis a hungry time of year, and men who have food to sell may find ready buyers. So the thief has not stayed from the tithe barn because there is no profit in his felony."

This conversation concluded just as the noon Angelus commenced. Father Thomas would be at the church. I might speak to him in the churchyard, far from open ears and prying eyes, when the rite was done.

"Nay," the priest said when I asked of Bartram's home. "Not of Bampton. From Burford. Wed Mariot and was to set up an inn here, in Bampton. His father was an innkeeper in Burford."

"He did not do so... the inn, I mean?"

"Nay. I offered him the post of cook and he accepted."

"Has Bartram family in Burford?"

"Aye. Sisters and a brother. Father died some years past, so his brother has the inn now. Why do you ask?"

"Nearly a fortnight has passed since we began the watch over the tithe barn. No man has come near the place. But when Arthur and I followed the thief who stole from the tithe barn ten days past his trail led us north. Toward Burford."

"But you said you lost the track at Brize Norton."

"Aye. And that may mean the thief resides there. But it may not. It may mean the malefactor outwitted me."

"Why do you ask of Bartram? You believe he may be the man of my household guilty of three murders?"

"I do."

"I should be shocked at your opinion."

"Should be... but you are not?"

"Some. Bartram is a fine cook, mind you."

"But..."

"Mariot owns a velvet cotehardie. I pay the man well, but not so that his wife could possess such a garment. Indeed, for her to do so is a violation of sumptuary law."

This was surely true. The law reads that no servant or member of a servant's family may wear silk, velvet, or gold or silver jewelry.

"Have you met any of Bartram's family?" I asked.

"Nay. I've heard him speak of them, but they've never visited and I've no reason to travel to Burford."

I wondered if there be a sister, or sister-in-law, who was tall and buxom and commonly wore a green cotehardie. There was but one way to know.

The proprietor of an inn would surely like to stock his larder with goods obtained at a bargain price. I decided that the nightly watch at the tithe barn should end. Did the thief suspect that he had been observed? Did Bartram overhear my conversations with Father Thomas? Or did some other man learn of the nightly watch and carelessly speak of it? Whatever the reason, the watch had been fruitless and seemed likely to be so for some time into the future.

I sought Father Ralph and Father Simon and told them that their servants were no longer required to spend one night of three watching over the tithe barn. I then went to the castle, found Arthur, and told him to have two palfreys ready next morning at the second hour. Or three, if Uctred wished to join our journey. "We will travel to Burford," I told him.

"You yet seekin' for the matron what wears a green cotehardie?" he asked.

"Aye. Keeping vigil at the tithe barn has been a failure. We will no longer do so. But there is now some reason to believe that the woman who sold Father Ralph's cresset in Oxford may reside in Burford."

* * *

A light mist dampened the dawn next morning, and low clouds barely rose above St. Beornwald's tower. I would have preferred to remain in Galen House before the hearth than set out for Burford upon muddy roads.

Arthur is always reliable, and had three palfreys ready when I entered the castle yard. Uctred would not remain at the castle when there was a chance of entertainment in leaving it, so when he learned from Arthur where I was bound, and why, he chose to accompany us. I did not look for conflict this day, or expect it, but if strife followed some discovery, a third dagger would be welcome.

We passed through Brize Norton before the third hour and as our beasts plodded the muddy road I found myself observing the mire for any sign of a handcart. There was none.

CHAPTER 17

Burford, being a greater town than Bampton due to the wool trade, has two inns: the Black Ram and the Stag and Hind. They are nearly across the street from each other on Swan Lane. I left Uctred with our beasts and entered the Black Ram with Arthur. I needed to go no further.

A tall, well-fed woman held sway over those who were consuming a peas and beans pottage flavored with thick slices of bacon. I wondered if the ingredients had come from Bampton's tithe barn. The woman wore a faded green cotehardie.

I asked for three bowls of pottage, and sent Arthur out with one bowl to Uctred, along with a spoon and a cup of watered ale.

Arthur and I emptied our bowls.

"Want another?" the woman said in a stentorian voice cultivated by years of making herself heard over raucous customers.

"Nay... thanks," I said. Then, assuming a bland expression: "What news of Bartram?"

The woman stiffened. "Bartram?"

"Aye. Your brother-in-law, is he not? Thought you might have news of him."

"Resides in Bampton, does Bartram," the woman said. "Haven't seen 'im in years. Last I knew 'e was well. You know 'im?"

The woman was surely curious about me. How would a man garbed as a gentleman, accompanied by a servant, know of Bartram and her relationship to him? I did not illuminate her, but changed the subject. She had been caught off guard by my question. I would ask another and watch her reaction.

The woman wore a ring. I pointed to it and complimented her on the craftsmanship. "I saw one much like it at a goldsmith's shop in Oxford, near the Northgate."

The woman's jaw dropped.

"Do you know the place?" I continued. "Is that where your husband purchased your ring?"

"Uh... don't know. Mayhap."

"Do you know the goldsmith I speak of? The fellow is in some trouble, I understand. Tried to sell a silver object which had been stolen. When he was told that the item was stolen goods he hid the silver away. But it was discovered and returned to its owner. The Sheriff of Oxford was quite angry. Last I knew Sir Roger had demanded the goldsmith tell him how he came to have stolen silver in his possession. The sheriff will have his answer, I think. His serjeants are skilled at prying information from those who would remain silent."

I had seen, through an open door, a man stirring a great bronze pot upon a hearth. The pottage I had just consumed, no doubt. The woman turned from me and strode through the door where I next saw her begin an arm-waving conversation with the man with the ladle. Her husband, and Bartram Thrupp's brother, no doubt.

After a moment of this agitated discourse I saw the man peer over his wife's shoulder. When he saw that he was observed he quickly looked away. What he then said I know not, but the woman turned and shoved the door closed so that they could continue their deliberations unobserved.

Arthur had listened and watched while I talked to the woman. Now he spoke.

"It's her what sold Father Ralph's cresset to that goldsmith, an' no doubt, eh?"

"I'm sure of it. And we may have filled our bellies with peas and bacon stolen from St. Beornwald's tithe barn."

"You think if you take 'er to Oxford that goldsmith will identify 'er as the one what sold 'im the cresset?"

"Perhaps, but with the proper threat we may not need to make such a journey."

As I spoke, the door to the kitchen opened slightly and I saw a masculine eye, nose, and beard through the crack. I stared back and assumed my most disagreeable scowl. The door closed abruptly. The noise of conversations obscured any words the couple may have exchanged, but I could guess the subject, even through a closed door.

A man whose cup was empty banged it upon his table and shouted, "Agnes! Let's be havin' more ale," toward the door.

Several other fellows joined him banging cups upon scarred tables before the kitchen door opened and Agnes appeared. She went to a ewer and, without looking to me, began to fill empty cups. I held mine forth, inviting her to approach with the ewer. Arthur saw, and lifted his cup also.

The woman made our table the last she visited. Other customers had turned from her to their own conversations and paid her and me no heed. I pointed to the end of the bench upon which I sat and invited her to be seated. She refused, at first.

"I am Sir Hugh de Singleton, bailiff to Lord Gilbert, Third Baron Talbot, at Bampton. If you desire a future which does not include a scaffold and a noose you will sit."

She sat.

"If I require you to come with me to Oxford, the goldsmith there, who has already described you, will surely tell me and Sheriff Roger that you sold him a silver cresset belonging to a vicar of St. Beornwald's Church. Nay, do not deny it," I said as the woman stiffened and opened her mouth to speak. "I know all."

This was not entirely true. I knew much, and suspected more. But what I did know and what I merely suspected were both unknown to Agnes.

"Your brother-in-law, cook to Father Thomas of St. Beornwald's Church, has provided you access to the tithe barn in Bampton. Your husband, or some servant, has been seen entering the tithe barn in the night and carrying off sacks and bacon. Where is the handcart he used when last he visited Bampton?"

The woman swallowed deeply. She looked toward the kitchen door as if seeking aid, or a place where she might find refuge. "My sister," Agnes said in a whisper.

"What? Your sister has the handcart? Does she reside in Brize Norton?"

"Aye."

"So the stolen corn and flesh were carried to Brize Norton in the handcart, then brought here, to be consumed at your inn, as you had need?"

A tear began to make its way down the woman's cheek as she nodded.

"Bartram has slain three clerks of the Church of St. Beornwald to keep this secret. Did you know this?"

"Three?" she said. "'E told us of but one."

"He slew three, and will hang."

"What will become of us?" Agnes whimpered.

"I cannot predict the decisions of the King's Eyre," I said. "If you give witness to Sheriff Elmerugg of what you and Bartram Thrupp have done you may escape with your life. The Bishop of Exeter will decide your fine and how much you will pay to restore the stolen goods, since your theft was against him, not the king. Have you horses?" I said.

"I have not."

"Then 'tis a long walk to Bampton and we'd best be started. Tell your husband to quench his fire, then send your customers away and close the inn. You will come with me to Bampton and reside this night in the castle dungeon, along with Bartram."

I might have sought the Burford bailiff and placed Agnes and her husband under his jurisdiction, but I did not know the man. Mayhap he and the innkeepers were friends. If so, when I returned to take them to Bampton to stand before Lord Gilbert they might be elsewhere.

The woman rose from the bench and set off to do my bidding. "Go with her," I said to Arthur. The kitchen surely had a rear door, and after the woman told her husband of my demand they might decide to vanish through it.

Arthur divined my suspicion and followed Agnes. Evidently the woman's husband required much persuasion. I saw through the open door as the woman spoke while Arthur stood, feet planted and beefy arms folded, close behind. No doubt flight entered the man's mind, but Arthur's formidable presence made the option seem undesirable.

The innkeeper said something in reply, then cast his arm about in a gesture that said, "Look here, at all this," to an onlooker. The man then peered through the door and his eyes rested upon me. I scowled, which I can do well, and assumed the same resolute pose as Arthur, which I do not do well. At least, not as well as a man who weighs fifteen stone. Even my Kate's cookery has not lifted me beyond ten or so stone. Kate has spoken of this as a shortcoming in her domestic competency.

The innkeeper glared at me through the open door, but then began to do as I had required. He removed the bronze pot from the fire, then vanished from view. He reappeared carrying a leather bucket and began dousing the blaze upon his hearth, to the accompaniment of billows of smoke and steam rising up the chimney and much hissing.

Customers heard the fire being extinguished, looked to each other with questions in their eyes, then two stood and moved to peer through the kitchen door to see what the proprietor was about. Conversations in the inn had ceased, so I heard the innkeeper clearly.

"Closin' for the day. All must depart," he said. The words inspired more curious glances between patrons, and some directed toward me. Then the innkeeper entered the room and spoke again. "We 'ave business elsewhere which cannot be delayed. All must leave."

Again some of those present looked in my direction, rightly guessing that my presence had something to do with this unforeseen event. There was some muttering, but patrons began to seek the door. The innkeeper, regardless of the delicate circumstances in which he now found himself, was quick to station himself at the exit to collect farthings and pennies from those who had consumed his ale and pottage. He would need the coins to pay the fines he'd be assessed. If he escaped a noose.

The inn doors had no locks – the innkeeper simply barred the doors at night. He complained to me that his establishment would be open to thieves if I required both him and his wife to travel to Bampton. I was not sympathetic to a thief who feared thieves.

Uctred knew little of what had transpired within the inn. I told him as our party departed Burford. He grinned as Arthur embellished the event and conversations. But neither Agnes nor her husband seemed entertained.

The misty rain had ceased, but the road remained muddy, so when we reached Brize Norton two hours later Agnes's cotehardie was caked with mud at the hem, and her shoes and those of her husband were heavy with mire. I asked which house was her sister's and she pointed to a house of two bays with smoke issuing from roof vents.

The woman who answered my knock upon the insubstantial door was unlike her sister. Shorter, and two stone lighter. Her mouth dropped open when she saw Agnes standing in the mud behind me.

"The handcart used to transport goods from the Bampton tithe barn some days past – bring it forth."

"Who are you to tell me so?" the matron replied.

"One who can send you to a scaffold for your felonies. Sir Hugh de Singleton, bailiff for Lord Gilbert Talbot, in Bampton. Now, fetch the cart."

The woman's attitude changed abruptly when she heard of her possible future associated with Lord Gilbert's name. She curtsied and said, "'Tis around back in the toft. I'll get it."

She was surely curious as to why her sister and brother-in-law were accompanying Lord Gilbert's bailiff, but did not ask. Nor did I tell her. She would discover the reason soon enough, when she and her husband were required to appear before the King's Eyre and possibly the bishop's court, and learn the fines they must share with Agnes and her husband. I doubted a king's judge would send her to a scaffold for her part in the thievery, but judges can be unpredictable. A magistrate whose wife has scolded him in the morning might not be lenient in the afternoon.

When we entered Bampton, the innkeeper hauling the handcart as evidence, I sent Uctred on to the castle with Agnes and her husband. I suppose they might have tried to flee when they heard me speak of the castle dungeon, but they knew already that this was their destination. And where would they go that Lord Gilbert's hounds could not soon bring them to bay? I told Uctred to seek Sir Henry, or Lord Gilbert himself, and tell them why the folk in his custody must be gaoled. I also told him to tell Sir Henry that a third prisoner would soon join the two.

'Twas time for Father Thomas's supper when Arthur and I halted our palfreys before the vicarage. A servant opened to my rapping upon the door and the priest, hearing my voice, appeared a moment later.

"Is Bartram within?" I asked.

"Nay," Father Thomas growled. "Not seen him since dinner. Cold pottage and a stale loaf for my supper."

"Did you seek him at his house?"

"Aye. Sent Roger to fetch him. Mariot said she'd not seen him since he left to prepare my dinner."

"He knows his felonies are about to be made known," I said, "and has fled."

"You now have proof he is the man who slew Odo?"

"Aye. And William and Ernaud also, surely. Bartram's brother and sister-in-law are at this moment entering the castle dungeon, where they will remain until I take them to Oxford and Sheriff Roger, there to face the King's Eyre. And after that the bishop's court will deal with them. I intended to seize Bartram and send him also to the dungeon.

"He knows I was close to proving his guilt," I continued, "so has fled. Likely he learned that I was on my way to Burford this day. There are yet a few hours of daylight. I will seek the castle fewterer and set Lord Gilbert's hounds after him."

I did so. Sir Jaket and his squire accompanied me, the fewterer, Arthur, and Uctred. Lady Joan's son heard of the chase and begged to participate. I could see no harm in the lad following along. Lady Joan had returned to Banbury, leaving

Charles with her brother to be instructed in the arts of war and knighthood and chivalry.

At Bartram's house I demanded an article of his clothing, unwashed. Mariot brought out an old, threadbare kirtle, which I passed before the hounds. The dogs knew what was expected of them and began a frenzied yapping.

They found a trail immediately and pulled on the leashes toward Bushy Row, thence across a fallow field which ended at Shill Brook to the south of the town. There the spoor ended. Bartram had guessed that we would set hounds after him and so entered the stream. The fewterer directed the hounds upstream and down, on both sides of the brook, but the animals never again caught Bartram's scent. We gave up the search when darkness fell, and stumbled back to the castle.

Next morn I called upon Mariot and demanded of her that if she received news of Bartram, she inform me or Father Thomas forthwith. Her expression said that she would rather chew upon broken glass than do so. I thought of taking her to the castle dungeon, and thence to appear also before the King's Eyre. But the woman would claim ignorance of her husband's felonies, and mayhap that would be true. Although I doubted it.

Two days later we placed Agnes and Rufus Thrupp – for that was Bartram's brother's name – into a cart and I, Arthur, Uctred, Sir Jaket, and his squire took the miscreants to Oxford Castle and Sir Roger's gaol. I left a signed affidavit with the sheriff's clerk, detailing the felonies Rufus and Agnes had committed, in hopes that the judges of the King's Eyre would deem the document sufficient and not require my testimony at the trial. They did so.

Rufus and Agnes escaped the noose, but were required to pay a ten shilling fine and make recompense to the Bishop of Exeter for the goods stolen from the tithe barn in the amount of two pounds. A great sum. They were required to sell their inn at Burford to pay, and I heard nothing more of them.

Agnes's sister pleaded ignorance of the reason for the handcart being secreted upon her property. I doubted her word – bailiffs learn to doubt most everyone's word – but the woman had little by way of this world's goods and if a fine had been settled upon her and her husband, she would be unable to pay.

* * *

Bartram Thrupp's felonies became known in Bampton and the Weald within hours of his disappearance. There followed much clucking and shaking of heads, and the opinion of most was that the man was twice a scoundrel – once for the murders he did, and again for absconding and leaving his wife to fend for herself. I wondered if the man might be not far off, awaiting an opportunity to return and carry his wife and children to some far place where he was unknown.

If this was his intent, he would likely send word to her and come some night to lead the family from Bampton. Must I organize a watch over Thrupp's house? I had spent too many nights sitting in the dark watching for felons, mostly with no result. Rosamond Wyle may continue to attract nocturnal visitors. I do not care, so long as they allow me to stay in my own bed, warm in the night.

Could I set some others to keep a watch on Bartram Thrupp's house and family? Perhaps. I thought I knew of a man who might be willing. The fourth day after Bartram Thrupp fled Bampton I entered the forest to the west of the castle and sought the holy man. I found him seated before a smoky fire, munching a stale maslin loaf. Well, I assume it was stale. Here was a man who seemed to enjoy watching over the village in the night. Why not put his ways to good use?

I have become adept through several exchanges with the man at asking questions that can be answered with a nod or a shake of the head. Within a few minutes I was able to explain what I wanted of him, and received his agreement in reply. I thought I saw a slight smile flash across his face as he consented to my request.

The hermit agreed to walk the village streets in the night as he often did, with attention to Mariot Thrupp's house. If he saw any nocturnal preparations which indicated the family's departure he would immediately seek me at Galen House, pound upon my door, and tell me of what he had discovered. I thought that if Bartram returned to collect his family the process of collecting what goods he wanted to take from the house, and herding wife and children from the town, would take long enough that I could apprehend the felon before he could escape.

* * *

Two days before Whitsunday came the thumping upon my door that I had expected. As usual, Kate snapped awake whilst I was yet trying to collect my wits. She knew who it must be at the door, for I had told her of the holy man's agreement. She called out to him that I would attend him immediately, and the pounding ceased.

A waning moon gave some light to the front of Galen House. When I asked the holy man if he had seen activity at Thrupp's house I could see clearly his affirmative nod. I thanked the fellow for his watchfulness and dismissed him. I thought that if there was trouble he should be far from the scene. His scrawny frame was not conducive to successful combat. And if he was with me when I confronted Bartram the cook might deduce who had informed me against him and attack the man.

But when I told the holy man that he might lose himself in the night he shook his head, and began to lead me through darkened streets to Thrupp's house.

It was as the hermit said. I saw Thrupp's stocky form loading a handcart with pots and blankets and other household items. I wondered if this was the same handcart which had been used to carry stuff from the tithe barn. Well, if it was, its days of use as a tool of wickedness were ended.

Bartram glanced about often as he loaded goods to the cart. I was careful to keep to the shadows as I drew near. I hoped that if I surprised him he would be so disconcerted that he would not consider fighting. I wished I had Arthur at my back rather than the hermit, but the groom was tucked away in his bed behind the castle drawbridge and portcullis. If Thrupp offered combat I would have to vanquish the man myself.

I saw Mariot leave the house with her two older children clutching her skirts. Bartram next left the house carrying the youngest child, whom he perched upon the loaded cart. The time had come.

I drew my dagger – just in case – and shouted "Halt" with as loud a voice as I could muster. I thought volume might serve to startle the man. If it did, the effect wore off quickly. I believe he almost expected to find his scheme upset.

Thrupp turned, crouched, and searched in the darkness to see whence the command had come. I saw the glint of moonlight on a blade the man held in his left hand. The hand at the end of an arm yet weakened from a deep slash.

I doubt that the man knew at the time who it was who had come before him, but he did know that he was doomed to end his life on a scaffold if he could not prevail against the one who had ordered him to halt.

I answered Thrupp's unspoken question. "'Tis Sir Hugh," I said. "And you are under arrest for three murders."

Mariot shrieked and fled back into the house. Bartram glanced at her as she ran, then with a yell came after me, dagger held before him.

The man was rotund but capable of quick movement. Of course, when a man's life is at stake he may discover abilities of which he was previously unaware. As with my reaction. I leaped to the side and Bartram's heavy body continued past. He skidded to a stop, turned, and prepared to come at me again.

Thrupp took one step toward me and suddenly collapsed to the ground. He roared in anger, and I saw the gleam from the blade of his dagger as it skittered through the dust. He had lost it from his weakened left arm when he fell.

And then in the dim light I saw why he had tumbled to the dust. The holy man had both arms wrapped about Bartram's legs below his knees, and clung to his kicking feet like a leech. This was no time to enjoy the spectacle. I leaped upon Thrupp's writhing body, held my dagger to his throat, and pricked him firmly enough that when I commanded him to cease his struggle he knew to obey.

227

I told Thrupp to stand, which he did after the hermit released his legs, then I picked his dagger from the dirt and placed it in my belt. One of the objects I had seen Bartram tossing into the handcart was a length of hempen rope. I fished about under the squalling child until I found it, and told the hermit to tie Thrupp's hands behind him. The fellow seemed pleased to do this, and when he had finished the job I tested the knot and found it tight.

The castle drawbridge would not be lowered for several hours, so I took Bartram to Galen House. Kate was nervously chewing upon a fingernail when I pushed my prisoner through the door before me. The holy man followed.

There was little conversation. I knew what Thrupp had done and why he had done it, so had no questions. He said nothing, for he knew no excuses or justifications would avail.

At the first hour I and the holy man took Bartram to the castle, where Lord Gilbert was pleased to offer him accommodation in the dungeon. Next day Sir Jaket, his page, Arthur, and I escorted Thrupp to Oxford, where he would face the King's Eyre. As before I left a signed deposition with Sir Roger which detailed the cook's felonies. Word came to Bampton a fortnight later that Thrupp was found guilty and hanged.

Lord Gilbert was impressed with the holy man's part in Thrupp's apprehension. He ordered the hermit's hut replaced. A small house with wattle and daub walls, nearly twice the size of the decayed swineherd's hut, was built. It had a hearthstone so the man might cook his pottage out of the rain, and a thatched roof.

Folk of Bampton would have nothing to do with Mariot Thrupp, for all suspected that she knew of her husband's felonies, and she certainly was aiding in his attempt to flee justice. So no one was surprised that shortly before Lammas Day she packed the handcart and set off toward Burford. She had kin there, some said.

Oswald Smith denied ever making a key for Bartram, but the vicars of St. Beornwald's Church changed the lock to the tithe barn anyway. Just in case.

Afterword

Many readers of the chronicles of Hugh de Singleton have asked about medieval remains in the Bampton area. St. Mary's Church is little changed from the 14th century. The May Bank Holiday is a good time to visit Bampton. The village is a Morris dancing center, and on that day hosts a day-long Morris dancing festival.

Village scenes in the popular television series "Downton Abbey" were filmed on Church View Street in Bampton. The town library became the Downton hospital, and St. Mary's Church appeared in several episodes.

Bampton castle was, in the fourteenth century, one of the largest castles in England in terms of the area enclosed within the curtain wall. Little remains of the castle but for the gatehouse and a small part of the curtain wall, which form a part of Ham Court, a farmhouse in private hands. The current owners are doing extensive restoration work. Gilbert Talbot was indeed the lord of the manor of Bampton in the late fourteenth century.

Mel Starr

Master Wycliffe's Symmons

**The fourteenth chronicle of
Hugh de Singleton, surgeon**

CHAPTER 1

Bessie was perturbed that she could not join the lads of her acquaintance in wrenching new boughs from bushes and shrubs with which to beat the bounds of St. Beornwald's Parish. 'Twas no use explaining to her that beating the bounds on Rogation Day was a thing boys did. Not lasses. To all such assertions my daughter had one reply. "Why?"

"Because," I said, "'tis the way of things."

This reply was unsatisfactory. As Kate, Bessie, and John followed me to the procession, I saw my daughter surreptitiously yank a tall weed from the roadside. She began to flick this stem at the trees, rocks, and stream which formed the parish boundaries, emulating the young males who were learning the boundaries of the parish. Their fathers and grandfathers had done the same for generations past, and their children and grandchildren would surely do likewise on the days before Ascension Day in years to come.

When the procession was completed, villagers gathered in the castle forecourt for the parish ale. Lord Gilbert provided the feast, and folk helped themselves to tables heaped with maslin loaves and stockfish from a barrel of salted cod. As 'twas a fast day there was no pork, to the dismay of the revelers. A few washed the meal down with too much of Lord Gilbert's ale and so, as night fell, wobbled unsteadily to their homes.

I am Sir Hugh de Singleton, surgeon, and bailiff to Lord Gilbert, Third Baron Talbot, at his manor of Bampton.

A golden sunset illuminated the spire of St. Beornwald's Church as Kate and I, with Bessie and John, made our way to Galen House. The night before a raging thunderstorm battered the village, but clouds had cleared at dawn and the day had been bright and washed clean by the deluge.

My son dropped a sleepy head to my shoulder as I carried him up Church View Street to our home. And Bessie walked quietly, fatigued by the long walk circumscribing Bampton and the Weald. I and my family would sleep well this night.

Men wish to know the future, and seek those who claim to see it. The stars foretell what is to come, some say. But to know one's destiny would be to see sorrow as well as joy, and perhaps more of the first than the second. Holy Writ says that sufficient to the day is the evil thereof. So I rested my head upon my pillow that evening with no thought of what was in store.

Thursday, at the third hour, I heard a rapping upon Galen House door and opened to two red-gowned youths. Scholars from Queen's College, Oxford, from their appearance. I soon learned that this surmise was accurate.

"I give you good day," one of the lads said. "We seek Sir Hugh de Singleton."

"You have found him," I replied. "How may I serve you?"

"I am William Sleyt. Here is Thomas Rous. Master John Wycliffe has sent us."

"Enter, and tell how I may be of service to Master Wycliffe."

"We are of Queen's College, and study with Master Wycliffe. Two days past another of Master Wycliffe's students perished."

I nodded, but did not reply. What was I to say of the death of a scholar I did not know? I felt sure I would soon learn more. I did.

"'Twas when a thunderstorm passed over Oxford," the lad continued. "We who lodge in chambers at Queen's heard a great crash, as if a bolt of lightning had struck the hall."

"The thunder was deafening," the other scholar agreed.

"When the storm had passed we emerged to see what damage was done. 'Twas then we found Richard."

"Dead, struck by lightning," the second youth said, "so we thought."

"What has this sorry event to do with me?" I asked.

"Master Wycliffe wishes you to attend him. He is not content that Richard was struck down by lightning and asks for you to investigate the matter."

"I serve Lord Gilbert Talbot. He does not pay me to inquire into matters at Queen's College."

"You will not come? Master Wycliffe has told us how you found his stolen books and unraveled other knotty incidents."

"Master John suspects this scholar's death due to the act of a man rather than a storm?"

"Aye, he does, and asks for you to investigate the matter."

"What of the sheriff? Can he not inquire into the death?"

"Master Wycliffe asked Sir Roger, but could not convince him that the death was suspicious."

"What has caused him to believe a murder may have been done?"

"He has not confided in us. We know only that he is troubled and sent us to you, begging you to come to Oxford and sort out the matter."

My Kate had heard the conversation from the kitchen, where she and Adela – her servant – were preparing our dinner. She appeared in the doorway and her words surprised me.

"'Tis an honor that Master Wycliffe seeks your aid," she said. "Mayhap Lord Gilbert will release you from your duties here."

"You wish to be rid of me?" I said.

"Nay. But I know the regard you have for Master Wycliffe. If you refuse this request you will fret about the decision for weeks to come. Especially if it is so that murder has been done. With Adela's aid I can keep Galen House in good order... I have done so in the past when you were called away."

"When do you return to Oxford?" I asked the scholars.

"As soon as we have your answer."

"You may tell Master John that I will come to him tomorrow, so long as Lord Gilbert is agreeable. If you depart Bampton now and make haste you may cross Bookbinder's Bridge before nightfall."

After a dinner of porre of peas with bacon, shared with the scholars, I sought the castle and my employer. Lord Gilbert, his household knights, his guests and servants, had but moments earlier finished their dinner. From the skeletal remains I saw that several roasted geese had been a feature of the last remove.

Lord Gilbert was about to depart the hall when he saw me approach. I lifted a hand to indicate a desire to speak and he waited at the screens passage.

"I give you good day, Hugh. Have you a matter for my consideration?"

"Aye."

"Then come. We will discuss it in the solar."

The day was sunny and warm so no fire burned upon the hearth. Lord Gilbert's solar has windows of glass, both clear and stained. Tapestries cunningly embroidered with hunting scenes cover two walls. Lady Petronilla and her maids did the work, before her untimely death, and I suspect that when Lord Gilbert looks at them he thinks of his lost wife. The lady has been deceased for several years, but he has not chosen another bride, although suitable candidates are plentiful. The solar is Lord Gilbert's favorite room, especially does he seek it in winter, when, being smaller, 'tis more easily warmed than the hall.

My employer bade me be seated, and dropped into a thickly padded chair. Lord Gilbert enjoys a good meal, and this delight has increased his girth since I first came to his service. He still sits a horse well, but the beast will not enjoy the experience.

"What matter do you bring to me?" he said.

"Master John Wycliffe has requested that I attend him in Oxford."

"Why so?"

"You remember the thunderstorm which shattered our repose two days past? The same storm struck Oxford, and when it had passed a scholar of Queen's College was found dead in his chamber. Struck by lightning, men said."

"So what has this death to do with Master Wycliffe, or you?"

"Master John is not satisfied that the lad's death came because of a lightning bolt. Your friend, Sheriff Elmerugg, disagrees and will not be bothered by sending a serjeant to inquire into the matter. So Master John asks me to seek the truth of the business."

"You wish my permission to leave your duties here?"

"Aye."

"You have it. Crops are planted, the harvest is yet months away, and, so far as I know, you have no local miscreants to deal with."

"Can you also spare Arthur Wagge?" I asked.

"Ah... your assistant in times past when apprehending felons required some brawn. Surely. His son is now full grown, you know, and is the image of the father."

Arthur's son serves Lord Gilbert at Goodrich Castle. I've not seen the lad, but heard that he is as sturdy as his father.

"Arthur has a brain to go with his brawn," I said. "Little escapes his notice."

"Aye, he does. I'll leave the matter to him, but I suspect he will be eager to assist you. And I'll inform the marshalsea to have beasts made ready. When? Will you leave tomorrow?"

"Aye."

Arthur was pleased to accompany me. Service as a groom to a great lord often requires onerous duties, mucking out the stables, for example, so a few days in Oxford appealed.

As Lord Gilbert said, Arthur is a sturdy fellow. His form resembles a wine cask set upon two coppiced stumps. He is not constructed so as to be able to chase down and catch a fleeing felon, but the miscreant who chases and catches Arthur will regret his success.

My Kate was pleased to learn that I would not travel to Oxford alone. King Edward is in his dotage, it is said, and cares for little but pleasing Alice Perrers. Prince Edward is ill, and not capable of governing in his father's place. So those who would do evil feel themselves unrestrained. Good and evil are always at war, and good men must decide what they will do about this conflict. Many seek the safety of home and hearth, for to oppose villains may be dangerous. I bear scars from Lord Gilbert's service to prove it so. I pray that I will never be found wanting when it is my duty to oppose miscreants.

The clear sky of Thursday gave way to clouds and mist Friday. I kissed my Kate farewell at the second hour, hugged Bessie and John, and extracted from my daughter a promise to be helpful to her mother whilst I was away. Bessie may have trouble keeping this pledge. She can be an energetic child. I would not have her be otherwise, although at some future time her husband might wish her less obstreperous.

The morning mist gave way to broken clouds and sun by the time we crossed Bookbinder's Bridge. I knew of a stable just off High Street where we might leave Lord Gilbert's palfreys, and from thence we sought an inn where we might consume a belated dinner. The Green Dragon served a pottage of whelks that day, which met with my approval but Arthur seemed to find the meal unappealing, unlike his usual robust appetite.

Master Wycliffe's dinner was not so toothsome. We found him in his chamber at Queen's College, munching upon a maslin loaf while he bent over a book open upon a table. His door was open, and when my shadow interrupted the light he looked up.

"Ah, Master Hugh... nay, 'tis Sir Hugh now. I forgot. William told me you had agreed to come. He told you why I have asked for your aid, did he not?"

"Aye. A scholar of the college is dead of a lightning bolt, but mayhap not."

"No mayhap about his death, but I suspect a bolt of lightning had nothing to do with Richard's demise."

"Why do you think this?" I asked.

Wycliffe pushed the remainder of his loaf aside, took a quick draught from a cup of ale, then said, "Come with me and I will show you."

For a decade and more after its founding Queen's was but a hall, with no building of its own. Its scholars, most poor lads from Cumberland, met with fellows in whatever chambers they could find. But now Queen's has a stone structure where its students and their masters may reside and study and dispute.

Wycliffe led us to a stairway, thence to the upper floor. A narrow corridor divided the chambers, each of these no more than five paces long by three paces wide. Near to the end of this passage Wycliffe stopped and pointed into a chamber. The door to this chamber stood open, and I saw that it was askew upon its hinges and likely could not be closed completely.

"'Twas here Richard lived… and died," Wycliffe said. "The chamber is as it was when Richard was found. I asked that it remain unmolested when I saw things which troubled me."

"What things?" I asked.

"I'll not say. To do so might influence your opinion. Examine the chamber for yourself and decide if it has the appearance of a place damaged by a lightning bolt."

I did so. As the damaged door was at hand I first inspected it. 'Twas not fashioned of oaken planks, but beech. The strength of oak was not required. The nails which held the upper hinge to the jamb had pulled loose, and one of the beech planks was split from top to bottom. Only a crossbuck held the plank together.

Straw from the scholar's mattress, and feathers from his pillow, littered the chamber. The wooden frame which had supported the mattress was splintered, and the desk upon which the lad had studied was tilted. One leg had been cracked away. The skin window above the desk was tattered and allowed the summer breeze to enter the room. Even so, the fresh air could not dispel the scent of burning and sulphur which yet permeated the place.

The walls which separated the chamber from those adjoining were of wattle and daub and flimsy. They were not made to resist the blast of a lightning bolt so were bowed out. The daub was cracked and some was scattered about the floor with the straw and feathers. The ceiling likewise was cracked with chunks of daub fallen away from the wattles.

Sunlight penetrated the chamber through the shattered ceiling, and where roofing slates were missing I saw sky and clouds between the exposed rafters.

Where were the missing slates? Was their absence from the chamber floor one of the things which troubled Master John?

"I would like to see the lane outside this window," I said. Arthur and Master Wycliffe followed me down the stairs and out into Queen's Lane. I looked up to the tattered window skin of the blasted chamber, then examined the ground. I saw there a few fragments of slate which had been dislodged from the roof. There had been no slate driven into the chamber, none which

238

I could see. Why would a bolt of lightning send pieces of slate outward, rather than in? Perhaps there may be a reason. I am not well-versed in the behavior of lightning, prefering to be elsewhere when it strikes.

But one thing I do know of lightning bolts is that they tend to strike the highest point close by. The hole in Queen's College roof was nearer to the eave than the peak, and across the lane was the squat tower of St. Peter's-in-the-east, which loomed above the scene.

Master John watched as I studied the fractured roof and the church tower, but held his tongue. Arthur was not so reticent.

"Seen a tree what was struck by lightning. Me uncle had a barn near, an' it was unmarred. Tree was taller, an' was split top to bottom. Blew the bark off ten paces. Wonder why that church tower didn't get the bolt."

I wondered the same.

"Strange, is it not," Wycliffe finally said, "that lightning would strike where it should not?"

"This is why you suspect that the scholar died due to some other cause?"

"Among other reasons. Did you notice the stink in Richard's chamber?"

"There was a hint of sulphur, I thought."

"Indeed. 'Twas stronger two days past, but persists."

"I've not heard of lightning producing sulphur," I said.

"Nor I," Master John agreed. "Come. Return with me to Richard's chamber. I will show you another troubling thing, which mayhap you did not notice."

We again ascended the stairs. I studied the place anew, curious as to what might have caught Wycliffe's eye that I had missed. 'Twas the mark upon the planks of the floor, under the remains of the scholar's shattered bed.

Master John saw me gaze at the blackened boards and said, "Bend low. The smell of sulphur there is yet great."

I did and it was. Upon the floorboards where the splintered bed would have rested was a circular black patch, with rays extending out from the center as far as my arm is long. Here was the place where the sulphurous odor originated, for the stink of rotten eggs was strong.

"Was the scholar burned upon his body?" I asked, "Where the lightning bolt would have passed through him to strike the floor?"

"Nay. Nor was there a hole burned through his blanket. See, here it is."

Master John went to a corner of the chamber and fetched the blanket. It was ragged, as might be expected of a poor scholar, but there was no blackened hole in it.

"What say you, Sir Hugh?" Wycliffe said as I studied the threadbare blanket.

"I have read *Opus Maius*," I said.

"As have I," Master John replied. "Has Roger Bacon told us from the grave what has happened here?"

"It may be so," I agreed.